READ ORDER

200
107 (7)
114
158 (10)

63 (15)
23
205

1
221

78
124
168

HAIR

BY FAITH MARLOW

THE BATHROOM TILE WAS COLD under Lucie's bare feet as she peered into the medicine cabinet mirror, partially reconsidering the decision she had made the day before. She ran her fingers through her shaggy pixie cut, nary a hair pointing in the same direction. The stylist had cut a full sixteen inches of pristine dark blonde locks for donation to charity and Lucie could not be happier with her new carefree, playful style. It was the decision to bleach and then change her color to a vibrant aqua blue that had her second guessing herself. She loved the color and was fortunate that her employer did not place any limitations on self-expression. So long as she wore black jeans with no holes in them and the company provided t-shirt, the owners of *The Sacred Bean* knew that an interesting and confident wait staff would only make the coffee drinking experience more memorable for their patrons. She loved the confidence boost and the smiles that had greeted her on the street as she walked home. But most of all she loved the grimace of disapproval she had received from Edith, the elderly lady two doors down from her, as they passed in the hallway of their apartment building. It was just a lot of change in a short amount of time. She loved it, but it would still take some getting used to.

After having long hair for so many years, she had learned how to use it to her advantage if she did not want to be seen, how to disappear on the subway or in a crowded store. Now there was nowhere to hide, no cover. Not only had she revealed herself to the world, but she had purposely chosen a color that was sure to draw the eye of anyone she passed if they liked it or not.

Lucie splashed some water on her face and rubbed her damp hands through her hair, ruffling it up even further. The occasional drip was chilly on her bare shoulders and chest. Her tank top and boxer shorts were going out of season. Her cool weather clothes would need to come out of storage soon. Just as she started to leave the bathroom, a tickle between her shoulder blades gave her a fright. Her irrational first instinct was some insidious spider had somehow crawled into her bed and then her shirt for warmth. She yanked her shirt over her head and vigorously shook it, watching to see if anything fell to the floor, but there was nothing. She sighed in relief and looked the shirt over just in case. Embedded in the threads of the tank top was a single auburn hair. She carefully pulled the winding hair from the shirt and held it in front of her. It was about five inches long and appeared to be color treated, judging by the silvery root at the end.

"Ugh," she groaned, dropping it in the wastebasket. Nobody she knew had that color hair and even if they did, how would one of their hairs get woven into the fabric of the tank she only wore to sleep in? "Nasty Laundromat machines."

Lucie dismissed the oddity, having no spare time to devote to something so inconsequential. The morning rush was always the busiest time at *The Sacred Bean* and today was the last day she would want to be late. Her hair would already be getting enough attention.

* * *

A sick co-worker calling out meant pulling a double shift and tired feet; Lucie was exhausted. She dragged through the door with a bag of fast food in tow, pausing to check her hair in the small decorative mirror that hung near the door. Thankfully the new hairstyle had held up, unnoticeably different from when she had left for work that morning. Lucie smiled at herself, finally certain she had made the right decision.

The greasy burger and salty fries seemed to take the edge off her nerves, warming her belly just before the frozen sweetness of the milkshake washed everything down. But after the day she had had, it would take a little more than a milkshake for her to relax. There was a bottle of cheap whiskey and a two liter of coke in the fridge that was calling her name. That would be more than enough to do the trick.

Settled in on the couch, drink in hand, she kicked off her shoes before propping her feet on the coffee table, careful not to knock over any of her dinner trash. Scanning her surroundings for the TV remote was fruitless, as was feeling under the couch. She regretfully knew the next course of action. Her face scrunched in disgust as she slid her hand between the couch cushions, brushing into every forgotten crumb and used tissue. Finally, she located the remote and drew it up from the darkness triumphantly. Her celebration was short-lived. Much to her disgust and confusion, several long, reddish hairs were stuck to her hand and the remote.

"That's disgusting," she grumbled as she pulled the hairs from the remote and her hand before gathering them into a ball. Thinking back to the morning, she returned to the bathroom and sat the wastebasket on the sink. There, laying right on top of an emptied tube of toothpaste was the single hair she had pulled from her shirt, trapped like a prehistoric insect in amber. Lucie carefully pulled it free of its minty trap and compared it to the hairball taken from the couch. The color was exact, and although the length was unable to be compared, she could see the roots at the end were the same. The same amount of natural, silvery roots was visible at the end of each of the hairs. Their owner had lost them at the same time.

Lucie grabbed a few squares of toilet paper and placed her strange collection on one end before folding the other side over it, and then folded it double. Returning to the couch, she was unable to focus on the show that was playing, instead staring off into space, trying to make sense of her discoveries. Considering that she often fell asleep on the couch, it was possible her shirt had picked up the hair and embedded into the weave of the fabric as she wiggled in her sleep. Her conclusion only led to a more complicated question. If she had gotten the hair in her shirt from sleeping on the couch, how did the hairs get inside her couch?

Lucie woke the next morning with a sore back and stinging eyes. Too much time working on concrete floors had taken its toll on her legs and back, leaving her stiff and slow. She had slept late, almost noon. The bright sun had seeped into her eyes through the lids, leaving them dry and swollen. She was thankful she had the day off, because if being worn out from the day before was not enough, she felt like she was getting sick. Her throat was dry and raw, and a horrid taste coated her mouth and tongue.

"I don't have time to be sick," she grumbled, dragging herself from the bed and toward the shower in hopes that the refreshing steam would infuse some resemblance of humanity with which she could face the day. She paused at the mirror, looking herself over. "At least my hair looks good. The rest of me looks like shit."

Standing under the water as still as a statue, the pounding droplets on her scalp seemed to echo in her stuffy head and ears. She breathed in the steam, felt it creeping up her nose and into her chest. A quick tickle was followed by a couple of sharp coughs, the vapor chasing out the invading gunk from her lungs. Lucie instantly crossed her arms over her breasts, squeezing her ribcage and lungs from the outside. She rubbed her throat and attempted to clear it, which was hurting more than before, and reluctantly accepted her body was under attack. She closed her eyes, fading out to the sounds of the shower and the heartbeat she could hear echoed in her ears. Another coughing spasm was working up, and she knew it was going to be worse than the last.

The water raced down her body in little rivers, traveling from her head to her feet. She shook one leg, assuming the tickle that she had felt on the back of her knee, and then on her ankle, was simply due to the water taking the path of least resistance. With her eyes closed, she was unable to see the red hairs that were making their way down her legs.

Another burning cough sliced through her chest and up her throat, dragging with it gravels of congestion. Her stomach turned, and she gagged, the thick knot of foulness that was creeping up her throat was nearly vomit inducing. She could smell and taste her sulfurous metallic breath with each ragged cough. The bathroom felt like a sauna as she leaned against the shower wall to steady her lightheadedness, dialing back the hot water in preparation for the next wave of coughing she knew would happen any minute. She dreaded the pain, but also welcomed it, knowing that she would be rid of the disgusting mass sitting right at the base of her throat.

Lucie held her chest and coughed, gasping for air in between. She crouched over, the warm water pounding on the back of her neck and shoulders. She coughed until she was certain that her throat was bleeding, but she was unable to move her phlegm adversary past the back of her throat. Then came the inevitable gag that moved the blockage on a scalding wave of bile but not quite far enough. She crammed her fingers into her mouth, desperate for relief, and gagged again. Looking down between her feet, Lucie saw a clump of red hair, matted with sickly yellow congestion circling the drain. Horrified, she felt more hair in her mouth. Crying, and nearly screaming, she raked at her tongue, and loose hairs tangled around her wet fingertips.

She nearly leaped from the shower, sliding on the slick floor to the sink. She grabbed the bottle of mouthwash and filled her mouth, gargling as she cried, trying not to swallow it or choke herself before she could spit it out. Desperate to rid herself of the taste, she swallowed a small sip of it. Like an industrial cleaner going down her throat, the burning rinse pushed down any remnants of the nightmare she had just experienced.

She grabbed her towel, unable to stay in the bathroom a moment longer, and retreated to the bedroom. She stopped dead in her tracks in front of her bed and screamed. Tears flowed down her cheeks, water dripped onto her shoulders and puddled around her feet. Her pillowcase and fitted sheet were covered in long, red hairs.

She crept closer, curiosity overriding shock and fear. The hair was distributed evenly, not in a clump. It almost looked like someone had gotten a haircut and the scraps had been swept up and sprinkled on her bed. She pulled a hair from her pillowcase, feeling the length with her fingertips, dry and brittle. At the end of the damaged strand, a silver root tip. She picked up another, and then more until she had a tiny bouquet of hairs. Each was almost the same length; each had the same amount of silver new growth. The hairs were not cut from their owner, but had fallen out.

Chilled to the core and still dripping wet, Lucie quickly dressed and left the bedroom. She sat on the couch and stared at her bedroom door, huddled under a blanket. Someone other than herself needed to see, needed to validate what she was experiencing was real and not her imagination. She picked up her cell phone and called the one person she could trust to tell her the truth, the one person she swore she would never call again.

The phone rang four times before the voicemail picked up, as she expected.

"I know I said I wouldn't call you again, and I'm sorry. But there is something going on in my apartment, and I'm scared. Can you please come over, just this once? I'm not trying to start anything. I don't have anyone else to call."

An hour later, as Lucie sat holding her phone, the sound of her door unlocking jolted her back into reality. She threw the blanket from her shoulders and rushed to the door. Tiffany still had a key.

"Oh my god, Tiff. Thank you for coming over." Lucie's elation quickly turned to confusion when she made eye contact with the strange woman who walked into her apartment right behind her ex-girlfriend. An awkward silence was immediately present amongst the three women, and for a moment, nobody moved or said a word. "I'm sorry, I wasn't expecting anyone to be with you."

Tiffany quietly scanned the room, her eyes not settling on anything for long. She was tense, tightly squeezing her companion's hand. Lucie had not even considered that asking her to come back to their apartment would be difficult for her, but given how painful their breakup had been, it wasn't surprising that she was behaving strangely. "I should have never got that call. Marissa, I am so sorry I dragged you into this."

"No wait, please! It's nice to meet you, Marissa. I'm Lucie. Thank you both for coming over." Lucie quickly gathered herself to extend a welcome, despite the prick in her heart. She wasn't surprised that Tiffany had already moved on, but seeing it with her own eyes was a different matter. However, her thankfulness to no longer be alone trumped the awkwardness. Both women took a seat on the couch, neither sure how to behave or what to say next. Lucie tried her best to be courteous and to hide her bruised feelings. "Do either of you want a bottle of water or a soda?"

Tiffany bit her lip and shook her head, attempting to speak at risk of breaking into tears.

"I don't know if you saw me the other day at work, Lucie, but I saw you. You were working late, I guess. You cut your hair *and* went blue. I would have never imagined you'd do that. You looked really good."

"Oh yeah, I just had it done a couple of days ago. I'm sorry, I haven't even brushed it today." She ruffled her disheveled hair, discreetly sniffing toward her underarm in the process. With everything going on, she had not even considered showering, not in that bathroom. It was impossible for Tiffany to think she looked good now. "You know how it is, nothing announces *back on the market* like an aqua blue pixie cut." Lucie cringed as she watched her ill-placed attempt at a joke fall flat.

"I don't understand what's going on, Lucie. I got a voicemail… it was just noise. I couldn't leave it alone, so we came over to check things out."

Tiffany's voice cracked and tears welled in her eyes. She caught her breath with a whispery gasp. "Lucie, do you hear me? Are you listening?"

"Yes, Tiff, of course I hear you. I didn't mean to upset you. It's been a strange couple of days is all," she answered as she nervously ran her fingers through her hair again, leaving it flat in some places and sticking out on end in others. She sat down on the nearby ottoman that faced Tiffany and Marissa, pausing for a moment to gather her thoughts. She wanted to reach out to Tiffany, take her trembling hands in hers and kiss them, smell them, but she dared not touch her. "I know this is going to sound crazy before I even start, but please just hear me out. I've started noticing these strange red hairs all over my house. The first one was in my shirt, not so weird, right? Then I found a clump of them in my couch when I was feeling around in the cushions for the remote. And now, they're all in my bed. They're still there, come look."

Tiffany leaned close to Marissa's ear, whispering to her. Finally, they walked into the bedroom and joined her by the bed, examining the evidence that was still scattered across it. Tiffany picked up the tiny bundle Lucie had gathered earlier from her pillow, presenting it to Marissa for investigation.

"Does she have a dog?" Marissa questioned.

"No, she never could have a pet because of allergies."

"See, that's what I was telling you. It's all over it." Lucie proclaimed as Marissa looked over Tiffany's shoulder, even more disarmed than she had been in the living room.

"There was more. I kept it. It all matches." Lucie searched over every surface, but to her frustration, she could not locate the folded squares of toilet paper that held the hair from her shirt and the tangle from the couch. Tiffany seemed bothered by her prowling, so she stopped and rejoined them at the bed. "I can't find them now, but they were all the same. I don't know anyone with this hair color. Tiff, you know that."

"So how did it get everywhere?" Marissa questioned, obviously harboring some doubt.

"I don't know." Tiffany wiped her hands on her jeans as if they were dirty, and crossed her arms around her waist. "It doesn't look like hers."

"Where are they coming from?"

"I don't know, Marissa. That's the thing. None of this makes sense."

The three women walked around the room, looking at the ceiling, the floor, the bed, trying to figure out a connection. Tiffany noticed a strip of snapshots from a photo booth pressed into the crack between the dresser mirror's glass and frame. She took the photographs and placed them in her purse.

"Yeah...sure. You can have that." The only thing stranger than what she had been experiencing was Tiffany's behavior.

They moved out from the bedroom and through the rest of the house. When they entered the kitchen, Lucie instantly felt embarrassed. The whole area was no less than three weeks overdue for a cleaning. The sink was full, mostly dirty cereal bowls filled with murky water that released a foul odor as they passed. The trash was overflowing, fast food cups spilling onto the floor. They quickly left the room and returned to the living room.

Tiffany looked around and rubbed her face, her gaze settling on Lucie, but improperly. Lucie realized that her former love could no longer bring herself to look her in the eye.

"Lucie, I ... I can't keep going on like this. This isn't going to help."

"I don't understand."

"A priest, or a therapist, hell maybe even an exorcist would know what to do, but I don't. I just know that I need to let go. I'm trying to. We tried, Lucie, but we weren't meant to be. We both have to accept that."

"That's not what this is." Lucie rebounded, embarrassed and hurt.

"She was at the salon just a couple of days ago, getting all her hair cut off and then magically there's hair all over her house. How are we not supposed to think this is connected, some sick joke." Marissa was more than skeptical. She was calling Lucie a liar. "This was just a last ditch effort at getting attention, to make you feel guilty for something that's not your fault."

"It's not my hair, Tiff. It's red. I don't have red hair. The roots, you can see silver roots. My hair isn't gray, not my whole head anyway." Tiffany shook her head, not accepting any of her reasoning. Marissa took her hand in hers, seeing she was getting upset. "Tiff, it was down my throat. I was choking on it in the shower this morning. I can't fake that, and why would I if I could?"

"Lucie, I don't understand what's happening, but I'm leaving now." They started for the door, leaving Lucie in the middle of her defense.

"Wait, please. Don't leave me here alone. I'm scared." She followed, hoping to stop them. Being alone in her apartment after dark was the last thing she wanted. Something bizarre was happening to her, and there was nobody to help her. She could see that her words had hit home by the grimace on Tiffany's face, that she still felt *something* for her.

"Bye, Lucie." She led Marissa through the door and out into the hallway.

"Please, Tiff. Both of you can stay, just please don't go."

Tears filled Tiffany's eyes and she pursed her lips, tightening her face to hold them in. "Please, let this be the end of it. I can't do this again. I won't."

Lucie watched them disappear at the end of the hall. She wanted to chase after them, leave with them. Instead, she closed the door and faced her apartment, as she would the coming night, alone.

The rest of the night was spent binge watching episode after episode of *The Joy of Painting*. The beautiful scenes and Bob Ross' gentle tone was relaxing, and for a few minutes, she forgot how terrified she was and how much it had hurt to see Tiffany with another woman. An hour past her bedtime, she turned off the light and wrapped herself in the blanket, as though the plush cocoon could protect her. She left the television on, sacrificing her data plan to keep the friendly voice streaming quietly in the background. She gave a final look at her closed bedroom door and covered up her head.

Happy trees, she thought to herself. *Happy trees.*

* * *

Overheated and sweaty, Lucie pulled the blanket off her head. Her T-shirt stuck to her skin, and she could feel dampness at the nape of her neck and trickling down her scalp. Her show had stopped streaming due to inactivity, and the TV had faded to a darkened screen. She rubbed her face, shifting on the pleather couch to find a position that was cool and comfortable. The light from the screen, even though it was muted, was irritating to her eyes, but she didn't want to be in the dark totally.

A deep, wet cough echoed through the silent apartment.

Lucie was shocked so completely that her entire body jerked like she had touched a live electric wire. Living in an apartment meant learning to be comfortable with the sounds of other people around her. Footsteps, slamming doors, coughing, sneezing, even loud sex were all things that she had learned to deal with, but this was different. This cough was loud, not muffled by the walls from next door, the floors from below, or the ceiling from above. This spongy, mucus-soaked cough was from inside her apartment, from inside her bedroom.

She held her breath, hoping that she would not hear anything else, but simultaneously straining to hear even the slightest hint of sound. She could hear nothing but sounds of life from outside, four floors beneath her at street level. The noise from a never ending river of vehicles, highlighted by the occasional cry of an emergency siren was constantly in the background of her life. Louder than the ambient roar, but only just, she could hear breathing, labored and muffled from behind her bedroom door. She wasn't dreaming. She didn't imagine it. It was happening. It was real. And she was alone, but unfortunately, not entirely alone.

Another cough, so loud and deep it was just as painful to hear it as well as terrifying. Lucie felt her strength drain out of her body and soak into the couch. She wanted to cry, to scream out for help, but that would alert them. If she made any noise, even breathed too loudly, whoever or whatever was in her apartment would know she had heard them. They would be aware of her.

Slowly she pulled the blanket back over her head, leaving the edge up just high enough that she could partially see the bedroom door. She heard the bed creak, the sound it always made when she got up every morning, and covered her mouth with her hands. Tears raced down her cheeks, leaking behind the gaps in her fingers. A moment of silence, and then she heard the bedroom doorknob rattle, attempting to open. Lucie's entire body was trembling, wrapped in her blanket cocoon like a caterpillar in metamorphosis, beyond her control.

The door slowly opened, but stopped halfway. Passing through the gap, and halfway through the door, the figure of an emaciated, elderly woman stood silent and whole before her. She was as solid as Lucie, or any inanimate object in the apartment, despite having just walked through the bedroom door. She looked frail, exhausted, and ill. Her nightgown hung loosely on her bony frame; her shoulders rounded, and her back hunched over. The apparition did not seem to notice Lucie's existence as she shuffled toward the bathroom, almost dragging her bare feet, wheezing and coughing.

It took every ounce of courage Lucie could summon not to bolt toward the door and run screaming down the hallway. Part of her wanted to, but most of her was too terrified to consider it. She did not want to draw attention to herself. She did not want *her* to know she was there. Her mind raced with a thousand questions. Who was she? Why did she linger in her apartment? Why had she only made herself known now? Why didn't she materialize when Tiffany lived there?

Her mind raced so quickly, overwhelmed with processing what she had experienced that a few minutes passed before she realized that the energy in the room had changed and she could no longer hear the dreadful wheezing. The woman had disappeared as completely as she had appeared in the first place. Lucie eventually sat up and huddled into the corner of the couch, still wrapped in her blanket with wide eyes. She did the only thing she could do. She clicked play on the next episode of *The Joy of Painting*, hoping that the happy, hippie painter's positive vibes would somehow leak out into the area and keep her unwanted houseguest at bay.

* * *

The dawn rose just like any day, as though the sun was unaware of what Lucie had experienced. She watched the bars of light lengthen across the floor as the sun rose higher in the sky. Her eyes hurt, and her neck was sore. As though protected by the power of the sun, Lucie slid from under her blanket and walked as quietly as she could toward the bathroom. It was empty, and nothing had been moved or seemed out of place. It was as though what she had experienced, what she knew she had seen with her own two, sober eyes, had not happened at all. But she knew better, and she knew if there were anyone in the entire apartment building who knew the identity of the spirit, it would be Edith. Lucie grabbed a hoodie from the back of the couch and set out in search of answers.

Notoriously known as the resident busybody, Edith had lived in the same apartment for eighteen years. She had outlasted an unknown number of surrounding residents, as well as three management companies, and two building name changes. The only thing living that was older than Edith on the entire property was the stately cedar tree that grew at the front of the building. If anyone knew who the spirit in her apartment might be, and what she might want, it would be Edith. Nobody came or went without passing under her eye, no event unnoticed. As much as Lucie hated to admit it, she needed Edith's help.

Lucie knocked on Edith's door and crammed her hands into the kangaroo pouch on her hoodie. The night's events had left her chilled to the bone, unable to warm up or fully recover. She had only heard the cough twice, but her mind had replayed it a thousand times. She constantly returned to the memory of watching the otherworldly figure drag past her and disappear into the bathroom. She was so frail, so obviously exhausted, that despite her terror, she felt pity for her.

Suddenly the door popped open, overextending the length of the security chain with a jerk, and Edith's wrinkled countenance filled the gap. Lucie's heart leaped out of her chest. She watched Edith's expression change from one of annoyance to morbid curiosity, surprised by her frazzled response.

"Dear god, what happened to you?"

"Can I come in for a minute?"

The door closed long enough for Edith's, shaking, knobby hand to unlock the chain and then opened again. Once Lucie was inside, she closed and locked the door behind them.

Edith's apartment was a time capsule of the 1970s. The sofa, drapes, rugs, and wall art, had all been carefully selected on a color chart, ranging from brownish rust up to a warm goldenrod yellow. The air smelled of dry-rotting, sunbaked polyester and mentholated chest salve. Edith studied her, her hands on her wide, drooping hips, her head gently nodding as she tried to figure Lucie out.

"Would you care for a cup of coffee?" she extended the gesture, not knowing what else to do with her. "It's not that fancy, eight dollars a cup stuff you brew, but it's hot."

"Yes, thank you. That would be nice." The sarcasm in her voice had not gone unnoticed, but Lucie had expected as much. She watched as Edith waddled to the kitchen and groaned as she reached up to eye level to retrieve coffee cups.

"I saw Tiffany yesterday," she called as she eyeballed the mugs for any spots, wiping them both with a dishcloth. "I haven't seen her in ages. Has she been out of town?"

"Tiffany moved out six months ago, Edith." There was the stab Lucie had been waiting for. "You watched us load her stuff into the moving van from your window."

"Oh yeah, that's right." She dodged, playing the age card horribly, but no less effectively. After a few more minutes and a couple more groans added in to emphasize her point, Edith returned with two cups of coffee, handing her a ceramic mug that had been molded in the shape of an owl, brown and yellow, with large judgmental, soulless eyes. "My old brain isn't what it used to be, you know."

"How much do you know about the people who have lived in my apartment?" Lucie changed the subject abruptly.

"Some, " her seemingly genuine response shocked Lucie."What do you want to know?"

"Who lived there before I moved in?"

"Well before you, there was a young couple there, a man and woman," Edith specified, "but they only stayed a couple of months."

"Do you know why they left?"

"Not really, didn't have much to say to anyone. One day they were both here, and then it was just the husband. Never saw the missus again, not even when they were moving out." Edith scratched at a long white hair growing from her chin as she spoke. "They were looking to have kids, so I just figured they moved to a larger place, someplace with a yard, maybe closer to family."

"Do you know who lived there before them?"

"Oh yes, I knew her quite well," Lucie thought she saw a glimmer of compassion in Edith's eyes as she recalled her friend. "Her name was Claudia, poor dear. At the end, she suffered so much."

Lucie's mind raced with a thousand questions, certain that Edith held the answers to all of them and more, but she refrained. That was Edith's friend, not just some vague idea of a person. She had no way of knowing if the apparition she had witnessed was Claudia or someone else, but either way, she wanted to proceed respectfully.

"What happened to her?"

"Cancer in her lungs, but it was all over her before she passed. They tried that chemo stuff on her, but it didn't do anything but make her sicker and lose all her hair."

Lucie felt her stomach drop to her toes. She thought of her bed, covered in hair that had fallen out. Her blood ran cold in her veins, the coffee cooling in her hands.

"Why do you ask?"

"I... I was just wondering."

"You didn't come here just to have a cup of coffee with me. What's the *real* reason you're here?" Edith stated, straightforward. She was too old to fall for such a shallow cover, and Lucie knew it.

"I saw something, and I can't explain it."

"What did you see?"

Lucie swallowed another hard drink of the strong black coffee that now seemed to be eating a hole out in her stomach. She didn't know how to best word it, how to avoid hurting Edith's feelings, so she simply started talking, rambling.

"I woke up yesterday, and my bed was covered in red hair. Last night,

I saw an elderly lady. She looked sick, like really sick. She had a really bad cough and was just skin and bones. I saw her walk *through* my bedroom door and into the bathroom, as solid and real as you and me, and then just disappear."

"You saw Claudia?"

"I don't know, maybe. It could have been. I don't know." She tripped over her words, fearing her attempts at tact had failed. Edith pulled herself up, groaning as her knees straightened out and shuffled to the bookshelf. She retrieved a gold picture frame and handed it to Lucie.

"That's Claudia and me at a Christmas luncheon a few years before she got sick."

Lucie stared at the woman's face, scarcely able to breathe. The woman she had seen in her apartment was an emaciated version of this woman, a shadow of her.

"It's her, isn't it?" Edith knew the truth, regardless of Lucie's response, which was eventually a silent nod in agreement. She couldn't take her eyes from the picture, could not even blink. Edith could see the young woman's heart beating through her thick sweatshirt. "Listen to me, dear. You have nothing to worry about from Claudia."

Lucie looked up, her face streaked with tears.

"She loved that apartment. She was so happy there, right up until the end. I think she would have liked you. Maybe liked you better without the blue hair, but still," Edith teased, possibly to help ease Lucie's nerves but perhaps not. Lucie chose to accept it as a positive with a halfhearted laugh and a sniff.

"Thank you, Edith. I really appreciate that."

The old woman nodded, looking out into the invisible distance. "So if you see her again, tell her I said hello, and she still owes me five dollars."

The air inside Lucie's apartment felt lighter when she returned. After speaking with Edith, and learning all she had about Claudia was encouraging. If this poor woman loved her apartment that much, if she had truly been so happy there, she didn't see why they couldn't find a way to coexist. Perhaps with time, her appearance would change to reflect the happier times spent there, instead of its unfortunate end. It didn't seem like such an abstract idea to Lucie, especially when she was already beginning to think of her supernatural houseguest as some sort of roommate. There was no reason why they both could not be happy there.

"Claudia," she whispered, wondering how loud she should speak for a ghost to hear her. Was she always there, invisible like the oxygen she knew filled the room, or did she come and go? Was there some portal, a place where her apartment was linked to the other side? Maybe their unusual arrangement would provide some insight into the mysteries of life after death. "I don't know if you can hear me, but if you can, I wanted you to know that Edith told me all about you. And I want you to know that I'm glad you're here. I'm glad this apartment still makes you happy, and you can stay here as long as you like."

Lucie looked around at the silent emptiness, the traffic outside the only sound she could hear. It felt like a burden had been lifted from her, like the pressure in the room had dissipated. She took it as a good sign that Claudia was happy with her.

* * *

Lucie woke for the first time in bed after having discovered it covered in Claudia's hair. After three nights of sleeping on the couch, a good night's rest had been long overdue. She stretched lazily, unconcerned that she had slept until nearly 11 o' clock. She was just happy not to be covered in her dead roommate's hair.

Stepping out of the bedroom, and briefly into the living room on her way to the bathroom, Lucie did a double take. The living room door was standing open, the curtains were gone, and the blinds pulled up to the top of the windows. The couch, coffee table, television, bookshelf, nearly everything in the living room had been removed.

"What the hell," she doubled back into the bedroom to grab her cell phone off the nightstand. Before she could take one step back into the room, Claudia appeared before her. She was solid, human-like. Her gray skin and sunken eye sockets were accentuated by the twigs of stringy red hair that still clung to her scalp. With unexpected strength, Claudia shoved Lucie backward.

"Get out! This is my house," she growled, a wheeze nearly overtaking her voice.

"Claudia, it's okay. I live here, too." Lucie backpedaled away from the angry spirit. She was more concerned with calming Claudia's wrath than whatever had happened to the furniture. Was that why the door was still standing open? Had the thieves run out in terror before they could take the rest?

"What have you done with my things?" she roared, her voice stronger than Lucie had believed possible. She shuffled toward her, just as quickly as Lucie could move backward.

"Nothing, this was my stuff. I don't know who took it."

"Who are you? Why are you here?" It was clear Claudia was reacting more to her presence than her words.

"Wait!" Lucie sprang to her feet. "Please, just wait a minute. Edith will be able to explain everything."

"Edith?" She could tell that her friend's name was still familiar to her, despite the years since her death. She stopped chasing her, looking around the apartment as though she were lost or confused.

"Yes, Edith from next door." She made a break for the door. "Wait right there."

Lucie raced down the hall at top speed, missing furniture now lower on her list of priorities. With Edith's help, maybe Claudia would be able to move on. Maybe the apartment being in such a state of confusion had made her realize that nothing was as she believed it to be. She stopped at Edith's door and knocked, loudly and quickly. Hopefully her hard of hearing neighbor would be sitting in the living room and not in the kitchen or worse, in the bathroom. If she delayed, the opportune moment to connect with Claudia might pass, and there was no way of knowing how long it would be before it happened again.

Edith yanked the door open with a huff, her wrinkles accentuating the fact that her skin was at least one size too big for her face.

"Why the hell are you beating my door down?"

"It's Claudia; she's upset." Lucie shuffled back and forth, impatiently waiting for Edith to unlock the safety chain. She opened it just enough for her to squeeze through. "Someone broke into my apartment and stole all my stuff. Claudia thinks it's hers and thinks I took it. Can I use your phone? I need to call the police. I can't get past Claudia to get my cell phone."

"Ugh, you young ones really wear me out, can never read the writing on the damn wall." Edith shuffled over to her favorite chair and sat down with a flop, her feet bouncing off the floor.

"What do you mean?" Lucie recoiled, insulted by her lack of concern.

"Have a seat, kid. We need to have a talk, and I would rather you sit down than fall down."

"Edith, I don't think you understand." She spoke slowly as if she was explaining the facts out to a child. "Someone broke into my apartment while I was sleeping and stole my stuff. Claudia is losing her mind because she thinks *I* took *her* stuff. I don't need to sit down. I need help."

"Okay, there's no good way to say this, so I'm just going to say it. Honey, you're dead."

"No, Edith. I'm not dead. Claudia is dead. Are you feeling okay?"

"Don't you remember anything, kid? Every time, it's always the same thing with you young ones. You off yourself or you crash your little smart car to smithereens, and then you come back here like nothing happened. You walk around lost for a few days and then when you start to notice the others, you lose your shit like you're the one that's being haunted. If anyone should be running around here screaming, it's me."

Edith's apartment spun around Lucie in a swirl of yellow and dark wood veneer. Her head felt light, her face hot. She realized she could not remember how many days had passed since she had last gone to work. When had she last eaten? The last thing she could remember was the last day she was at work. Double shift. The table under the light of the streetlamp. Tiffany. Too much to drink. Can't sleep. Sleeping pills in the bathroom cabinet.

"No, you're wrong. I found Claudia's hair in my bed. I talked to Tiffany. I'm talking to you now. I'm *not* dead."

"Think back to Tiffany's visit. Did she talk to you or *at* you? Did she answer a direct question, make eye contact?"

Tiffany and Marissa's visit flashed through her mind. She had not answered her call or understood her voicemail, and didn't knock when she arrived. She had not touched her or looked her in the eye, or even ask if she could have the strip of pictures from the mirror. She didn't think much about it at the time. The situation was already so strange, but Marissa had not even acknowledged her presence. Why would Tiffany bring her there in the first place? It wasn't like her to strike out in an attempt to hurt her. Tiffany had *never* tried to hurt her. She would never have brought Marissa into her home knowing she would be there. Tiffany knew she would not be there. She knew she was dead. Lucie grabbed the sides of her head, crumbling down into a ball under the weight of Edith's words. It was too much; she could not accept it. She would not accept it.

"I didn't mean to... I don't think... This can't be happening. I don't want to die."

"Not die, honey. Dead. Past tense."

Lucie broke into wailing sobs, balling up on Edith's couch. She wanted her to be wrong. She wanted to wake up from her nightmare. She wanted to go back in time, back to the day she cut her hair, passing smiling faces on the street.

"Okay, so I can see you're not taking this very well. So let me try to explain to you in a way your little hipster brain might understand. Back in the day, we had boxes that sat on our TVs, and you could tune in channels that you didn't pay for. Sometimes the picture was just scrambled, blended with the channel beside it. It was right there, but both pictures would overlap, and you couldn't make any sense out of either one. That's what's happening with you and Claudia. You see, she can't accept it either, that's she's dead, and that's not her apartment anymore, and neither can you, so your channels are scrambled together. She's watching pieces of your show, and you're seeing pieces of hers."

"What about you then? How come you can see me and Tiffany couldn't?"

"Well sometimes, if you were really careful, you could tune your TV just right, and you could see that scrambled channel. Your show or movie would be just as clear as if you were meant to see, maybe even get to watch something your parents didn't want you to see. Something you weren't *supposed* to see. Do you think it's an accident that you spirits keep showing up at my door? Do you think I like living in eternal 1975? No, I'm sick of yellow, but I keep it the same because it's familiar to your little ghost brains. Everything around here changes but me and this apartment. That's what brings you back here to me instead of roaming the halls, scaring kids, and aggravating my neighbor's little Chihuahua. God, it pisses me off when you guys do that, get that big rat to yapping. You need to tell the others to cut that shit out. I'm too old for all that noise."

"What do I do now? How do I move on? Everything I love is here. There's nobody waiting for me." She wiped her face on her sleeves, her mind beginning to accept what her heart already knew.

"For starters, you've got to let go of Tiffany. You have to accept that she's alive and you're dead, by your own doings." She pointed her finger at her, accenting her words in a no-nonsense type of way. Lucie felt like she was being scolded by a parent again. "You have to settle up with yourself on that, nothing I can say to help you there. But what I can tell you is that you have to cut ties, kid. This life's not for you anymore."

"What if I can't?"

"Then you'll stay here, or wherever it is that you decide to haunt, but don't even consider trying to find Tiffany. Even if you do, that will just make you and her miserable. You understand? You leave that girl alone. Let her live."

"Can I stay here?"

"Hell no. I'm eighty-four-years-old. I might die in my sleep tonight, and I don't want the first thing I see to be you moping around in my apartment, get *my* ghost brain all confused like yours." Edith peered down her bifocals that sat on the end of her nose, inspecting the buttons on her TV remote. "Now get on out of here. My soaps come on in fifteen minutes."

* * *

Lucie walked slowly back to her apartment, unsure of what to do next. How could everything be so different and still look the same? The door to her apartment was still open and as she turned to walk in, she could see moving men carrying her mattress toward the door. Unlike willfully using her cell phone or holding Edith's coffee cup, she simply sighed and allowed it to pass right through her, effortlessly, like she wasn't even there. Like most of the living, they could not see her, but a shimmer of warmth on her side and arm from one of the men's hands passing through her presence highlighted the interaction of the living world and spirit world.

The energy of his life was electric and hot, and she wondered what he had felt, or if he had felt anything at all. Had he experienced the infamous "cold spot" that all the paranormal researchers had claimed to be the presence of a spirit? As she walked toward the window, standing in the empty room, Claudia shuffled up beside her. The paranormal was normal now. Death was now life. As she looked out into the bright sun, she could still feel the warmth through the glass. The river of vehicles still flowed. The sirens still called out. Her life had ended, but life had not. It all still sounded the same, looked the same, everything but her.

BAD RELIGION

BY LAURENCIA HOFFMAN

MELINA COLLINS TILTED HER HEAD as she looked at her reflection in the mirror. Her lipstick was smeared and her hair was a disaster. She looked more like a prostitute than a lady, but that was bound to happen when she fed. Vampires couldn't help the mess they left— blood tended to spray, pour and pool wherever it pleased. If she was home then she would have to do the clean-up herself, but since she hadn't had a proper home in a very long time, this particular mess would be left for the hotel to sort out.

She fixed her appearance and then turned to the company in the room. One was dead; that was unavoidable. What kind of vampire would she be if she picked up a couple and didn't eat at least one of them?

The man was sprawled on the bed, his dull eyes wide open. Melina had tried to drain him as cleanly as possible, but blood had still oozed onto the sheets. The woman was beside him, her knees pulled up to her chest.

More often than not, she had a soft spot for women and children. The older she got, the more compassion she felt for them. Men, however, were not given the same courtesy. It didn't matter if the men were genuinely good people— she had been hurt by too many to trust any of them. If she saw anyone of the opposite gender, she saw red. She couldn't be objective when she was blinded by hatred.

"Relax," she told the woman. "I'm not going to kill you. Your boyfriend was enough to satisfy my hunger."

The woman was no threat to her, so Melina grabbed her handbag and left the hotel room. On her way back to her antique shop, she made a stop— the same stop she made every day. The Pulse Nightclub was owned by her estranged fledgling. She had been tempted to enter the building many times, but when she tried to imagine what she would say to him, and what she would do, she couldn't think of a damn thing. Clearly, she was not yet ready to face him, nor to forgive him.

"Nope," she said with a sigh. "Not today."

Besides, she gained a little bit of satisfaction knowing that she was so close in proximity, but he hadn't the slightest idea.

She yawned, more so out of boredom than exhaustion, and continued down the sidewalk. Driving was almost useless at this time of day in this part of town. Walking wouldn't kill her. It might make her hungrier though, so a few miles down the road, she walked into the bar where she found most of her victims. It didn't take much convincing for the man to agree to take her back to his place, but that wasn't out of the ordinary– in her experience, men didn't need much convincing.

To her surprise, he directed her to a limo, and she gave him a once-over. He didn't look particularly rich. What kind of person went around in a limo picking up women at a bar? Maybe he was a little too big for his britches. She didn't want to get involved with someone well-off; she needed to remain low-key, so her victims couldn't be anyone of importance.

"Do you give the royal treatment to every woman you meet?"

"No," he assured her with a smile and a shake of his head. "I own a limousine business. But it doesn't hurt when I do have a date."

He didn't seem too impressive. She was a vampire, so what harm could he do to her? Deciding to take the risk, she got into the limo.

"I hope you're a wine drinker." He was eager to offer a glass of red liquid.

"Honey, I'll drink anything." She took the glass from him and gulped it down. Business wasn't exactly booming, so alcohol wasn't on her list of priorities. Like most humans who were low-income, the bills came first. She relied on the kindness of strangers to be able to indulge in her vices.

As she set the glass down and stared at her company, she smacked her lips together. Something about that wine didn't taste quite right. It wasn't spoiled or sour, but it left a bad taste in her mouth. She started to feel like she was going to be sick, but vampires didn't get sick.

"What was in that drink?"

The man was no longer smiling. His friendly demeanor had changed. "Dead man's blood. Have you had it before?"

It had been forced down her sire's throat, but she had been lucky enough never to have experienced its unpleasantness– until now. "Can't say that I have." She didn't want to give him the satisfaction of knowing that she was afraid, but she was already feeling the effects of the bad blood. She was nauseous, her hands were getting clammy and her energy was fading. She was becoming weaker by the second.

Though she knew it was a risk, she lunged for the door and managed to open it, but the man grabbed her by the waist and threw her across the limo like a rag-doll. The fucking prick was going to pay dearly for that one.

She heard the clicking sound of the doors locking automatically and the stranger sat back comfortably in his seat– watching as her eyelids fluttered. She felt so hazy. "What the hell do you want from me?"

"To save you, of course."

Melina furrowed her brow, but she didn't have time to argue. Though she didn't think she'd lost consciousness, she was in a complete daze and couldn't remember how she'd gotten from the car to the room she was in now.

It was dark, save for a few candles near the walls. She swallowed hard and blinked rapidly as she tried to get her bearings. The more she came to, the more she felt the burning of her wrists and feet. She was sitting on a cold stone floor, chained to a wall.

"Hello?" she called out. "Where am I? What is this place?"

It was times like these when she really wished she had friends. Then they would be there to rescue her when such situations arose. But no one knew who she was or that she was missing; no one cared. And she was too stubborn to call for her fledgling. She hadn't called for him the last time she'd been tortured, so why should now be any different?

A man who didn't look much older than fifty entered the room. It wasn't the same man who had talked her into the limo, but they were probably around the same age. Apparently, older people were assholes. After tonight's fiasco, she would start looking for much, much younger dates. They would be too stupid to try and kidnap her.

"What do you want?" she asked the man she assumed to be her captor.

He took another step forward, just enough for her to see that he was dressed as a priest. What kind of holy man kidnapped people?

"Who the fuck are you?" she demanded. "What the fuck is this?"

He took in a deep breath and let it out slowly as his gaze wandered over her. "You attacked my daughter and murdered her companion."

"You mean her booty-call?" She rolled her eyes; there was no point in showing any respect or politeness to this idiot. "Well, that's the last time I'll ever try to be nice to someone."

The priest pointed to her which she thought was a silly action; she knew very well that he was addressing her. "I saw the marks on your neck. I know what you are."

"Congratulations. Would you like a medal?"

"No. I don't want recognition of any kind."

"Then what do you want?" She tugged on her chains and it made her skin sizzle. Grimacing, she looked back at him. "I'm sure there's a reason for all this."

The priest, his stance casual and calm– as if holding a vampire hostage was a perfectly normal thing to do– raised his hand, and in it was a Bible. "I'm going to perform an exorcism."

A fucking what? "Excuse me? Are you fucking mental?" She had a difficult time believing that he was serious, but then she remembered how thick-headed some religious people could be. And she laughed. "You can't pray the evil away, Father. This is what I am. Nothing you do can change that. You'll just have to kill me." Not that she wanted to die, but that might be better than having to sit in this dank basement for God knew how long.

He clicked his tongue. "That is a sin."

He had to be joking. Was he taking himself seriously? Because she sure wasn't– he was being hypocritical. What was with the double-standards? "But kidnapping someone is a-okay in God's book, huh?"

"If I'm doing his work, then yes." He seemed unaffected by her laughter; he was just as calm as he'd been when he walked in. "I'm going to expel the monster from your body and save your soul."

"I don't want to be saved. You can't expel anything from me. I *am* the monster." Still, his expression was unchanged, and it bothered her. She couldn't read him, couldn't figure out what he was going to do to her or what his end game really was. Gritting her teeth and pursing her lips, she asked, "What are you going to do?"

Turning his back to her, he walked to the door and placed his hand on the knob. "I intend to keep you here until I'm satisfied that there's nothing more I can do."

Knowing that he would never be able to accomplish what was in his mind, she scoffed and rolled her eyes. "Then I guess I'm in it for the long haul."

He was about to leave the room, but she stopped him. "Wait! Let's say you do, you know, save me and all that. Does that mean you'll let me live?" She wanted to see just what his intentions were and what she might be able to get away with.

For the first time, he smiled, and it sent chills down her spine. "Of course not, my child. I intend to kill you either way."

Growling as he exited the room, she tugged on her restraints. "I'm not your child, you sick fucker. I'm *God's* child, remember?"

Screaming, clanking, and making as much noise as she could, she gave it her all until her wrists and ankles had been rubbed raw from the silver. It burned like fire on her skin.

"Goddamn you, God! No offense." She looked up at the ceiling as if the man could hear him. "No, you know what, *lots* of offense! I blame you for your crazy fucking follower. If he kills me, I swear to...well, you, that I'd better get a get-into-Heaven-free card!"

* * *

Melina groaned as hunger burned in her stomach. By her count, she'd been there three days. No food, no company, and no indication of what was happening on the other side of that door.

She'd been shouting so much that she'd nearly lost her voice– it was better to save that in case she had a chance to use it. How she wished she had been given a book or something; she needed entertainment. If the priest had intended to kill her with boredom, he was succeeding.

She was about to resign herself to another less-than-restful slumber when the door creaked open. She didn't want to seem too eager for company, but she sat up as much as she could.

"I was beginning to think you'd forgotten about me."

"The world doesn't revolve around you," he said. "I have the church to run, a family to watch over, and other souls to save."

Did that mean that this sick freak had other vampires somewhere in the building? Maybe if she could find them, they could all help each other escape. "Have you come to preach? Do I get my very own show?"

"I'm glad you think this is a joke, but this is my calling and I take it very seriously."

He may have been convinced that he was one of the good guys, but his actions proved otherwise. He couldn't save any evil person by simply praying for their souls, especially not vampires. Words changed nothing.

"Do you even know my name? Do you know who you're saving?"

"Would you like me to know your name?"

"No. But I'd like to know yours."

Now that he came closer to her, he appeared to have a Bible in one hand and a bottle of something in the other. "Very well. Call me Father Matthews."

"Really? I would have thought your name would be Dick. You know, short for Richard? But the nickname would suit you."

Sighing exasperatedly, he opened the bottle and poured it over her head. "Let's see if the holy water cleanses that mouth of yours."

For a moment, she pursed her lips. Then she bit her tongue. She was trying not to laugh, but she couldn't help it. "Is that what that was? Holy water? It kinda smells."

He furrowed his brow. "So it's safe to assume you're unaffected?"

"Of course I am, you moron. Holy water doesn't do anything, not even to normal vampires." That was a slip of the tongue; she didn't want him to know that she differed from the average of the species. "And just for the record, crosses don't hurt us either."

"Then let the word of God burn your ears." Confident in his ability to harm her, he set down the bottle, opened the books, and began spouting verse after verse. When Melina continued to laugh, he turned to the back of the book where he kept pages of other verses– specific to his cause.

He chanted the words for what seemed like hours, his voice rose and he recited the lines with vigor, but all it did was put Melina to sleep.

Angered by her ability to make him feel irrelevant, he pulled a small cross made out of silver from his pocket, pressed it to her forehead and then proceeded to chant again.

Melina screeched as the silver burned her skin. She tried to push Father Matthews away, but it only caused her binds to eat away at her flesh as well. The harder he pushed the cross against her head, the more she screamed and tried to fight him off.

Father Matthews, looking extremely pleased with himself, pulled the cross from her forehead and got to his feet. He was smiling all the while.

Blood from her forehead trailed down her nose and mixed with her tears. "What are you so smug about?"

"You were so certain that I couldn't do anything to move you. And you said that crosses couldn't harm you."

"I'm not crying because your ridiculous chanting got through to me, I'm crying because it fucking hurts! And of course that cross hurt because it was made of silver– which you've clearly discovered is a weakness."

He looked a little disappointed, but it would not deter him from trying again. "Perhaps I chose the wrong prayer to help you."

"Oh my God, I'm not possessed by anything, you goddamn nutcase! An exorcism won't work on me because there's nothing to exorcise!"

"Do not take the Lord's name in vain!" He raised the cross in a threatening manner, his eyes filled with disdain.

Melina couldn't decide whether or not she was afraid of this man, but it was clear that he was unhinged, and that he took pleasure in harming her. Or, at least, he was so desperate to believe he was all-powerful that he couldn't admit defeat. She loathed men on power trips. "Your Lord has done nothing for me. I'll speak of him however I goddamn please."

Apparently, she'd struck a nerve, because Father Matthews stormed out of the room– though it didn't take long for him to return. She recoiled as he came toward her with a mug. He forced her mouth open and poured the liquid down her throat. She choked and gasped; the taste was atrocious– more dead man's blood. And judging by the flavor, that blood had been sitting around for quite some time.

It rendered her practically useless and he was able to unchain her without fearing that she would fight back. He dragged her down a hallway and into a room that smelled even more horrid than the blood had tasted.

She was tied to a metal chair in the center of the room, and thank goodness it wasn't made of silver because it would have hurt like hell. Of course, the clasps he used to keep her hands and feet bound were made of silver, but she was already used to that pain.

The blood was already doing a number on her stomach and now the smell of this room was making it unbearable.

"This is where your Godless life will lead," Father Matthews spat. "Think on your sins and decide if it's worth it."

With a slam f the door, he was gone, and Melina was hit with the aroma of decaying flesh. Though she was afraid to look around the room, she knew that it would be worse if she didn't.

On each side of the wall, there were three people on crucifixes – she assumed that they had all been vampires at one time, but now there were mere skeletons with bits of flesh hanging from the bones. She wanted to vomit, but since the dead man's blood was the only thing she was being fed, she thought it was best to try and remain calm. She didn't want to lose the little nutrition she had.

There was one body that still looked somewhat human, and when its eyes opened, Melina screamed. When the shock wore off, she knew that she needed to pick his brain. It might help her find a way to escape. The more she knew, the less power Father Matthews held over her.

"How long have you been here?"

She had to wait some time before the man on the cross could speak to her. She wondered how long he'd been without food– it was a miracle that he could move or speak at all, but he looked mere days away from death.

"Two months…I think."

Melina heaved a sigh and immediately regretted it– she felt as though she could taste that rotting flesh on her tongue. "And the others?"

"None were alive when I came here."

So the priest liked to tackle one vampire at a time. Did he really think he was changing the world? Perhaps if he was actually saving souls, it would have been worth it. But he was torturing, murdering, and saving no one. "Has Father Matthews said anything to you other than Bible-talk?"

"No," the man croaked. His voice sounded so dry– it must have been agonizing for him to speak, and Melina felt guilty for making him do so. "Day after day, it's all the same. But after he got bored with the torture, he decided to let me starve to death."

Death wasn't an option. She had survived too much to be taken down by a priest– she wouldn't let him have that satisfaction. "Well, I'm getting out of here one way or another. I don't care what he does to me."

"Will you take me with you?"

Although she knew that the vampire who looked like a prune would slow her down, how could she say no? If their positions were reversed, she hoped that someone would have helped her. "If I can."

* * *

Had she fallen asleep again? It was a wonder that she could feel safe enough to sleep in this place, but the tainted blood acted as a sedative. She groaned as her eyelids fluttered open and she was disappointed to see that her situation hadn't changed. But it seemed that someone else's had.

She looked up at the man on the wall, the one who'd been speaking to her. He was a vampire, and it was difficult to tell when they were alive or dead because they didn't have beating hearts, but something told her that he was gone.

Though she felt sorry for his passing, at least now she wouldn't have to worry about factoring him into her escape.

The door opened and Father Matthews's voice rang out through the room, "Are you hungry?"

He'd said it so loudly that it caused her to wince; she felt like she was recovering from a hangover. "That depends on what I'm being served."

"Only the best for Satan's followers."

"Look, I may not follow your God, but it doesn't mean that I follow Satan. Neither of them have done me any good, so I'm neutral."

"What a selfish person you are to expect things from your creator."

Her hands clasped the arms of her chair as he came toward her with what she could only assume was another cup of dead man's blood. "Please, not that again."

Father Matthews paused his actions and smiled. "So you do have manners. I'm impressed." Then, once again, he forced her to open her mouth and drink the blood.

She did her best not to swallow, but it was unavoidable. There was some left in her mouth, so she gathered it and spat in his face. Laughing at the sight of the blood dripping down his cheek, she sat back in her chair.

Father Matthews stood up straight and threw the cup to the floor. He didn't look amused. "I thought you might be willing to cooperate today, but I can see that you're going to need a little more convincing."

He waited until the blood had taken the fight out of her, and then he unlocked her chains and dragged her to the door. She had a difficult time seeing anything except blurs, but she could smell him, and while he was distracted she took a bite out of his leg. She tore into his flesh as much as she could through his clothes and he yelped– trying to kick her off.

When she showed no signs of releasing him, he reached over to the wall where there was an assortment of stakes and plunged one into Melina's shoulder. She screamed and let go of his ankle before falling to the floor. The stake was made of silver. Blood trickled down her back and collarbone. She was certain that this was the end, that he would use the stake and stab her through the heart or the head.

But he simply continued with what he'd been trying to do before she'd attacked him. With two other stakes in one hand, he dragged her by her neck up to her feet and thrust her against the door.

He took one of her hands, placed it above her head, and with all the strength he could muster, he shoved a stake through it. Melina cried out in agony as the silver went through her delicate skin almost as a knife would through butter. She barely had time to process the pain before he forced her other hand next to the first and pushed the second stake through that one.

How could no one hear her screams? She wasn't being quiet– anyone within a mile should have heard her at the very least. Had the walls been soundproofed? Or were the other occupants in this place simply ignoring her? She had a hard time believing that Father Matthews was doing this alone.

Taking a deep breath as he stepped backward, he gave a small nod, admiring his work. "Perhaps now you will listen to reason."

With blood dripping down her arms and tears streaming down her face, she tried to look at him through her mangled hair. "You think that by hurting me I'll become more receptive? You're insane! How can you do such things and still call yourself a man of God?"

"I never hurt real people, my dear. Only monsters."

"Monsters?" Through her pain, she still managed to see the humor, and laugh. "You think that you're good and I'm evil? Didn't God create me in his image? I thought we were all God's children. He loves and forgives us, doesn't he?"

"Yes," he answered with a firm nod. "He forgives those who repent. Are you sorry for your sins?"

After everything he'd done to her, he expected her to ask for forgiveness? To repent for *her* sins? She would never ask for anything from a man like him. He was no more in touch with God than she was. "No, I'm not sorry. This is what your God made me."

Furrowing his brow, he took a step closer to her, now with a limp. "What good does it do for you to take vengeance on the innocent?"

"*I* was innocent! No one showed me mercy, especially not your God. Why should I show any sympathy for mankind when it hasn't done the same for me?"

He stared at her in contemplation. As was his usual source for answers, he pulled a small Bible from his pocket and opened it, but he couldn't seem to read from it. Father Matthews stared at the pages for a long time before he closed the book, put it away, and turned his attention back to her. "You are truly lost, my child. I cannot help you."

Melina gritted her teeth. If he had given up on her, did that mean that he would leave her in this room as he'd left the other vampires? "What does that mean?"

She wanted him to tell her exactly what would happen to her, but he did a far crueler thing. He opened the door– the one she was now attached to –and closed it with a thud. He left without saying a word, leaving her imagination to conjure up whatever fate he was condemning her to.

Her entire body was shaking, not just from the pain, but with anger. She was cold from the loss of blood, nauseous from the tainted food, and weak from being drugged, starved, and tortured.

But she would not resign herself to death. Not yet.

"You...goddamn, motherfucking cocksucker! I'm going to tear you limb from limb if it's the last thing I do!"

It took a while for her to calm down, but the burning, aching in her palms made her stop struggling. She thought that she might have been able to wriggle free, but it wasn't working. So what was she going to do now– how was she going to get away?

Father Matthews had given up on her. He wanted nothing to do with her. But did that mean that he would never visit this room again? If he really wanted to help her, to save her poor soul, how could he give up on her so quickly?

There had to be a way to coax him back. If she could make him believe that she was sorry then maybe he would come into the room again. All she had to do was convince him to let her down, even if it was to put her out of her misery. And that was when she would strike.

So she waited what she considered to be an ample amount of time to make it believable. Two days. Anything less and it would just be stupid. Anything more and she would be too weak to do anything.

She cried and screamed; she begged to speak with him. There were no guarantees that anyone would even hear her, but someone must have been nearby.

After almost a full day of shouting for attention, she finally heard footsteps coming toward the door.

"I-I have to talk to you," she said in a pleading tone. "If I'm going to die then I have to confess. Surely you can give me that courtesy."

It was quiet. Too quiet. She thought that whoever was outside the door had abandoned her, but then the glorious sound of the clicking lock filled her ears.

The door swung open and her along with it. She had been fake-crying for hours. She was exhausted and dehydrated, but she still managed to produce tears.

Father Matthews closed the door and stared up at her. "I thought you had forsaken God."

"I thought so too," she said with a quivering lip. "But if I'm going to die then I should make my peace with Him."

He was hesitant to trust her– she could see it in his eyes –but she hoped that his superiority complex won out. "God speaks to me. If you want to talk to Him, you can go through me."

She took a deep, unnecessary breath, and squeezed as many tears from her eyes as she could. "I've done so many terrible things, hurt so many people…I know that it was wrong, but I couldn't help myself. Can there be redemption for people like me?"

"Of course," he said with hope in his voice. "God forgives all who repent."

This would be a hard pill to swallow. She didn't want to submit, but if she didn't, it would cost her her life. So she lied through her teeth. "I beg forgiveness…from you and from God. I want for all my sins to be washed away."

Father Matthews stared at her in awe, and strangely, with pride. She couldn't wait to wipe that look off his face. It took some effort, but he pulled the stakes from her hands, and with a scream, she fell to the floor.

"There, there, my child. I knew you'd come 'round."

She was shaking terribly. She had felt pain before, but this was the worst state her hands had ever been in. "Will I be allowed to enter the kingdom of Heaven now?"

"I will make you no promises. I can only try."

He pulled his cross and Bible from his pocket, but before he could begin his usual schpeel, Melina lunged at him. She cupped her hand over his mouth to muffle his screams, and then she plunged her other hand into his abdomen and tore out the biggest amount of skin and organs as she could. Part of his intestines were hanging out of his body, and she was tempted to reach for his spine next, but was worried that it might kill him. She didn't want him to die before she'd said her piece. "Your faith has blinded you. Where is your common sense?"

"You will be punished," he cried as he writhed beneath her, no doubt in excruciating pain. "God will give me justice!"

A few days ago she might have laughed, but she was too pissed off to find any of this humorous. "For a man claiming to be a pure Christian, and a good man, you are far from either of those things. You kidnap living beings, torture and murder them!"

"You're dead!"

"We are *un*dead! And you were so desperate to believe that you had power over me that you let your guard down. Guess what? You're not that special. You don't have the power to save souls and absolve sins." Smiling down at him, she forced open his mouth, just as he had done to her these past several days. "I am a vampire, you fucking stupid little man. And your God won't save you."

Though her hands with bleeding and shaking, with one sharp tug, she separated his tongue from his mouth and threw it aside.

Father Matthews howled and she relished in the sound. He had caused her so much grief; it was only natural that she should take pleasure in his suffering. She clapped her hand over his mouth once again and chuckled as he began to choke on his own blood.

"How do you like it, hmm? Blood being forced down your throat. Not so fun, is it?"

While she would have loved to torture him further, she needed to heal and get out of there. So she– as savagely as she could manage –bit into his neck, making a much larger wound than she needed, and drained every last drop of his blood.

Feeling exhilarated, she sat back up and smiled as she felt her hands and shoulder begin to heal. The holes were reduced in size – not as patched up as she would like, but she would need to feed more for them to look normal again.

It would be a nuisance to lug the body around, but she wanted to show it off to whoever else was in this place. So she decided to make it lighter for her to carry. Grabbing hold of his head, she twisted it until she heard the definitive crack and pop that meant that his head was free from his neck.

With his severed head in hand, she opened the door and walked into what appeared to be a hallway. If there was anyone nearby, she couldn't sense them, so she continued with caution. Leaving a trail of blood behind her, she walked up several flights of stairs until she heard voices.

As she came to what looked like the main part of the church, she saw a man– another priest – giving a sermon. Mass was in session.

Gasps and murmurs erupted in the crowd as she walked to the podium. The priest turned to face her and she saw that it was the same man who had lured her into the limousine. Her gaze narrowed and her nostrils flared. She wondered how many more priests were in on this.

"You," she hissed. "How many of you are there? How many religious men have taken it upon themselves to *save* the souls of vampires by means of kidnap, torture, and murder?"

The man stared at her in shock, his mouth wide open. "I...I..."

"Spit it out!" she spat, and flecks of blood flew from her mouth to his face. She laughed– she had found her sense of humor again. "If you lie to me, I'll kill you. If you're honest, I'll spare you."

Swallowing hard, he looked from the severed head of his friend back to the female vampire. "It was just the two of us. Father Matthews wanted to expand our group, but I was hesitant."

She believed him, but that didn't mean that she wouldn't go looking for more of them– just to be sure. Stepping in front of the podium, she tossed the head and it rolled down the floor between the pews. "Let this be a lesson to you! Never try to convert a vampire." She had made herself laugh again, but while she doubled over in a fit of giggles, the priest tried to attack her.

Luckily, she sensed his movement in time, and she spun around and grabbed him by the throat.

"Wait!" he choked. "You said I would be spared."

"I lied."

She did away with him with a quick twist of his neck. The screams of the families in the pews made her grin. But even with all her anger, she felt merciful today. After all, these people hadn't done anything to her.

"I'm feeling generous. Women and children are free to go. I'll count to ten. Anyone left in the church after that time is up will die."

Families– men, women, and children –scrambled for the door, but there was so much chaos that not all of them could make it out in time.

Melina was true to her word; she allowed the rest of the women and children to leave, but then she stood at the large wooden doors, grinning mischievously. "So...who's next?"

It was a smart move– and probably what they thought was their best chance –attacking her all at once. But she was still stronger than them. And, unlike their dearly departed Fathers, they didn't know about her weaknesses.

When she was finished with them, their limbs were scattered on the floor and she was covered in blood from head to toe. She had drunk as much blood as she could and her wounds were healed. All the damage Father Matthews had done to her was put right.

She was so happy to finally be free. She had been kidnapped more than once, and people had tried to kill her more than that. It was so satisfying to be the victor. It was a small battle to have won, but it felt wonderful all the same.

* * *

Here she was again, staring at The Pulse Nightclub. If there was ever a time to reach out to her estranged fledgling, it would have been now, after she'd had such a close encounter with death. She could boast about her accomplishments and listen to his. It sounded nice in the moment, but was she really ready for that?

It had been many years, but she couldn't imagine that Blake Auckley had changed much. The more she stared at the club, the more she thought it was still a bad idea.

If she went inside, what then? It wasn't as if he'd welcome her with open arms. And after she had just murdered men who had desired to put her in her place, she wasn't interested in seeing a vampire with the same ideals.

Heaving a sigh and turning away from the building for what seemed to be the thousandth time, she began the long walk back home.

"Nope. Not today."

CALL OF THE MOON
BY NICOLAJAYNE TAYLOR

Nicolajayne Taylor is a British, Erotic, Fantasy horror writer. She has authored novels such as the international best-seller The Curse of Mary, All Legends, The Chronicles of being Isisti and has penned a couple of short stories, The Fallen Ones and Berlin War. All her works are well written, researched and are grippingly addictive. Her dark worlds are not for the faint hearted, these worlds are intricate, colourful and the reviews say it all.

CHAPTER ONE

THE NIGHT WAS STILL AND had only just begun. A sunset on the horizon, dissolving into a brilliant vibrant purple sky, looked very serene as Lindsay Delfino walked the pavement listening to the flat slap of her own footsteps. She walked past shuttered shop windows that wouldn't be opening anytime soon. They were closed, abandoned and a reflection of the world's financial despair. On the other side of the street there was a park usually teeming with people, but like the street seemingly empty of life.

A stray dog scampered past the entrance to the park, sniffed at a lamp post and then at a bin over flowing with trash. Lindsay stopped walking for a moment to watch the dog pick out its evening meal from the paper wrappers and discarded fast food boxes. The dog looked up and saw her as it munched through a leftover burger. She thought the dog to be very beautiful with a long grey coat and a black stripe down its flanks with patches of white on its underside. The dog had startling blue eyes that seemed intelligent, humanly so. She wasn't sure of the dog's breed, a Husky-cross, maybe. Lindsay also considered that it may not be a stray, but a runaway as it looked groomed and well fed.

Carrying on her journey, she left the dog to its adventures. She was heading home and wanted to rid herself of the day, and it had been a long ass day at that. Having woken up at four-thirty in the morning, showered, dressed and caffeinated, she had walked to work. At work, her office had been immensely busy. The mounds of data she had to input had appeared unreal and felt like it was never going to end. She had taken a few quiet moments during her lunch hour to call the garage where her car was being repaired, only to be told it would be at least another three weeks before they could get the parts needed. Now she reached her garden gate. With a frustrated sigh at the thought of walking to work for the foreseeable future, Lindsay reached for the front door keys within her handbag as she walked down the path towards the door.

As she fumbled around, something caught her eye at the garden gate. She turned to see that it was the dog, Lindsay gasped. For some reason the sight of the dog and those eyes so close, startled her. The dog gave her a long, knowing, strange glare before looking away, and then continued its journey. She went back down the path to the gate with the keys in her hand, the dog had gone and there was no trace of which direction. Confused as to why the dog had followed and not approached her if it thought that she may have food or could find its owner, she went back to the front door and let herself into the house.

The small house, nestled in a small suburb of Chester was a little run down and in need of redecorating and refurnishing. It would have been a little cosier, if it wasn't for the litter of her ex-boyfriend Steven's stuff. He left it when he walked out on her, a week ago now. She hadn't been able to get in touch with him at all after that night of violent arguing. Message after message and he hadn't returned any, not even to yell at her. Lindsay felt relieved to be out of Steven's control and laziness. He had been unemployed for almost a year and sunk into deep depression. He began to drink heavily and stay up all night. Jealousy plagued him and everything came to a head a week ago when she went out with her girlfriends for drinks.

Making her way to the kitchen, she pondered trying to call Steven again and then changed her mind. She put a light under a pan containing the remains of some chicken stew that she had cooked a day ago. She wasn't the obsessive type and knew that she was giving Steven more thought than he deserved. Ten years they had spent together and this past year proved more of a nightmare with every passing argument. Lindsay read her mail, listened to her answering machine and still not a word from Steven— she shook her head as she made a pot of tea and buttered bread, trying to dismiss him from her thoughts.

The evening ritual began, this was her time and she relished being able to wind down over supper at her laptop on the kitchen table, her social networks were just as de-motivating as life seemed to be at that moment. Finding things to feel good about had become hard, but she was never the sort of person to give up. Her friends and family complaining about work, kids and the weather as well as each other, she was interrupted by the phone ringing and went to answer it.

"Hello?"

Silence...

"Hello?" she repeated.

Then Lindsay heard a dragging and a scratching sound from the receiver. She pulled the phone away, stared at it with confusion and then returned the receiver to her ear. "Hello?" Lindsay repeated again and just as she was about to hang up, she heard a voice.

"The moon will be high, the moon will be bright and it will call on you upon the night." It was a harsh whisper and sounded like a creepy lullaby that belonged to a horror movie or game.

"Who is this?" she asked irritated.

The phone line went dead and she had to hang up. Lindsay held her head beneath her chin and clutched her hair with one hand as if it was too heavy for her body to keep upright. She gave a heavy sigh, she didn't need prank calls after the week she was enduring.

Lindsay cleared the remains of her meal now that she was no longer hungry. She poured a large glass of chardonnay from the fridge and took it upstairs. She would drink it while taking a bath. She was so tired and the climb up the steep stairs hurt her calves. Wearily, she got to the top and entered the bathroom. Lindsay perched her wine glass on a small wooden stool beside the bathtub and then began to run the taps, she shook in some bath salts and lit a couple of vanilla scented candles.

Getting into the bath, Lindsay laid back in the hot steamy bubbles and let them soak her aching muscles. She found it hard to be in the moment as she lay there with her mind swimming with thoughts of work, the car, Steven and the phone call. She washed her face and tried to quiet her mind. The loudest thoughts were about the strange caller's words—nagging at her and rattling around her mind. She took a sip of wine and rinsed her hair. She massaged a soaped up sponge around her shoulders, neck, then her chest and breasts trying to rid her muscles of stress and tension. *The moon will be high, the moon will be bright and it will call on you upon the night,* floated through her mind like a nursery rhyme, loud and clear. She felt like the rhyme was outside of her head for a moment, the words and voice seemed next to her ear. She felt dizzy and a cool breeze drifted over her. She shook her head hard. *Why can't I rid myself of that call?*

Heaving her body out of the bath, she slid on her bathrobe, wrapped her long ash blonde hair in a towel and took her glass of wine with her into the bedroom. She lit her bedside lamp, perched the wine glass beside it and then flopped upon her bed.

Lindsay picked up her kindle and began to find her place in the book that she was reading. It was an anthology called *'The Curse of Mary'* by Nicolajayne Taylor...the phone rang out from downstairs. With an effort, she ignored it. She was too tired and wanted to relax and answering the phone at this time of the night wasn't something she relished, especially if it was another one of those prank calls.

CHAPTER TWO

LINDSAY COULD HEAR THE SOUND of a clock ticking loudly, but there was no telling where the sound was coming from, her heart pounded and her skin felt like it was on fire. She ran fast through woodland, barefooted, wearing just her night shirt and shorts.

She didn't want to look at what she was running from, but knew it was fast on her heels. Rain lashed down, a gale wind blasted at her and all the while she felt as though she was running towards the moon. It was bright and huge on the horizon.

Suddenly she fell hard, her breath caught in her lungs and then, as she turned on to her back, Lindsay screamed. She saw teeth and those eyes— crystal blue eyes and recognised them. The dog that she had seen on the pavement and again at her garden gate was now pinning her to the ground of a dark mist ridden woodland. The dog's teeth were so very sharp and glistening with saliva that dripped onto Lindsay's chest. She could feel the wet slime as it drizzled onto her face. It growled at her fiercely, then opened its jaws wide and quickly came down on her face...

Screaming and struggling with the bed covers, Lindsay jumped out of bed. She stared around her room and saw that the glass of chardonnay had been tipped over and was dripping remnants onto the polished floorboards. Her lamp also over turned and her alarm clock was beeping away by the door at the other side of the room.

The rest of the room looked like chaos as everything was turned upside down, draws were open with clothing hanging out and her dressing table contents were scattered all over.

Lindsay became aware of a cold breeze coming from behind the curtains. Shivering, she quickly went over to them, drew them back, and saw the window wide open. Looking down into the cloudy dawn and rain washed street, at first she saw nothing. Then she saw the dog across the road and staring up at her.

Shivers of fear rippled down her back, her scalp and her hands tingled at the memory of her dream. She rapidly shut the window and closed the curtains. Stepping away slowly from the window, she then turned on her room. Lindsay began cleaning up the disarray of mess that had seemingly happened during her sleep and looked to be as confused as she was.

She felt exhausted as she made herself some coffee, a toasted bagel and sat eating her breakfast. The answering machine on the kitchen wall blinked red at her. Having decided not to listen to the message, she finished her breakfast and then went for a shower and to get dressed. Realising that time had run away with her that morning, she rushed out of the door.

When she left the house, she felt nervous. Walking hurriedly along the pavement, she kept looking frantically around and behind. The dog was nowhere to be seen, but somehow, she knew it wasn't far away.

Having decided to take the bus, she arrived at work twenty minutes late. Her boss's growling eyebrows and frown told her that he wasn't pleased as he watched her enter the office and take a seat at her desk. Lindsay started to get to work as soon as her computer fired up and was logged in. She jumped in fright as a hefty pile of data slammed onto her desk. Lindsay looked up and saw her boss.

"You're late, Delfino," he told her in a flat tone, his slight London accent hinted through, "don't make a habit of it." And then he hesitated for a moment as if he was going to say something else, but didn't and went back to his office.

Thumbing through her day's work, she organized it into alphabetical order and then Lindsay began inputting data with a sigh...she only turned once and saw her boss watching her. He had a strange expression etched across his face. She didn't know him all that well. He usually didn't say more than the occasional 'hello' to her and now his full attention appeared to be on her.

Lindsay looked up at the plain digital office clock and saw that the screen blinked 12:30, she felt disheartened that her lunch hour was still half an hour away. The desk phone bleeped and she looked around the room to see if anyone was on their phone. All the calls she got were usually from somebody in her own office too lazy to come up and ask for something so they called— nobody waved or indicated for her to answer their call. On this occasion the office was quiet and everybody seemed focused on their tasks or daydreaming as they stared into their computer screens.

Her fingers began to tingle and the icy waves of fear began mounting as last night's prank caller's words floated through her mind. She grabbed the phone...

"Hello, this is Lindsay Delfino. You are through to Waterman Accounting."

"The moon will rise, the sun will die and the world...and the world... will never be the same... and you won't see another soul the same way again." The feminine voice sang out loudly and with giddy insane tone, it sounded like her voice had come from a crackling radio station and an old song played from vinyl was there in the background.

Lindsay slammed down the phone and stood. She felt her co-workers eyes burning into her as she trembled and began to look around for help.

She saw her boss coming towards her, his face angry, but concerned and his voice a little more gentle than his expression, "What's wrong Lindsay?"

"I had a phone call..." She saw him scowl at the statement. "I had a prank call last night at home and now here."

His tone of voice changed to a more urgent stutter, "What did it say, di... did you recognise the voice?"

She quickly answered, "Some song or rhyme about the night, the voice was quiet last night. This time it was loud and just now it sounded like a woman, it also sounded like a threat." She then began to sob.

Her boss ushered Lindsay into his office and sat her down on the sofa. "I will get you some tissues and some water. Stay here."

* * *

Lee went to the staff room and found some napkins, a bottle of water in the fridge, and a cookie that was still in the plastic as an afterthought. He turned, and saw his personal assistant, Matilda hovering by the door.

"Is everything okay, Lee?" She began to play with a stray strand of hair between her fingers with one hand and in the other was her beloved cell phone.

Lee watched as she forcefully tried to keep her expression concerned, but when it wavered, he saw a slight smirk on her face and this made him cold towards her.

He hated fake people, gossipers and rudeness and somehow he felt it hypocritical seeing as he was no angel, but felt he had good reason. He liked to run a tight ship within his small company just as he had in his personal life, but his life at that moment was a sinking wreck. Waterman Accounting, a wealthy business which had been offered several times to be bought out by bigger corporations, but he'd refused. If he couldn't control his personal life then he was damned if it would affect his business. Being the top of the food chain of his company meant doing the hiring and firing himself. Lee had given Matilda a job as his personal assistant only for her father's sake that also worked for the business and was a good man. Her father always looked extremely apologetic every time Matilda came in late, took longer than allotted time for lunch breaks and paid more attention to her phone than to the tasks that she had been hired to do.

Right now, he had no time for her. "Everything is fine thanks, get back to work." He waited for her to step aside.

When Lee re-entered his office, he saw that Lindsay bent forward with her arms stretch out and her head in her lap. She was openly sobbing and lifted her head as he ventured towards her. He saw her grey eyes surrounded by long black lashes, clouded with tears, black streaks ran down her porcelain pale face and her neck reddened.

"Here, drink this," he said and gave her the water then plonked the rest of the items down beside her.

"Thank you," she replied after a long gulp. "I am so very sorry that I freaked out. I have been under too much stress lately and I think it has finally got to me."

"No need to apologise. Tell me, what has been going on?" He felt concerned, but began to notice to his surprise how very pretty if not sexy she was. He got up, went back to his desk and sat in his chair to observe her.

"I broke up with my boyfriend, my cat went missing and my car broke down all within a week. I can't get hold of my ex to give him his stuff. My car won't be ready for three weeks and god only knows what's happened to Suki," she said between gasps and sniffles.

Lee rested his elbows on the desk and placed his hands prayer like as he pressed them against his lips. He wondered what to do. Should he let Lindsay go home? She could be in danger. Should he, keep her at work? Her co-workers would be having a field day with the break in routine and it seemed that if the calls were here at work then she may not be safe here either.

"Hmm... Let us go and have some lunch," he announced and saw the look of surprise on her face. "We are all human, one of the many things that we have in common. Another thing that we have in common is the need to feed ourselves." He smiled at her.

Lindsay smiled back at him. She seemed relieved not to face being sacked, going home or staying in work. "Thank you, I would like that," she said, and her voice sounded weary.

Lee gathered his things and watched Lindsay collect her handbag and a few papers. He saw her co-workers tensely trying to concentrate on their work and fighting the urge to look and watch. He shook his head, straightened his tie and flicked off his computer, people were so...he couldn't find the words to describe how he thought of people, but they just irritated and frustrated him. He hadn't always hated people, but due to his personal issues and misfortune, he found them ignorant and arrogant more so now than ever before, if they only knew what he did...

As he left the office, Matilda stood to attention and came rushing over.

"I will be out for the rest of the day, delegate all Lindsay's work load to everyone and take down all messages and leave them on my desk," he told her abruptly and rushed onwards toward the elevator to where Lindsay was waiting.

Lindsay still looked very nervous and upset and Lee found it hard to think about what to do to help her. He couldn't explain to himself why he was suddenly cared, so very attracted to his employee that had barely spoke to him in the whole time she'd worked for him, his desire for her had started a few weeks ago now and he'd hoped to control it or at the very least hide those mounting feelings towards her, but that nagging feeling was back.

They rode the elevator in silence that was broken every now and then with a sniffle from Lindsay.

* * *

Lindsay made a stop by the ground floor bathrooms to clean up her face. Peering at her brightly lit reflection, she began to wipe away the streaks of mascara and replace her foundation. The lights flicked off for a moment, she thought nothing of it and waited for them to blink back on.

She screamed in terror, the reflection, a totally different being. It was still an image of herself, but very different. Bloody tears ran thickly down her face, her skin cracked as if it were made of dried mud— her mouth, like the jaws of a wolf, snarling and with bared teeth. Her eyes were spheres of crimson light and a clawed hand reached out of the mirror slowly and came towards her.

Lindsay scurried away and felt her shoulder collide into somebody... "Ah!" she cried out.

* * *

Lee grabbed and dragged her out of the bathroom and into the lobby. He was shaking and sweating. He had heard her scream and run in to see what had happened. When he entered the bathroom, he then saw Lindsay so very frightened and the image in the mirror had been something out of a nightmare. Still the mirror's image was etched into his mind and now felt like his entire soul obliterated. He knew he had seen it, he knew it was real.

He looked around at the reception and for the security staff. Bobby Riley, head of security was walking towards him.

"You ol' right, sir?" Bobby asked. He looked bewildered and oddly amused.

"I think there is somebody in the bathroom that shouldn't be there," Lee told him.

He watched Bobby push out his chest and click his fingers in the air. Another security guard came over, he was new, Lee had only seen him a couple of times and he hadn't known his name until now and looking at his nametag that stated Alan Rochet. Lee nodded to him.

"Looks like somebody may have gotten past us," Bobby told his partner. The two of them made for the direction of the ladies bathroom without ceremony.

Lee turned his attention back to Lindsay, she looked terrified and timid. If it was one thing that he had noticed about Lindsay over the past six years, it was her independent, confident and easy-going nature. To see her looking scared and panicked was just as disturbing as what he had seen in the mirror. He gently took her hand and pulled her toward the lobby doors that led out on to the busy town street.

* * *

Lindsay let her boss lead her out of the building. Feeling as though she was floating and that he was the only thing weighing her down. It was as if he to let go of her hand, she would drift off into nowhere.

They walked down the street and the fresh air cooled their flushed frightened faces. Lindsay heard so much noise that it began to make her head pound with pain and dizziness. She heard the bin wagon beeping and bins clanking and banging as they were emptied. Dogs barking loudly from all directions and people, their footsteps on the pavement sounded like thunder.

She had to stop and stay still for a moment. Lee tugged at her before he must have realised something was wrong. She felt his arms wrap around her shoulders, holding her close as if they were lovers and like it was the most natural thing in the world even though she knew that it wasn't, his embrace did quiet her mind and the noise. Her head still felt ready to explode, but the dizziness began to sink away. She couldn't figure out why she felt so indifferent to the world all of a sudden.

Lee appeared to sense her become steady again and then he looked around to find somewhere to go. "We need somewhere quiet, secluded and away from this chaos that seems to be surrounding us." He kept his right arm around Lindsay's slim waist and navigated the busy pavement. He had spotted and pointed towards a small bar across the road from where they were and guided Lindsay towards it when the traffic gave away.

He chose wisely, the place was nearly empty. Behind the bar stood a Goth woman, looking bored with black and purple hair in high bunches, her pale face decorated with piercings and her limbs had all manner of tattoos. She wore a black leather vest, a short black skirt and she black and purple striped stockings that matched her hair, black ankle boots. Lindsay found her fascinating to look at.

Looking over into the back bar she saw a couple of large men playing pool, they were also covered in tattoos, leather clad and all seemed friendly as the men nodded at them, the bartender gave them a friendly smile. "What will it be?" The woman looked them up and down.

"Can we have two shots of whatever and two beers?" Lee hesitated and turned to look at Lindsay. "Do you want something to eat?"

Lindsay nodded. "Anything, just order anything."

Lee turned back to face the bartender. "Along with two house special sandwiches," he ordered and threw two fifties down, "keep the change."

The bartender smiled a little brighter and wider at him. "Please take a seat," she told them with a customer friendly tone that hadn't been there moments earlier.

Lindsay sat and slid into a booth at the far end of the bar. She dry washed her face and hands. She sensed Lee slide in across from her. Feeling his stare just as much as she felt his fear for what happened in the bathroom earlier.

It was the same way for her. She couldn't fathom what had happened. Letting her hands fall flat on the table, she stared back at him. Her boss had been a distant acquaintance who clocked her time and paid her salary every month. He gave her mountains of deadlines and he was what she had assumed to be a power mad controlling asshole. Now she saw him as her saviour or at the very least a good friend. His handsome face, pure green eyes with long lashes and his dark floppy hair was sleek and had fallen into his eyes and gave him a boyish look. She saw him brush it back and noticed his clear sun-kissed skin was smooth and subtle.

Lindsay blinked and shook her head. *There is no way on this Earth that I could begin to fancy my boss.*

* * *

Lee reached across the table and laid his hands flat on top of hers. He felt compelled to touch her. There was a need to protect her even though he felt that Lindsay was far stronger than she realised. One more puzzling piece to this entire situation was his desire for her affection and acceptance, feelings he couldn't figure out which were growing like wild fire.

"I need..." He was started to say something about his feelings when the bartender brought over the drinks. "Two more shots please," he said and then slid one of the glasses of tequila over to Lindsay.

"Of course and your sandwiches will be about half an hour. We have a new chef and he is on the slow side," she replied with a shrug and walked away.

Lindsay and Lee downed their shots and then took a long gulp of beer to wash away the burn. Lindsay began to speak, her voice now measured as if she was thinking aloud, "I don't know what that was in the bathroom. I feel strange now and I am having a hard time trying to figuring this all out."

"Do you think it could be related to those prank calls?" He had to take another long gulp of his beer as the mirror image came blasting back into his mind.

"I don't know. The calls were strange, but I hadn't thought anything scary about the first call until that second call. I even had a nightmare this morning and it felt connected somehow to the call." She took a drink.

"Tell me everything, maybe there is something that has happened in the past week that you are over looking and that may have led to these events."

Lindsay told him all that had happened that past week and of her dream, she even told him about the dog as it seemed to be part of it all for some strange reason, unless she was just imagining it and then she told him about the upturned bedroom.

* * *

Lee listened intently, he was becoming mesmerised by her voice and by the way her smooth pink lips moved with her words. He saw the irritation in the expression of her face whenever she mentioned her ex. He was also surprised that there was nothing unusual about the events prior to the phone calls that seemed odd. He would have thought there would be more to it.

The bartender returned with their sandwiches and shots and he was grateful for the food as well as the alcohol. "I don't want you to be alone tonight, my place or yours?"

Lindsay smiled back. "Your place please, I am just reminded of unfinished business when I go home."

Lee's smile grew bigger and brighter at her decision. "That's really great. Should we swing by your place to collect a few things or are you okay?"

"I will get some things from nearby stores before we head off," she replied and her tone now was defeated and tired.

CHAPTER THREE

LINDSAY WAS IN AWE AT Lee's large penthouse apartment that over looked the city skyline. She stepped out onto the balcony and allowed the fresh cool evening breeze to blow the trauma of the day away. The sky was clear, the stars blinked at her and there was the sliver of a new moon. Lee came up from behind and wrapped his arms around her shoulders, she would have normally felt this inappropriate, but on this occasion it felt more than right and so she let him comfort her.

He too watched the skyline and saw the flashing lights of police helicopters in the distance. When Lee looked down, he saw the street washed in amber light. He leaned his head against Lindsay's cheek and kissed gently at her shoulders. Lee felt her body pressing against his and saw her neck leaning away. He took it as an invite to kiss her neck and heard her deep intake of breath as he did so. His hands brushed over her arms and down her sides. He massaged her hips through the thin blue cotton maxi dress that she wore. He caressed the tops of her thighs and then ventured slowly upwards to her breasts. All the while his kisses turning ever more urgent and before he knew it, his desire for Lindsay burned through his veins.

Lindsay turned around to face him. She had to have him and wasn't going to even think about it. She hadn't been with anybody for over a year, not even her ex before splitting up, and now Lee was overwhelming in his appeal. Ripping open his shirt to reveal well tone, defined muscle, his broad chest, shoulders, and his abs were tantalisingly pleasing to her eyes. She pressed her body firmer against his, feeling his solidarity and warmth. He tore down her dress and then unleashed her breasts from her bra without fumble. Lindsay shimmied out of the dress now at her waist. She felt his tongue sink into her mouth. It made her hungry for him. His kisses left her mouth and traced his tongue down to her breasts. Her nipples stiffened and tingled as she felt him sucking and nibbling. His lips went down her ribs and then to the rim of her panties. His breath on her moistened panties made her tremble and aroused.

Lee tugged off her panties and threw them aside. She saw his eyes light up and a smile cross his lips as he saw her neat pussy with little hair and a little shine from her wetness. He lifted her leg up over his shoulder as he parted her labia and began to lick heavily and slowly at first, pressing his tongue against her clitoris. She ran her hands in his hair and tugged at it gently. Lee sucked at her clitoris and quickly delved his tongue into her grooves. Panting and feeling ready to burst with enraptured passion, she grabbed the balcony rail. Tracing his kisses back up to her mouth, he lifted and perched her against the baloney wall. He guided his cock to the entrance of her juicy wet pussy. Then held her close as he ploughed deeply and slowly into her and they both groaned in harmony.

Lee could feel his cock sliding inside and her pussy pulsed with orgasm around him. She bit then sucked at his neck and shoulders, hungrily. The sensations of his heavy, slow thrusting took on a life and soul of its own locomotion. He could hear her heaving breath in his ear and felt it on his shoulder. Feeling her desire for him was more than a deep rumble of excitement in this carnal moment. He let her legs down and turned her around before leaning over her balcony railing. Reuniting his cock with her pulsing pussy, he slammed into her fast and hard, panting as his arousing hunger grew. He wanted to howl, his veins felt ablaze and he pulled her back from the baloney wall. Still coupled, he guided her to the floor and she went on all fours. He crouched behind her, grabbed her breasts hard and tugged at her nipples as he quickly and deeply fucked her as though his life depended on it. He felt her trembling the same way as he was. He instinctively knew that she felt what he was feeling. He heard her growling and he became ever more excited, more aroused and it felt primal.

The more Lee pounded into her the more he wanted. The new depth of his thrust was painfully pleasurable and the way he was tugging at her breasts and his desire to suck them, kiss and even nibble her breasts made his mouth water. He then heard himself growling and this made his body take over his mind. The feelings of lust, fear and desire were just as arousing as her body being ravished from the inside out by his rough, deep and fast penetration.

Lindsay felt him clawing at her back and she made the primitive sound of a hound. Feeling the hotness of her blood drizzle down over her ribs made her howl again and then she felt him lick at her wounds. She lent her head down to the floor. Lindsay felt submissive and wanted to show him that she was. Lee knocked her to the ground and kneeled above her and she felt his cock at her lips. She opened her mouth and allowed him to thrust into her.

Lee seemed elated, his cock was submersed into her mouth and she felt the ridges of her teeth gently glazing his skin. She could feel he was close to orgasm. He stiffened further and held her head back. He kissed her and then laid himself over her, ploughed into her pussy once more and they growled, snarled and panted through a pulsation of ecstasy as his orgasm spilled over.

* * *

The sun broke the horizon, Lindsay looked over for Lee. He was just waking up and stirring just as she was. She couldn't remember having fallen asleep and couldn't work out why they were still on the balcony. Feeling cold, damp and stiff, Lindsay tried to cover herself with her dress that she had slept on. The memories of the night before flooded back and she blushed. Lindsay had never had hot, passionate, hungry sex before, her sex life up until last night had been plain and uneventful. Lee looked just as embarrassed and confused.

Lee looked around and saw the litter of their clothes, over turned plant pots and patio chairs. He became aware of his aching muscles, scratches and bite marks and they weren't just on his body, but also Lindsay's too. He prided himself on being a good lover, gentle and generous. Last night's passion felt too good, selfish, and unreal and he still felt very aroused. He got up and helped Lindsay to stand.

They were staring at one another in tense silence. They both began picking up their clothes and made their way indoors. Lee began to organise some breakfast and Lindsay headed for the bathroom to wash and clean up.

The phone rang, Lee went to answer. "Hello, you have reached Lee Waterman's residence." He heard music crackling away...

"Lee, help me. Please..." ropey and whiny music began to play loud and clear, "the moon will be high, the moon will be bright and it will call on you upon the night."

Lee slammed the phone down with a shaky hand. He was sweating and fear gripped him. He turned off the gas on the cooker hob, threw the frying pan and eggs aside and went to see if Lindsay was okay.

He heard the shower running and saw the bathroom door ajar. Lee opened it and pressed it flat against the wall. He heard Lindsay humming. It reminded him of the music he had just heard on the phone call. Lee held his breath to quieten his rising fear as he approached the shower.

Gently he pulled back the shower curtain and quickly jumped back as a dog with gray, white and black long fur rushed at him. Lee saw the dog's crystal blue eyes looking down at him as if looking into his very soul. It snarled at him, and then it was gone.

Lindsay was on her knees, naked and dripping wet beside him. She looked frighten and concerned, her voice almost a cry, "What happened?"

"I saw a dog leap out at me from the shower. It was the same dog as you described and it came at me." He heard his voice shaking and weak.

"I didn't see the dog. I saw your reaction though. Then I saw you fall onto your back," she said looking around for the dog.

Lee got up and though he felt terrified of what might be lurking in his apartment, he was also aware of Lindsay's naked wet body. All he could do was to pull her close and wrap his arms around her tightly. He quietened his hunger for her and his fear of the unexpected. He didn't want to let her go, in that moment, she felt like the safest place to be.

Lindsay felt him trembling in her arms and felt saddened by the thought that this whole situation was her fault. Now it was affecting a person who had meant nothing but a pay-check less than twenty-four hours ago. She felt that they were both in danger and didn't know what to do about it.

As they went back to the kitchen and Lee struggled to finish making breakfast. He was still visibly shaken, he told Lindsay about the phone call.

"This is crazy. How do we find out what is going on, how to stop the phone calls and the dog?" Lindsay played nervously with her cup and cutlery.

He shrugged and then dished out scramble eggs and shoved some toast on to the plates. "I think we ought to go to the police about the phone calls. At least they can look into it and maybe trace it back to who-ever is making the calls."

Lindsay tugged her plate towards her, she felt famished and very thirsty. "I agree, should we do that after work?"

Lee checked the clock. It was still only eight-thirty in the morning. "Are you sure you want to work today? I sure as hell don't."

Lindsay thought for a moment, maybe it wasn't a good idea to work with these strange occurrences. "Yeah, you're right. Let's just go and talk to the police."

CHAPTER FOUR

CHESTER POLICE AT CLEMONDS HAY on Oakmere Road Winsford, CW7, Lindsay and Lee walked into the police station holding hands. They weren't surprised to see a busy office. This area of the country wasn't a high crime area and it was apparent as to why, seeing all the officers were hard at work and focused on their cases.

Lee took the initiative and went to the front desk. A young officer with thin rimmed glasses and a thin moustache stood from his chair and held out a clip board.

"Please sign in and can I have your name?" He observed Lee and then lent to one side to see Lindsay, who was stood a little way behind.

"My name is Lee Waterman and my friend here, is Lindsay Delfino. We work together and until yesterday we were just boss and employee. We had a bad experience...prank calls and they were threatening calls... and we would like to report it." He stumbled upon his words as he knew it sounded crazy and didn't know if he ought to tell the officer the whole situation.

"Okay, take a seat and I will get someone to take a statement," the young officer told them. "My name is Alan Sparks, Officer Sparks," he said with a chuckle as he did what appeared to his take on a James Bond impression.

Lee grinned as he handed the clipboard back, he didn't share the officer's humour. He was too stressed and tensed for jokes. He and Lindsay took their seats across from the front desk and watched officer Sparks go about his reception duties.

Lindsay watched as the police went in and out of offices and the main doors. She saw a drunken scruffy and dirty middle aged woman was being guided to a desk by two officers.

Prickly fear circulated between Lee and Lindsay as the drunken woman began singing loudly. "The moon will raise a whole. It will light the dark... The moon will be high, the moon will be bright and it will call on you upon the night!" She cackled loudly and all the while, staring at Lee and Lindsay.

A sob escaped Lindsay as the rhyme was repeated and Lee put his arm around her.

A female officer came over to the woman. "Come on Nancy. Let's get you some coffee and some food and then you can sleep off that gin."

"Nah...get off of me. They need to know," Nancy told the officer and then pointed at Lee.

Lindsay stood up abruptly, she was shaking and trembling. Her face felt drained of blood as terror was rising from within her. "What should we know!" she yelled and heard her own voice as a panicked screech.

Lee stood and got between Lindsay and Nancy. "Calm down, now isn't the time for losing it." He stood aside and pulled Lindsay further away.

Nancy began clapping as if she was joyous, like she had been told some good news. She smiled and revealed her blacken teeth or what was left of them. "The mists will come upon the next full moon. The world for you will change forever!" she squealed at them. Then she repeated the rhyme as the officer guided her away towards the cells, the officer looked over her shoulder at the couple and mouthed an apology.

The pair of them was left looking at each other dumbfounded. They looked over back towards the cells in time to see a big man in a suit walking towards them from one of the offices. He looked very serious and annoyed.

"I am detective Marshal Anderson, please follow me." And then he walked back in the direction the he had come from.

TO BE CONTINUED...

The full book will be released later this year. Thank you for reading and I will see you for part two of chapter four.

Nicolajayne Taylor

CARD TRICK

BY P. MATTERN

"SERIOUSLY, DON'T PUT TOO MUCH thought into it, just pick one," Boone was telling Maisie as he fanned the deck of cards out in front of her. Along with Maisie's older sister Carrie, they were waiting outside of the entrance to the Blue River Karstland Caves waiting for the last tour, the one Boone had shelled out $30 for—and that was with a discount code he'd found online.

Maisie, who was fifteen-years-old, studied the backs of the cards in front of her. After hovering over for another moment, she reached out and selected one on the left as she popped her gum.

"Don't look at it," he told her after she'd pulled one from his deck. "Just put it in your pocket and prepare to have your young mind blown."

"Haha," Maisie answered.

Carrie, his girlfriend, snorted and stretched her arms over her head. The rustic bench they were sitting on was placed before one of the few notable natural wonders the flatlands of Indiana boasted. It was rough hewn and uncomfortable.

"I don't like the way the sky looks," she said. "And I don't want to get a splinter in my ass. Maybe we should just get a refund and come back another day."

Boone gave her a patient expression. He was remarkably nice looking for a geek— thick brown hair that was a little too long, nice arms, copper colored brown eyes that were fringed with thick lashes and lips a bit too full for a white boy.

He nodded his head toward the cut out space where they'd purchased the tickets and said, "See the sign? No Refunds. And the snack shop is about to close."

"Weird. It's only the three of us then?" Maisie asked, looking around them. A couple families holding drippy ice cream cones were walking away from the site and several other tourists were climbing into their cars in the gravel parking lot.

"No— look," Carrie said pointing to the third bench down. She crossed and uncrossed her perfect, golden legs. They were one of her best features and the tiny pink shorts she was wearing drew attention to them. She was also aware she had a nice rack. And long blonde hair she had just dyed in the hombre style.

The lady sitting on the next bench was middle aged and mousy looking and kept pushing her glasses back up on her nose as she studied a tourist brochure. She had an open backpack beside her that was trying to move. A small lapdog stuck its nose out of the opening and started to lick his owner's thigh. The woman absentmindedly reached over and scratched the mop topped miniature behind its ears.

"What about my card?" Maisie asked, "Do you know which one it is?"

"Which one do you want it to be?" Boone answered with a smirk.

"Hmmm...seven of hearts," she answered.

"Your wish has been granted," he said with a wave of his hand. "Check and see if I'm right."

Maisie pulled the card from her pocket with difficulty. Her jean shorts were tight.

"Hah! I don't believe it! How did you do that, Boone?" she asked. Her eyes narrowed, but still held a glimmer of admiration.

Her older sister snorted again. She shielded her eyes as she glanced up at Boone.

"You want to tell her or should I?" she asked. When he hesitated she turned to Maisie.

"Ask to see the rest of the deck," she said.

"Boone give me the deck!" Maisie demanded.

Boone smirked, reached into the pocket of his cargo shorts, and handed it to her.

Maisie rifled through it, then handed it to Carrie saying, "It doesn't *look* like a trick deck or anything sissy, see?"

Carrie and Boone exchanged a glance. Carrie smiled.

"Well you're right! It's not a trick deck after all!"

"Nice!" Maisie said with a joyous smile. "You got any more?"

Boone returned her smile.

"I got a million of 'em, trust me!" he said.

A balding man dressed in khaki came out of the front of the Tourist trap. He stopped and ran his eyes over the benches for a moment before frowning in disappointment.

"You folks all there is?" he asked.

Carrie pointed around Maisie at the next bench down.

"I think that lady with the dog is coming…" she said.

The khaki clad guy who was wearing a nametag that said, "Burt" walked to where the solitary female figure was sitting.

"Ma'am," he said, "Are you aware that no pets are allowed on the underground tours?"

The lady looked up at him for a moment, then pushed her lapdog's head back into the recesses of her backpack, smiling up at the tour guide.

"What dog?" she asked.

Burt wasn't having it.

"I'm sorry, ma'am," he told her, "No dogs allowed on the tours. Period."

"In that case," the woman responded, as the three teens one bench down looked on, "you can shove this up your *ass!*"

She threw her ticket at the tour guide's face and, getting up, shoved past him in a huff, her dog yapping at Burt as she stormed off.

Burt turned, looking up at the sky, which had grown darker in the last five minutes. He smiled at Carrie, Maisie and Boone.

"Well...feel like getting out of the weather?" he asked with an awkward smile. "I know a nice cave close by."

Boone chuckled and the trio hoisted their backpacks over their shoulders. Maisie had a pink furry one.

"Love to see the animal that one came from." The tour guide smiled, motioning them back to the main building.

"I think it was Sasquatch's girlfriend," Maisie joked, searching for a reaction from Boone.

Carrie learned up and whispered into Boone's ear.

"I know how you did it, Boone. But I won't tell for now. You can offer me a service later for keeping your hero image intact."

As they all backed into the freight elevator going down, they had a panoramic view of the souvenir shop and the snack bar beyond by the reflection of the convex security mirrors.

"The elevator will take us seventy-six feet straight down into the main cave chamber known as the Magician's Cathedral," the guide told them. "These caves are not as deep as some that are literally several stories underground, and some portions of the caves run uphill and quite near the surface..."

Boone smiled at Carrie and slipped his arm around her. Maisie leaned back on the far wall of the elevator.

The elevator jolted to a stop and opened. Even Maisie gasped at the view.

Many lights, some of them in colors, highlighted the stalactites, stalagmites, and numerous formations that resembled bejeweled stone flowers. It was a wonder of sparkle and shine in shades of amber, red, orange, and white. Several large crystals, some several feet tall, stood in clusters.

Maisie bounded out of the elevator, slipping on the muddy cave floor as she landed.

"Be careful there, young lady," the guard told her. "No running in the caves, it's mighty wet and you could take a tumble!"

"I'm fine!" Maisie said, pushing her hair behind her ears and shrugging. She had managed to catch her balance. Boone and Carrie followed with caution.

"Okie dokie," Burt the Tour Guide said, transitioning back into official mode. "I want to give you a little background on the caves before I give you a choice of which passage to explore today. You may have heard this, but bear with me. I like to hear myself talk."

"That's pretty evident," Maisie muttered under her breath. She seemed to have it in for Burt since he crabbed at her.

"The Marengo Caves located near the scenic Red River were discovered by three schoolchildren who were chasing a rabbit. Because the countryside is full of bogs and sinkholes, one of them, young Johnny Marks, eventually slid down an entrance while chasing the rabbit. His sister Blanche and their classmate Ben Fuller caught up with him. They helped remove the debris that had fallen behind him.

"They couldn't really see anything, so Ben, who lived the closest by, ran to his cabin to fetch a candle. The inside of the small cave was narrow, and Johnny and Blanche went in single file, holding the candle up, not knowing what they'd find.

"After several yards, the low tunnel opened up into a magnificent stone cathedral that glittered in the light of the candle as if it were festooned with diamonds. The siblings thought they had discovered a diamond cave!"

Boone, Carrie, and Maisie could well understand why the children had thought this was a diamond mine. Sparkling trails of crystals glittered in all directions.

There was music playing overhead, but the group could still hear water dripping from the rock formations. Burt searched his pockets for something while the group walked around a pillar of quartz and archway covered in rubellite crystal.

He then came over holding a map of the different underground trails.

"Depends on how much time you want to spend, really," Burt told them as they gathered around him, "I got a thirty minute, a forty-five minute, and one kind of off trail, but it takes an hour."

Boone perked up.

"Off trail? What does that mean?" he asked.

Burt scratched his head.

"Well— end of the day and all —the most magnificent formations are all off the beaten path. They are off trails that haven't been tourist-proofed yet. Some have a few small sinkholes. Fixing that costs money and time, so the owners haven't pursued opening them to the public yet.

"But I do know that the owners take private parties down when we are closed— like during the holidays. So you know it's probably more exciting, right? But it's up to you."

"Consensus?" Boone asked with a lopsided grin. "Being down here gets my inner explorer going. How about we take a walk on the wild side. Girls?"

Carrie and Maisie looked at each other.

"We're in," Carrie said.

Maisie nodded.

Boone just looked at Burt and said, "Yep."

"Okay, the Gargoyle Court it is!" Burt said. "You won't believe these formations. Never seen anything like it and I've been in caves all over the U.S. The stalactites are formed differently— almost a totem pole effect, like faces stacked on top of one another. You'll see!"

There were several passageways leading off of the open cavern they were standing in. Burt made a beeline behind a row of natural columns.

"Everybody got flashlights?" Burt called out, his voice echoing as he entered a dark hole in the rock about six feet high. "You'll need 'em!"

The air was thicker with the humidity of the tunnel, and the floor was more slippery. Boone and Maisie were both wearing boots, but Carrie had opted for sandals and was hanging onto Boone as they passed through the tunnel.

The only lights were naked bulbs encased in metal. They were hooked onto metal anchors that had been hammered into the rock high on the tunnel walls. The tunnel was opening up, with a ceiling of at least fourteen feet above them, and had widened by a similar margin.

"Quarter of a mile," Burt called over his shoulder, "Anytime now!"

Boone was the first to step into the cavern. It was not well lit, but its arcane beauty still superseded the previous cavern.

Carrie and Maisie gasped, both of them had phones in hand, snapping pics in rapid fire.

"Oh my GAWD," Carrie said. "Unbelievable. Creepy, but unbelievable. The faces in the rock formations look like gargoyles!"

"There's nothing wrong with gargoyles," Boone said with a smirk. "Did you know that originally they were considered good luck totems—the hideous faces were sculpted to ward away evil."

Carrie was quiet.

"Awesome," she said. "What's that rushing sound?"

Burt turned to her.

"Up ahead, there's a stream running through one side of the tunnel. Waters run all through these caverns— that's how they were formed. A few twists and turns beyond here is a cavern that makes this one look dull, believe it or not. Like I said, the nicest ones haven't been opened to the public."

Boone was getting hungry. He pulled a granola bar out of his pack and offered one to Burt.

"Don't mind if I do," Burt said, taking it.

They were on the move again, this time the passage wasn't as narrow, but they had their flashlights switched on because the lighting was even more sparse. They came to forks in the path several times, and had a sense they were descending. There were dark passages in between each wall lantern, and the narrow path fell off to their left, facing a fast moving stream.

"Why couldn't we see the stream on the way in?" Maisie asked. "Where does it start?"

"Probably up near the backside of the mountain," Burt told her. "There is an underground waterfall another mile up ahead. Like most of the underground streams and rivers it disappears at some point, likely carving out caves underneath us."

Carrie's legs were getting tired.

"Here," she said, handing her backpack to Boone, "You carry this," she said.

"What a little hothouse flower you are," Boone teased. "An underground Diva!"

"Wait!" Maisie said from behind them, "I have something in my boot..."

That was when all the lights went out.

They all went silent. The lights flickered on for a second and they looked at each other. There was a booming sound that shook the cave floor and caused several loosened pebbles to shower down upon them.

And then it was black again.

"Don't panic," they heard Burt say. "There should be a backup generator kicking in very soon. In the meantime get out your flashlights—"

This was followed by a cracking noise and a large splashing sound.

Then more silence.

Maisie moved closer to Carrie's body in front of her.

"Don't move!" said Carrie. "Boone? What was that?"

Carrie and Boone both flicked their flashlights on. Boone's face looked sweaty in the glare of the flashlight.

"Yours is better," Carrie said. "I'm turning mine off to save the battery."

"Where did Burt go?" Maisie mewed, "Where is our tour guide?"

There was a moment of stunned silence. Boone shined the light all around them in a panic.

"Burt!" he called out, the girls echoing him.

A few more pebbles fell from above their heads, but there was no answer.

Boone shone the flashlight to the ground and they saw him.

Burt was bobbing face down in the underground stream, his clothes caught on sharp rocks as water rushed over him. A gash could clearly be seen on the top of his bald head with rivulets of blood running down in a star pattern.

"Burt!" Maisie shrieked.

"Do we have anything to use as rope?" Boone asked in a panic. He was taking off his boots in preparation for a dive into the stream.

"What the hell are you *doing?*" Carrie demanded, grabbing his arm. "You *know* we don't have any rope! Burt probably had some, but it's not going to do *us* any good! Don't you *dare* think of going down there! Neither of us are strong enough to pull you out! What the fuck are you thinking!"

Boone stopped and shone the flashlight down into the stream again.

Burt's body was gone. Or at least out of sight. The cavern curved up ahead as did the stream.

Boone gave a sigh that sounded more like a shudder.

"Oh God. How did that happen? He was just a few feet in front of us."

Maisie, who had situated herself between them, started to cry.

"I'm scared Carrie," she said. "H-how are we going to get out of here without Burt? We must have walked miles by now. I'm hungry. And it's getting colder."

Carrie's voice was low and firm.

"Your jacket is in your pack— put it on. One problem at a time. I think I have some snacks in my pack. We can find our way out, Maisie, just be patient."

"Okay," Maisie agreed. She unzipped her bag as Boone shone the light on it and slipped her jacket on with Carrie's help. Maisie started crying again, wiping away tears on her sleeve.

"Don't cry," Carrie told her, giving her a hug, "Or I'll cry too..."

"But Burt!" Maisie said, "What if he's still alive? We don't even know where he went!"

Boone looked uneasy as he shone the flashlight upward, then to either side, then back behind them.

"We have a decision to make. Do we keep going on ahead, to wherever Burt was taking us? The alternative is to backtrack and try to remember which passages we took to get here. I think there were two forks and a three-way— do either of you remember how that went?"

"Not really," Carrie said. Her stomach grumbled audibly, but she said nothing.

"We were going down for a bit," Boone said, "But I think Burt said this trail went back up eventually— after the waterfall. We just need to keep going until we hit fresh air."

"No signal on the cell," Carrie fretted, putting her phone away, at least it's charged, so we can use the flashlight, right? Better than nothing!"

Boone revealed the light up ahead of them.

"Well let's start walking. We should be able to tell if we're descending...it would get warmer for one thing. If it stays cool and we follow the stream we might find an outlet. Or, if and when we reach the next open cavern, we might be able to climb up and get out. Carrie, you and Maisie are pretty good climbers, right?"

"We don't have rope," Carrie pointed out, "and not a lot of light. This isn't practice, there are no safety ropes...we could break our legs!"

Boone shone the flashlight under his chin. "Okay, fine. *You* come up with something better, princess. And by the way, nobody is going to die. *Lots* of people knew we were headed here. If we elect to stay in this one spot even, *guaranteed* we will be getting out of here in twenty-four hours. So that's my second question— should we just stay here?"

Carrie and Maisie looked at each other and then back at Boone.

"I don't wanna just stay here," Maisie said, "But we should leave something to mark the trail we took just in case we need to backtrack! Look– I have a notebook! We can just leave a trail of crumbled paper on the dry side of the path. That way we can find our way back."

"Smart kid," Boone said. "Okay then...onward and, hopefully, upward!"

They were able to walk two abreast at first, and then finally three abreast when the trail widened. It was pitch black except for the flashlight Boone was shining in front of them. The darkness was oppressive, and no one was talking.

Carrie was wearing a vintage Joe Boxer watch that had an Indiglo feature that allowed her to check the time. After they'd been walking for twenty minutes the trail forked again.

"Oh crap," Boone said shortly, "Now what? Do we remember? Do we toss a coin? Ladies?"

"Left," Carrie said, "Take the trail that continues along the stream. Maybe the stream will lead us outside at some point.

"The cavern might too," Boone pointed out. "But of course Burt isn't here..."

The words were barely out of his mouth when Maisie screamed and pointed at something hanging around a rock formation in the stream below them.

It was Burt. He was facedown, the gash on the back of his head had been wiped clean of blood by the stream. The wound looked like an open mouth. The more vigorous movement of the stream was making his body twist and turn as the current hit it. As the three teens stared stupefied, he rolled over in the water, staring right up at them with opaque, unseeing eyes and a slack mouth.

Maisie buried her face in Carrie's shoulder.

Boone cleared his throat.

"Maybe we should try the other way," he suggested. "Come on, let's try it for about fifteen minutes. We can always come back. Maisie you're still dropping paper, right?"

Maisie didn't answer, but Carrie said, "Maisie, give me the notebook. I can do it."

Carrie still had her arm around Maisie as they turned.

Fifteen minutes later, the path they'd chosen had narrowed and everyone but Maisie had to stoop to walk through it.

Carrie tugged on the back of Boone's shirt.

"Hey!" she said when he turned. "This doesn't seem like it's going anywhere. I vote we double back and get a drink from the stream."

"I thought you had the rest of your energy drink in your pack," Boone answered.

"I was saving it," Carrie said, annoyed, "It's all we have to drink!"

"I would think given the circumstances, *now* would be a perfect time to share," Boon said in irritation. "You don't know if that cave water is safe to drink. It might have weird microbes or dead guy funk in it or something."

"Fine!" Carrie said. She dropped her backpack off one of her slim shoulders and swung it around to rummage in it, pulling out the bottled drink and handing it to Maisie.

"Savor every sip," she told her, "This has to last...at least until they find us."

Maisie took the drink and twisted the cap off, taking a few tentative sips before returning it to her sister.

"Just a little further now," Boone said, adjusting his backpack. He moved more closely to Maisie.

"Hey Maisie— don't be upset! Everything will be fine, I swear!"

Maisie looked at him.

"I know you cheated with the card trick," she said. "Why should I believe you now?"

Boone's face went instantly red.

"Because I'm all you've got, that's why! Now stop moping and keep up!"

Carrie wasn't taking it well.

"What the fuck, Boone," she shouted, her voice echoing throughout the cave. "We should have stayed where we were. Or followed the stream. Now we're totally fucked!"

"Shhhhhhh, Carrie," Boone said. He was trying to sound calm, but there was an unmistakable note of panic in his voice. "Please, baby. I know we are going to find the other cavern soon. We're right on track. I can feel it!"

Boone mentioning time caused Carrie to remember her Joe Boxer watch. She lifted her arm and pressed the light up feature. It cast a steady bluish tinted light on all their faces.

Boone learned forward and kissed her.

"Stop yelling at me, my darling bee-otch," he said. "Let's keep going. Ten more minutes, I swear. Then, if you want to go back we'll go back, I promise...okay?"

He turned and his flashlight dimmed.

"Boone turn it back on high beam," Carrie complained, "I can hardly see to follow the trail."

"I didn't turn it down," Boone answered. "The batteries are getting low. Let's just keep going."

Fifteen minutes later, the utility flashlight went out.

Carrie scrabbled in her backpack and a narrower beam of light illuminated the dust motes in the cavern.

She exchanged a desperate look with Boone.

"I think we should go back. It's getting narrower in here and it doesn't feel right."

"Don't you feel it?" Boone asked her. His face was unreadable.

"Feel what!" she answered. She felt exhausted. All she wanted to do was sleep.

"Air," Maisie answered in excitement. "I can feel air moving! Boone's right! Let's keep going!"

Carrie wasn't feeling their enthusiasm. A sense of dread crept over her.

"Okay," she agreed, hoisting her backpack up over her shoulder again.

They'd only traveled another fifteen feet when the wall on their right disappeared, the ceiling clearance shooting up cathedral style at least fifteen feet. When Carrie shone the flashlight into the immense opening in the rock wall, they were all dumbstruck.

The cavern was three times the size of the initial cavern they'd encountered. The stalactites and stalagmites had an earth-covered base and tapered into long opalescent crystal cylinders with rounded tips.

Everywhere they shined the flashlight, rainbows danced as if the stalagmites were prisms.

For a moment they gazed in awe at their surroundings.

Then for the second time, there was a sharp cracking sound.

Maisie turned around startled. Boone was standing over Carrie. She was lying on the stone floor at the entrance.

"Why?" she wailed, looking up at Boone with a dazed expression. Blood flowed down the front of her face from a gash in her forehead.

"Maisie help me! Help me!" she screamed at her sister.

Maisie looked down at her, then turned again.

"Finish it," she whispered. Her voice echoed in the cavernous room. "I don't want her to suffer."

There was a short scream and another sound, this one more of a crunching sound, as stone impacted skull. It was heard twice, then a third time.

"It's done," Boone said, wiping the blood spatter from his forehead.

"Good," Maisie replied in an even tone. "I hope you're sure about the stream exit."

"Yep," Boone said, catching her around the waist and bending to kiss her for half a minute before he finished. "I told you I was here last week. I grew up here. All we need to do is follow the stream and go out the back mountain side."

"And how old do we have to be to get married in Kentucky?"

"Fifteen," Boone told her, grabbing a handful of her ass and pulling her close. "I think it's time I made an honest woman of you, Maisie!"

Maisie stopped looking at Boone in adoration for a moment and cast her eyes toward the dark spot where she had last heard her sister's plea.

"Cover her with rocks or something before we go— I don't want to think of her like that...okay?"

"You got it 'Jailbait'," Boone teased. "And lucky you— you don't have to be jealous anymore... I'm all yours!"

Their passionate kiss was interrupted by another sharp cracking sounds and the rumble of earth shifting.

"What the hell, Boone! Is this a cave-in? You told me it was safe!" Maisie shouted.

"I'm sorry, baby..." Boone said as he backed away, moving the dim light to his apologetic face for a few seconds.

Abruptly, he shifted his flashlight to the surrounding cave and again the light cast prisms through huge crystals— but the crystals were moving and glowed with an arcane light all their own. The totemic pillar had faces glowing in amber, red, orange, and white. The mouths moved as roars like shattering stone erupted through the chamber.

"I told you I'd make your wish come true, just like I can with the cards. Unfortunately for you, the price for the power of a god is the lives of his followers."

Maisie shrieked as two glowing red crystal wings ripped themselves from a ceiling and a monumental gargoyle crashed into the earth before her. Boone cast the light on her as she scrambled toward the exit. A crystal claw pierced her calf with a tight grip and lifted her high in the air. Blood gushed down her leg as she hung upside down. She looked into the light and cried, "Boone... I love you."

The words echoed back to her through the cavern, "I can see you do. Your jealous love shines like a diamond. My magic has its own raw appetites...

"...And all magic feasts on beauty."

THE END

CRIMINALLY UNDEAD

(A Paranormal Detectives Series Short)

BY LILY LUCHESI

Manhattan, NY

February, 2013

"WHAT'VE WE GOT?" DOCTOR VIVIENNE O'Neal asked as she stepped onto the crime scene, otherwise known as "work". This crime scene was a hotel room in Manhattan.

"Female, between twenty-five and thirty, looks like exsanguination. Won't know for sure till we get her to autopsy," replied homicide detective Nick Falcon.

Vivienne looked over the poor girl whose throat and wrists were precisely sliced. Blood surrounded her, thick and congealed. Even Vivienne could tell that she'd been dead for at least two days. If the stench hadn't been enough of a clue, the flies eating out her eyeballs were a dead giveaway. The blood only had a single arterial spray that hit the wall to the left of the bed. The rest was pooled beneath the corpse.

"These look similar to the murder last month," she said. "The cuts where she'd bleed the most, leaving her in the same position on the bed, she's young and beautiful, and if she died from exsanguination, it'll be almost identical to the previous murder." She bent down, ignoring the smell. The wrists were slit vertically and horizontally. The neck wound was made by a thin blade, but the killer had held the wound open, so it looked like she had a second smile two inches below the chin.

"If the coroner says that she has more blood missing than we can see on the floor here..." Detective Jack Corrie trailed off. "We don't need a serial killer on the loose during election season."

Vivienne, who was twenty years younger than Corrie and ten years younger than Falcon, couldn't believe how callous they were. "Don't you think you should be more worried about the safety of the people in your jurisdiction than your captain getting reelected?" Shaking her head, she made notes on her tablet.

Vivienne was a criminal psychologist. She usually worked for the FBI, but she was on loan for the next year to the Major Crimes department at the NYPD. A child prodigy, she'd graduated from medical school when she was twenty-two, got her PhD at twenty-eight, and joined the FBI that same year. Now she was thirty, working on a novel about criminal psychology and was the only reason that Manhattan PD had even solved a case since December.

She waited for hours till the coroner called her and the two detectives down to autopsy to give them her findings.

"Facial recognition confirms: your victim was twenty-five year old Sarah Brimley, originally from London. She died between eleven P.M. Saturday night and three A.M. Sunday morning. Cause of death: exsanguination."

"Was there blood missing?" Falcon asked.

"Yes. I can't be completely sure, because a lot of it was on the bed and wall of the hotel, but as close as a total of one pint is missing." She heaved a sigh. "I can't confirm that you are dealing with the same killer both times, but it looks like it was the same weapon, like a doctor's scalpel, that was used on both victims."

"Of course you can't confirm it," Vivienne said. "That's why I'm here. Email me copies of the report, including photos." She walked away and Falcon followed her. He was always interested in her life, and could be friendly when he wasn't busy being Corrie's tool, but he wasn't her type. He was on the short side, blonde, with a heavy Hampton's accent.

The fact that he'd grown up a privileged Congressman's son was another turn off, as was his tendency to be a follower as opposed to a leader.

"Where are you off to tonight?" he asked.

"My old roommate is opening her gallery in March. I offered to help her fix it up a little. She gets scared being there at night." Vivienne put on her favorite leather jacket and gathered her things. "I'll go over the report and have my preliminary evaluation by noon tomorrow. Goodnight."

* * *

Vivienne had been good friends with her college roommate, Clara White. While she was serious and analytical, Clara was artistic and free-spirited. They bonded over a love of literature and *Supernatural* and never lost contact after graduation. She'd been ecstatic when Clara had finally bought her own art gallery, and now she was ready to have her first show.

"Hey, you're hard at work," she said, coming into the bright room and wincing. The harsh lighting was going to be great for viewing art, but terrible on the pale complexion of someone who spent most of her time at a laptop.

"Hi, Viv. Grab a hammer and join the fun." Clara was an endless optimist whose bubbly personality couldn't be burst.

Despite still being in her slacks and nice, black silk shirt, Vivienne shucked her jacket and heeled boots to help out. She wasn't great, but she could fix a wall decently enough. She put her phone on speaker for some music and they got to work.

After half an hour, there was a knock on the door. "Expecting someone?" Vivienne asked. It was a bit late for callers to an empty art gallery.

"Shit! I forgot, the artist wanted to stop by and see the room, so he knows how many pieces to put out on display." Clara went to answer the door as Vivienne shut the music off.

The two voices carried in the empty room: Clara's high, musical tones and a male baritone with a sexy accent. The man that entered was just as sexy as his voice. He was tall, with styled black hair, fair skin, and the brightest blue eyes she'd seen. His smile was pleasant with a hint of mischief hidden just below the surface. He might've been about ten years older than Vivienne.

"This is my best friend, Dr. Vivienne O'Neal," Clara said when she came into view. "She's helping me fix the place up. Viv, this is John Francis, the artist whose work I'm showcasing for the gallery opening."

"Pleasure to meet you, Doctor." He took her hand in his large, strong one.

So unusual for an artist, she noted. *Their hands are usually delicate.*

"The pleasure is mine," Vivienne replied. "I read an article on you in a magazine. They called you a cross between Monet and Gorey. I'm interested in seeing your work in person."

"Thank you." Hands behind his back, he turned to survey the room. "This is a wonderful gallery. It has some twists, perfect for a surprising piece here and there. And the lighting is so harsh, it's perfect to showcase the brutality of my work."

"Wonderful! I'm expecting to have it ready for a media showing on Valentine's Day, and for public viewing March first. Does that timeline work for you?" Clara asked.

Vivienne, trained to see subtleties in a person's countenance, saw something akin to panic and worry pass across John's fair features.

"Well. I assumed I'd have a little more time. I suppose I need to paint a little faster then." He grinned, and the panic was gone. "You'll display what, ten of mine? I should be able to manage that in two weeks. I've already got six finished and an idea for the seventh."

He turned around, surveying the room a final time. His eyes were sharp, a bit calculating. Vivienne had never been more attracted to a man. Something about him drew her like a lodestone. What was it about him, hidden in the depths of his pretty eyes that was so alluring, so mysterious? She didn't know, but she had a sudden desire to discover it for herself.

Evidently, John found something equally intriguing in her, as he made her his next study. His eyes roamed over her long brown hair, her round cheeks, hazel eyes, and full lips.

"Dr. O'Neal, may I presume on so short an acquaintance and ask you to dinner tomorrow night?" he asked. "Forgive my bluntness. I'm normally not so forward."

"Blunt? They must do things differently in England. That was calculated and polite, not blunt. Believe me, I know blunt." Vivienne smiled, thinking of Falcon's attempts at flirtation. She reached into her purse and pulled out her business card. "Here. Give me a call tomorrow afternoon." His fingers deliberately brushed hers as he took it, giving her old-fashioned chills.

He read the card and then put it in his wallet. "I will call. Till tomorrow, Doctor." He turned to Clara. "A pleasure doing business with you, Ms. White."

He gave them both a wave and left, and Vivienne saw that the view of him was just as tempting from behind as it was from the front. *What on Earth is wrong with me? I never do this,* she thought, confused. She always knew what she was doing and why. Work surprised her at times, but her personal life never did; she made sure of it. Every movement was analyzed before it was implemented. Agreeing to a date with an artist she'd only known for half an hour? Not part of the plan.

"Viv? Are you okay?" Clara asked. "I've known you twelve years and I think you've dated twice. And that was after talking my ear off with pros and cons. What just happened?"

Vivienne was silent for a moment. She then answered as honestly as she could: "I have no clue."

* * *

Vivienne distracted herself all the next morning by reviewing the crime scene photos and autopsy report in her office.

The killer was precise and methodical in every move he made. Another thing that should be noted that everyone was forgetting was that, despite the victims' being young and beautiful, neither one had been sexually assaulted before or after their murders.

One pint of blood taken, she thought. *What's so special about one pint of blood?* She tapped her pen against her notebook, where she made preliminary notes before writing her final report. All she could think of was that he had a vampire fetish or, depending on his level of insanity, thought that he *was* a vampire. *I hope I'm not dealing with a murderer and a schizophrenic. I don't need to deal with someone like that again.*

She began to type up her report, which contained more speculation than usual, because this was a whole different kind of killer than she'd dealt with before.

Of course, instead of reading her report, Captain Lopez asked her to read the key points to him, Corrie and Falcon. Why didn't he just read her report? Why make her write it up and then waste her time in explaining it all to them? Oh, right...because none of them properly understood the medical terminology she used and needed it explained in layman's terms.

"This killer is most likely male, between the ages of thirty and fifty. While I can't confirm that his weapon of choice is in fact a scalpel, I find it best to go on as if we are certain that it is, unless proven otherwise. He's very precise, making slow, sure cuts where the most blood will be expelled from the body in the most timely manner possible. That also seems like he might be a doctor or even a medical student.

"He's either careless about leaving a pattern or knows exactly what he's doing. More likely he has a reason for his obvious patterns, because he seems too smart and careful to accidentally leave a trail for us to follow. It doesn't fit the profile.

"He targets women in their mid to late-twenties who are physically attractive, the typical targets of serial killers in media. I can't say he's following what is considered the norm for killers, but if he's just starting out his murderous career, this might be just a stepping stone or a way for him to test the waters, so to speak.

"The most unsettling thing, and what confuses me the most, is the missing pint of blood from both victims. Is it a signature, like his perfectly placed cuts? Does he have a vampire fetish or even think that he *is* a vampire? I highly doubt the latter, because vampires are usually associated with sex and, again, the women weren't assaulted and there were also no bite marks. Not even needle marks to resemble vampire bites. So, what does he do with the blood he steals? If it's a souvenir or trophy, where would he keep it? What would he do with it? Find the answer to that, and you'll find the killer."

"So, where do you suggest we start looking for suspects?" Corrie asked.

"Medical records," Vivienne replied. "See if they visited the same doctors' offices or hospitals recently. If not, see if they dated doctors or med students, if they were acquainted with any, things like that. If you strike out with doctors, I'll reevaluate my hypothesis, though I do believe I'm on the right track."

"For everyone's sake, let's hope you're right," Corrie said.

Vivienne sighed. She despised doing all of the work and getting none of the credit, which usually happened here at the sixteenth precinct.

"Hey, don't get yourself down," Falcon said, placing his hand on her arm. She immediately shrugged it off. Before she had to remind him she wasn't fond of being touched uninvited, her phone rang.

"Dr. O'Neal," said the smooth, cool voice on the other end of the line. "I'm glad you picked up."

She couldn't stop her entire countenance from brightening. "Mr. Francis, I'm glad you called. Please, call me Vivienne."

"Only if you call me John," he replied. "I wanted to ask you if you wanted to dine with me this evening?"

"I'd love to, John. When were you thinking of? I leave work at six."

"Okay. How about we meet at the restaurant? There's a nice place on Madison I've been meaning to try. Are you averse to French food?" he asked.

"Averse? I *am* French," she said. "I'll see you tonight."

"Wonderful. See you soon, *ma cherie*." He hung up, leaving her in a rare state of emotional disarray. She couldn't recall a man ever making her feel this weak in the knees, or so flushed.

Falcon overheard her end of the conversation and looked envious. "Friend of yours?"

"I hope so," she replied. She went back into her office and left Falcon standing there like an idiot.

Why did he feel jealous? In the short time Vivienne had known him, she had never once alluded to thinking of him as anything more than a temporary coworker. He carried a torch for her regardless of her aloof attitude. It was annoying, to say the least.

* * *

Vivienne arrived at the upscale French restaurant at the exact moment John did. He looked impeccable in a slate grey suit, white shirt, and undone tie. It was cold, but he wore no coat.

"*Bon soir*," he said, kissing her hand playfully.

«*Bon soir, monsieur*,» she replied. "Do you speak French or did you learn a few phrases just to impress me?"

"Don't flatter yourself," he said, his eyes alight. "I'm multilingual." He pulled her chair out for her before seating himself.

They ordered drinks and hors d'oeuvres before beginning to converse. "So, what kind of psychology do you specialize in?" he asked.

"Criminal," she replied. "I'm an FBI liaison with NYPD in Manhattan."

"Really? That must be exciting," he said. "Which department?"

"Major Crimes. I'm currently on a homicide case," she explained. "I can't say much more than that, since it's an ongoing investigation."

He held up a hand. "I understand. I'm actually quite interested in criminology. I had toyed with the idea of being a bobby in London, but art is my passion and I couldn't deny it."

"And you paint beautifully," she said. "What will your show be like?"

"Actually, you might enjoy this: I'm basing the paintings on famous murders. Like I said, I enjoy criminology; I wish to find beauty in death." He toyed with his wineglass. "These things are portrayed in the media as terrifying. While the murders are deplorable acts, I'd like to change the idea of death being horrible and grotesque."

Vivienne was intrigued. "I like the sound of that."

"Why are you interested in criminal psychology?" he asked.

This was a difficult yet inevitable question. She'd been through a terrible childhood trauma, went to plenty of doctors, and was now as fine as could be expected. However, she preferred not talking about it if she could help it.

"Well, did you ever hear about the serial killer Samuel O'Neill— not spelled like my name —who was caught in 1996?" she asked.

John nodded. "Yes, I read a book that mentioned him. He had killed seventeen women that they know of, and kept their legs as souvenirs in a meat locker below the building his family lived in. His wife found the legs and confronted him. He killed her and their child saw it. The kid turned him in, isn't that right? They claimed he drank the victim's blood like a vampire."

Vivienne confirmed he was correct. "Right. I lived in that building. I was ten."

"My Lord, that must've been awful for you," he said. He put his hand on hers. "I'm glad you're using your trauma for good."

Despite not liking being touched uninvited, she shivered at his touch. Was this what the novels she'd read talked about? Were these warm feelings indicative of an emotion Vivienne hadn't felt in twenty years? She avoided dating if she could, and intimacy was out of the question. Why now? Why him? Just because he was handsome? Because of the accent? Because of his talent and sensitivity? She might be a psychologist, but she couldn't analyze this feeling.

He smiled at her. "Your nervousness shows. You have nothing to fear from me."

"I'm not afraid of you," she said. "I'm afraid of how I feel."

"Why's that?" he asked, tilting his head and making a lock of raven hair fall over his brow. She wanted to run her fingers through it.

"What I saw...a husband doing something so unspeakable to his wife...I have never considered a romantic relationship. Feeling the way I do frightens me," she admitted.

His smile widened. "Really? It flatters me that I have this sort of effect on you." He reached out and brushed her cheek with his forefinger. "Do not fear your emotions. Embrace them."

"I can only try," she said.

He walked her home. Standing outside her apartment building, he gently took her hand in his. Another unwelcome touch that Vivienne found she actually did welcome.

"*Bonne nuit, ma belle*," he said, leaning down and placing the gentlest of kisses on her lips. "I look forward to seeing you again." He winked, walked away, and was swallowed up by the night.

* * *

"I need to talk to you," Falcon said, running up to Vivienne as soon as she got off the elevator. "And I don't want anyone else to hear. You are the only person I can trust with what I am about to say."

She arched her brows. "All right. In my office." She led him into the sterile room and locked the door. She gestured for him to sit, but he instead began to pace about the small room. "Falcon, are you all right? What is it?"

"I know what the killer does with the blood," he said. "And you know, too."

"Excuse me?" she asked, bristling at the accusation that she would withhold evidence or even a theory from the police.

"April of 1996: Samuel O'Neill was murdered by the FBI after resisting arrest for the murders of eighteen women. He drank their blood like an animal while they lived and kept their legs as souvenirs," Falcon began. "His daughter, one Vivienne Caitlin O'Neill, was the one who called the FBI. But it wasn't *just* the FBI. These people were the fucking *X-Files*, shooting him down with silver bullets. Of course, silver bullets couldn't kill him, so he was decapitated. You changed your name after that, to distance yourself from him as much as possible."

Vivienne was stunned. "How did you know any of that?" she asked, her voice shaky and low in her throat.

"My father is one of the Congressmen who voted to keep this secret FBI affiliate, the Paranormal Investigative Division, running. Their HQ is in Chicago, but they have agents here, too. I am training to join them," Falcon explained.

"You're crazy," Vivienne said. "Vampires don't exist. There is no Paranormal whatever you called it in the FBI. Don't be ridiculous. Now, please stop wasting precious time talking about Count Dracula when you have a serial killer on the loose!"

Falcon leaned over the desk and looked her in the eye. "You know I'm telling the truth. You know what you saw when you were ten."

She lowered her gaze. "The doctors told me I was imagining it."

"Of course they did! The less mortals know about the paranormal, the better," Falcon scoffed. "Please. Help me catch this son of a bitch. You know it's real and it's gonna kill more people if you don't help me stop it."

Vivienne stood up, her eyes red with angry tears. "If you believe this, then go and call the PID and tell them to get on it! Why bother with me?"

"Because the FBI, legally, can't take this case yet, even the PID. It's up to us."

She sighed, placing her hand over her eyes. She didn't want to be thrown back into the dark past she had gone through Hell to forget. "Don't make me go back to that place in my psyche," she whispered. "I can't take it."

"You can." Falcon's voice was as soft as she had ever heard it. "If anyone can do it, you can. I know it. Don't let any more women wind up like your mother did."

"Fine." She sighed, and then said a phrase she had never expected herself to say: "Let's go vampire hunting."

Later that day she sat at her desk, trying to be sure she was not dreaming. Her father had been a good man, until he started working the night shift at the local hospital. He had changed, become...a vampire. His Sire was either in the wind or killed by the PID and he was ravenous. Why he kept souvenirs she never understood, but he fed as little as possible and never fed on her or her mother until he had been found out as a vampire. Working the graveyard shift in a day-loving family, it was easy for his appearance and lack of appetite to be overlooked, which was why it had gone on for seventeen long months.

She had gone to many shrinks, and they had finally drugged her with the right meds and told her there was no such things as vampires. However, her dreams told her the truth.

In her nightmares, she heard her mother shriek when she went into the meat locker; she saw her mother wake her father and tell him to call the police; she saw her father rise up from the bed, eyes red and a mouth filled with sharp, protruding fangs, and attack her like a wild animal.

She had screamed and cried, watching those unearthly fangs pierce her mother's jugular. The blood had gushed up like a fountain, splattering her father's face and the wall. Not much was lost, however, as he began drinking like a dehydrated man at a fountain. The blood was dark and thick. She could clearly recall the smell of it as she ran off and dialed the number in the speed dial that was supposed to be 911. How it connected her to the PID, she did not know. It was now something she needed to think about.

How had her mother known about the PID? Her father hadn't been a vampire his whole life, so how had her mother known about a secret government agency to fight against the paranormal? Had she known that Samuel had been turned? She needed answers, and she needed them fast. Unfortunately, she wouldn't be getting them fast enough.

Another body had been found, not far from where she had been having dinner the previous night.

The crime scene was typical and the kill was exactly the same, except more blood was gone from the body than just a pint, and the cut was just on the neck, not the wrists.

Corrie looked sick. "She's lost so much blood, she looks like a husk."

He was right, she seemed shriveled. Her eyes had deep hollows, as did her cheeks and collarbones. The gash was so wide, the vampire must have been drenched with the blood. Unless it turned into a bat, there was no way it could have gone unnoticed. Even in Manhattan, that would be considered conspicuous.

It's getting hungrier. That could have been me last night, she thought, and then she did something unprecedented: she threw up.

"I thought Goths like you loved blood," Corrie joked.

"I was having dinner here last night, you asshat," she said. "That could have been me!"

"At least you turned away and didn't contaminate the body," Corrie muttered.

Falcon led her away, pretending that he was going to get her some water. "What do you think happened? It never killed this quickly before, and it took more blood than usual."

Vivienne shook her head. "I don't know. I'm not familiar with the feeding habits of the Undead!"

"Don't get snippy with me. I didn't make it come here!" Falcon sighed. "What do we do?"

Vivienne, looking back over at the bloodless corpse, said, "Pray."

* * *

"You're joking."

John had called Vivienne that evening to talk, and was shocked when she'd told him about the murder right where they had been dining the previous night.

"I wish I was," she said. "It's the same killer we've been tracking. It seems he is escalating and I'm starting to get nervous."

"Do you have any leads?" John asked.

"Not as to who, but we have more details than we did before. Detective

Falcon and I have put together a...more precise profile. The only thing now is to find the one who fits it," she said. She rubbed the bridge of her nose. "What I wouldn't give for a vacation without any murders. I'm terrified he's going to escalate...or worse."

"What's worse than escalating?" John wondered.

"Disappearing. Turning up somewhere we won't hear about and maybe never getting caught. More women dying at his hands," she said. "Anyway, onto better topics. How's the painting going?"

"Wonderfully," he said. "I've done two in three days. Might be a record for me. I need three more and I will have my newest showcase completed. You know, it is quite fortunate that I found Clara's ad when I relocated here. I think it was meeting you that inspired me to keep painting so much."

"Well, I must say I always desired to be someone's muse," she joked. "I can't wait to see what you've been working on."

"In six days you will be able to," he said. "I have to bring the paintings to Clara's show. Did she tell you she wants to open it early for the press?"

"Uh-huh. It's going to be a zoo. Cameras flashing...too many voices in that small space. Ugh." Vivienne shuddered.

"I think I'd much rather spend time with you instead of in that Hellish nightmare," John commented. "The cameras alone make me shudder."

Vivienne's ears perked up at that one. Indeed, she looked almost cat-like in her attentiveness and curiosity as she leaned forward in her chair. "I never asked, how long have you been here?"

"A month. I was visiting Chicago before this, and before that I was traveling in Europe. I admit, I have not been home to London in quite some time," he said.

Like a century? Vivienne thought. *It can't be!* Could the man she was falling for, be a vampire? She needed to think. She needed to make a list of facts to help her keep things in perspective. Most of all, she needed to stop listening to his smooth, sexy voice. It was distracting.

"I'm sorry. There's another call," she said, interrupting him in the middle of his talking about a haunted convent in France.

"I'm afraid I've been prattling on too long. Would you like to go for dinner tomorrow?" he asked.

"I'll let you know." *And make a plan, too.*

She hung up and went to her desk. She ignored her shaking hands as she got out her notepad and a red pen. She marked everything of a personal nature in red. Like blood. She began writing, her usually unreadable script even worse due to nerves.

I've never seen John in daylight, however, I have only seen him twice.

I've never spoken to him on the phone before twilight.

I can't recall what he ate at the restaurant. I only remember he had wine.

He's paler than I am, and his lips are thin but undeniably a darker pink than anyone's I've seen.

I've never seen a photo of him, just a well-done portrait.

His ears have a point to them, like a vampire.

He came here around the time of the first murder.

She stopped writing and shook her head. How could John be a vampire? She'd be dead by then, wouldn't she? No vampire would leave prey alive for so long. He would've eaten *her* after their date, not a waitress. So she was making a mistake. She was jumping to conclusions out of fear and desperation. As a doctor, she should know better.

Then again, as a doctor she should also believe that vampires weren't real, and yet there it was, proven to her thanks to her own father.

"I'm being silly. If a person were to look at me, they'd think *I* was a vampire! I can't judge until I get to know John better," she said, going back to her phone. She text him, asking if they could do lunch instead. In a few minutes, he replied.

"Sorry. Daylight is my painting time. Dinner?"

She bit her lip. Perfectly plausible. "How about Patsy's on 56th? I'll make a reservation."

"I'll do it. See you tomorrow at eight."

Patsy's was an Italian restaurant. Garlic City. If he went there, he was obviously mortal. She felt her muscles relax. It was okay.

* * *

The chef at Patsy's was closing up for the night, proud of the clientele they had brought in that night. More celebrities and politicians than ever, and they all went online to rave about his food. He considered this a good night. They had reservations booked solid for the next month!

As he went around back to check the locks, he heard a throat clear. He jumped, frightened, but calmed when he saw a well-dressed man standing there. He recognized him from his self-portraits, an artist from London.

"Hello, sir. May I help you?" he asked, thinking he might have been a patron.

"Ah, yes, perhaps you can," the man said. "You are the head chef, correct?"

"Yes. I know you: you have a gallery showing next week," he said. "My wife loves your artwork. We bought tickets to it already."

The man smiled. The chef imagined that many women found him sexy and charming. He was putting a spell over him, and he had never looked twice at another man. Something in the back of his mind went to a priest he had met when he was a child. He warned him about "unearthly charming" people. He said they would lead him astray. At the time, he had thought he meant that pretty people would make him sin. Now he was remembering how Count Dracula had charmed his prey.

"What can I help you with, sir?" he asked, his hands clammy.

"My girlfriend wants to come here tomorrow. Obviously, I cannot do that, and since I can get a reservation anywhere, I've no reason to tell her why we cannot dine here. I'm afraid I must dine myself, however," he said.

"...We're closed now, as you can see," the chef said, his stomach doing flip flops.

"I care not for your restaurant's food," the man said. "My palate is more refined." He stepped closer, and the chef was too frightened to move. His knees felt as if they would give out at any moment. "A pity your wife will have to attend my show alone. Perhaps she'll join you afterwards."

In the blink of an eye, the handsome man's eyes turned red and black, his jaw extended and revealed a mouthful of fangs, two of which were about three inches long. His hands at his sides twitched, and his nails elongated. They looked as sharp as his fangs. A little squeak left the chef's lips and he felt urine trickle down his leg as the vampire advanced on him.

"I wonder if you will taste as good as the food you feed the human waste," he said, his voice a low hiss. "I can't use you in my art— you really don't embody feminine beauty —but that means I can enjoy more of you."

When those disgusting fangs pierced his throat, the chef felt them go through his skin like a hot knife in butter, like someone had stabbed his very soul. The tiny fangs all through the vampire's mouth also pricked him, like tiny needles dipped in rubbing alcohol. No pain could compare to this agony. The chef felt his blood spurt out before the mouth came back, drinking and draining him of his life.

The vampire's appetite knew no bounds and the chef had to watch as his life was taken, he felt himself grow weaker as he heard the vampire hungrily slurping up his blood, until he passed into blissful death.

* * *

As soon as Vivienne walked into the precinct, she saw everyone running around like madmen.

"Did the killer strike again?" she asked.

Corrie shook his head. "Nope. Not unless he suddenly switched teams."

"What?"

Falcon rolled his eyes. "The victim was a man. And Major Crimes was called because he's a bit of a known personae. Ever watch Food Network?"

She rolled her eyes. "All the time. Bobby Flay's divorce got messy?"

Falcon was surprised into laughter. Vivienne never made jokes. "It was the chef from Patsy's. He was once a guest on one of their shows. I'm actually glad that this is a new murder. I was starting to become too obsessive over...Viv? What's wrong?"

Vivienne had sunk down into the nearest chair, her already pale face ashen. "It was him. God, I can't believe this!"

"How do you know it was him? It doesn't fit the profile. Alone that this is a man makes it seem unlikely," he said.

"You don't understand." *Maybe it's a coincidence,* she thought.

"We'll go to the crime scene. There's no way the vamp would change his style. They're creatures of habit. You'll see." He got his things and she rode with the two detectives to the crime scene on 56th.

The coroner was already there and she said, "Definitely not your serial killer. The only similarity is the loss of blood. I know you two have seen a lot, but this one is brutal, so she might need a minute."

"First, I don't approve of being spoken about as if I were deaf or not present. Second, you have no idea what I have witnessed in my life." Vivienne was bristling at her impertinence. She wondered if the coroner would be able to handle watching her father murder her mother for food. Doubtful.

The body in the back of the alley by a garbage bin like trash, was certainly in a bad state. This was not a prettily laid out corpse like the women. There was no art in this murder. It was brutal.

The throat was not cut, it was slashed with what looked like a serrated blade and was gaping wide, a jagged hole that should have had congealed blood around it. Instead, it was stained at the edges, but there was no blood to congeal. The man's blood was on the ground beneath him, but there was not enough blood to have filled a grown man.

"Well, I don't think this is our killer," Corrie said, bending down to examine the body a bit closer. "Now we have two cases to solve."

The sight of the mangled and bloodless body made her think that this couldn't be the same killer. No killer, mortal or not, changed their patterns so abruptly. Maybe this was another vampire, or just some psycho. Either way, it wasn't John. Which meant she had been overreacting.

Thank God, she thought, trying to hide a relieved smile.

* * *

Valentine's Day was not just the deadline for John to have his paintings at Clara's gallery, but also the day of a special press and industry professional preview show. John invited Vivienne as his date. They had not seen each other since their abruptly canceled date, and when she saw him again she wondered why she had ever thought he could possibly be a vampire. Vampires were ugly, accented creatures who ripped your throat open and smelled like grave dirt. They did not wear fancy cologne, silk suits purchased on Savile Row, and Giuseppe Zanotti shoes. Nor did they kiss you sweetly on the lips as a hello.

"I can't wait for you to see my work," he said as they walked to the gallery.

"I'm sure it will be wonderful. Though I wish the paintings weren't based on murders. I've been surrounded by far too much death the past week," she admitted.

When they approached the gallery, it was just opened and Clara was waiting impatiently for them outside the door. Press was already inside, as were the elite clientele who had advance access to the opening.

Clara gave Vivienne a big hug and kiss and shook John's hand. "I can't thank you enough for doing this opening with me," she said. "Everyone is already tweeting about your art."

"Are the restrictions I set in place?" he asked.

"No cameras? Of course. I made sure of it, and the security I hired are on the lookout tonight for any wayward cell phones," Clara said.

"I didn't want them taking photos of the art till the official opening on the first," John explained to Vivienne, who nodded. "It's not fair to the public who will pay to get into the gallery that people will be able to peruse the work online for free before them."

Entering the gallery, Vivienne took a breath. This was a huge crowd, and she had no trouble imagining a vampire hiding among them, ready to bite when the mood struck them. She knew vampires could hide amongst society, and events like these probably drew them like a lodestone.

John had to leave her side to go and talk with press and other important people, letting her view the art without him hovering, waiting to see what she thought. She recognized some of the bigger murders, some real and some fictional. All were beautiful women, and he only used three colors: black, white, and a lot of red. He really did create beauty in death.

She was still looking when the press conference started. Clara spoke first, talking about her hopes and dreams for the gallery, and how much she loved art.

John spoke second, talking about the brutality and beauty of his art, how he mixed the two ideas to create something wholly unique. His voice mesmerized the audience, even Vivienne. But something kept drawing her attention away from John. Something in the painting she was standing next to. She struggled to drown out his hypnotic voice and focused on what she was trying to get in her mind. Was it the scene? Not really. She had known he was using murders in his art, and finding a murder she was a consultant on was not surprising. No, it was the way the blood was painted, the way the paint smelled...

What *was* it? It was driving her crazy. Something had triggered a sensory memory. She recalled the first murder from the serial killer she was tracking. Beautiful dark haired woman in her bedroom. Laid out like a model. Blood covering her naked body. She remembered putting on a glove and touching the small spray on the headboard, thinking that the blood flaked away like paint. She recalled the coppery smell of it.

No one was looking. She reached and touched the paint. It wasn't paint. It was blood. Without thinking, she ran from the gallery.

* * *

"I think John Francis is the killer."

Nick Falcon had been watching *Hannibal* on his tablet on Netflix and had to adjust the phone, making sure he heard correctly. After all, there was a killer on that show named Francis. "The guy you're dating? He's the killer? How the Hell would you know?"

She proceeded to explain about the paintings in a rushed breath.

"Okay. Okay. Let me get in contact with the PID. We need to turn this case over to them now that you've got a suspect. Are you okay? Where are you?" he asked.

"At home. I called Clara and left her a voicemail, leaving out the vampire stuff. I told her we had it under control and to not say anything," she replied.

"Are you sure we can trust her?" Nick asked. "One slip, and not only could she die, we could lose the vamp, too."

"Yes. I'd trust her with my life. She questioned me when I decided to date John, and I should have listened to her. My God, I was this close to being his fucking dinner!" He heard her take a calming breath.

"The thing is, you weren't. You got us to catch him. You're a hero, Viv. Let me go. Let me take care of this so we can all sleep easy tomorrow."

* * *

They might sleep easy the next night, but Clara White wouldn't. She was sleeping permanently. The PID hadn't gotten to John in time: he had killed her. They found her in her gallery the morning after Valentine's Day, laid out like the others, but not carefully drained of blood. Because John didn't need anymore blood for his art. This had just been for food.

Her pale, gaunt face was peaceful, as if she were asleep. Only the holes at her jugular said otherwise. It was a classic vampire bite, just like in the movies. When Vivienne saw what had happened, probably because of her, she burst into tears. She was no longer the cold psychologist, but the grieving friend.

Nick put an arm around her shoulders in comfort and she did not shrug it off, which was a first. Right then, she needed all the comfort she could get.

"They're going to get him," Nick whispered. "Tonight."

"I hope they torture him before they execute him," she said.

As they left the crime scene, Corrie ordered her to go home. She looked awful, he said, and he was right. She felt awful. She might have been the cause of death for her best friend! She felt dizzy and sick, she ached from the stress.

Nick caught up with her as she left. "Do you want me to take you home? You really shouldn't be alone."

While his solicitousness was a nice change from his slightly pervy way he looked at her, she didn't like him enough to invite him into her home. Despite his humanity, she just couldn't bring up any extra trust for any male at that point: species notwithstanding.

"I'm fine on my own."

"If they catch him, I'll let you know," he said.

"You better. I want to see him pay for what he's done."

At home, she laid on her couch beneath a throw blanket, watching a movie, but not really seeing it. There was something nagging at her mind about the latest crime scene. It was too...perfect. Too staged. Too "*I vant to suck your bloooooood*" worthy. Did vampire bites really look like that? Perfectly spaced? No bruising? Bites bruised. Or was it just the lack of blood that didn't make Clara's bite bruise?

Was there even a lack of blood? There had been a lot of it splashed around the gallery. Had he drank *anything*? Or was this just a warning to her? Was she next? Too many questions. Not enough answers. She wanted to sleep, to pass out into oblivion until this nightmare was over. She called it a nightmare, yet this was reality. Thinking about the Paranormal Detectives who worked at the FBI, she wondered how they could live this life day in and day out. How did they not go crazy? She felt like she was losing every vestige of sanity she possessed.

As she let her mind go down the rabbit hole, she was startled by her phone ringing.

"They got him."

She made her way down to the FBI building and went into the basement offices. She was glad it was so late that there was no one around who would recognize her and ask her what she was doing. How on Earth could she explain it?

She met Nick outside an iron and silver door that led to a room with no windows facing the halls. He was grinning like he had won the lottery...or her heart. Both were probably equal to him.

"What's that?" Nick asked, gesturing to the file in her hand.

"Crime scene photos. I said I want to question him and I still do," she replied. "Vampire or not, this was still my case and I've a right to all the information I desire."

He nodded. "Can you do it alone? I'm going to the gallery with the PID to make sure there's nothing Corrie and I missed."

"Go on. Not like I haven't been alone with him before," she said, feeling sick at the thought of how close to being dinner she had become.

"Good. Well, they'll be outside if you need any help. Someone from the Chicago office will be arriving soon to take him there for execution." Nick gestured to two burly men outside the door. They looked like security. "The werewolves are great guards against vampires because vamps can't bite them."

Werewolves. Those two guards are werewolves. God help me, I need a vacation, she thought. "Okay. Thanks for...bringing the reality of this to my attention. The doctors made me believe what I saw as a child was my imagination. Frankly, I wish it had been."

He walked away and she took a breath before entering the room. Sitting at a desk, chained from his wrists to his legs with blessed silver cuffs and leg irons, looking as calm as if he were at a cocktail party, was John. The first man she had let herself think might be decent, the first man to attract her attention in years and the second man to turn out to be a devil is disguise.

He certainly didn't look like a monster facing execution: his hair was perfect, his face was elegant and sexy, his blue eyes hinted at mischief, and he was smiling. Smiling!

"Vivienne," he said, his voice so alluring she felt weak. "Congratulations. The strongest vampire in the world has been tracking me for nearly two centuries, and you managed to capture me in two weeks. An impressive feat."

"You got careless. Killing the chef at the Italian place we were supposed to eat at? Not even TV writers would have made that kind of mistake," she said, trying to force her emotions aside and be just the analytical doctor. It wasn't working. "I have a few questions for you, John. And it looks like you're in no position to refuse me answers."

"Well, if that's the case, I suppose you should know my name isn't John Francis," he said.

"What's your name, then?"

He smirked, and she saw the flash of his eyes for a quick second. "Does it matter? They're holding me because I need to go to Chicago for execution. Dead men need no names."

"Why did you keep me alive? Why not drink from me like you did everyone else?" she asked.

"Because I have watched you. Since you were a little girl. You always showed such...life. Such vivacity. Such bravery. I knew your parents, you know. Your mother's parents were killed by a werewolf when she was about twenty-five, so that's why she had the PID's number on speed dial. I know you were wondering that.

"I was a night time colleague of your father's at the hospital. I ran the blood bank." He smirked again, but Vivienne didn't see the humor. "One night, there was a terrible car crash. It was a truly bloody mess. Mangled bodies everywhere, many of them still alive and pumping that sweet nectar all over the place. Of course, I couldn't drink any of it.

"I was so hungry and I needed to feed. Your father happened to cross my path on our break. He was covered in blood and I lost control. I realized I couldn't leave his dead body there, so I turned him. Managed to keep him civilized for quite some time, too. I can't comprehend why he kept souvenirs of his kills. No self-respecting vampire would ever do that. His humanity was his downfall."

Vivienne felt weak. "*You* turned my father? You made him a monster?"

"No. I *was* your father's Sire. I did not make him a 'monster'. You know, there are many vampires who follow the law and never kill mortals. Your father could have easily become one of them. But he didn't. He became a killer because, apparently, he already had the killer instinct inside of him when he was a mortal," he explained.

"Bullshit," Vivienne replied. "My father wasn't a killer until you made him one. And besides, what do you mean you watched me? What kind of pervert are you?"

He chuckled deep in his throat. "I saw how calm you were in the face of a true nightmare. No child would act as you did. So I watched you. And when I realized it was you who was investigating my case, I decided to get a little closer. Not as close as I would have liked, however." His eyes flicked appreciatively over her curves, lingering on her long, pale neck. "I wanted to make you mine, Vivienne. Mine forever."

Her mouth fell agape. "You wanted to *turn* me?"

"Don't sound so disgusted. This life isn't so bad," he said. "You mortals...you live in a blink. Some of you not even a whole day. I have all the time in the world to enjoy."

Vivienne felt her tears rise in her eyes. "If you value long life so much, why do you take it? Why did you take my only friend from me?"

At that, he looked up, surprised. "I don't understand. What friend? I left that little detective alive, even though when the PID caught up with me, I could've killed him."

"Not Nick, you asshat. Clara. Why did you kill Clara? She never did anything to you!" she cried. She opened her file and slapped the photos down, hardly able to look at them. Her best friend, slaughtered like a lamb.

"John" looked down at the photos, his eyes scrutinizing.

"You don't have to study them. They're not art, like your blood paintings! That is my best friend's corpse, you son of a bitch!" she cried, letting her tears fall.

"Vivienne, you need to listen to me and you must believe me— I didn't kill Clara. You can ask anyone in this godforsaken organization, these aren't even vampire bites," he said.

"Yeah right."

"Why wouldn't I own up to it? I killed everyone else you accused me of, and more. Many more. I did not kill Clara White. And I think you know that. Deep down, you know there's something not right about this murder scene." His eyes were clear. There was no glamour in them. Was it possible he was telling the truth?

"How do you know it's not a vampiric murder?" Vivienne challenged.

"The blood on the walls. Yes, I splashed about some blood when I killed, but never this much. No vampire would ever waste that much blood! Finally, the fang marks. Have you ever seen a bite that didn't bruise? You saw your father's fangs."

She remembered what a vampire really looked like: the black and red eyes, the elongated nails, the stretched jaw and the mouthful of long, twisting fangs. Two of them were longer than the others, but there was no way a vampire's fangs would leave only two little puncture wounds in

Clara's neck. Real vampire fangs were the stuff of nightmares, not vampiric romance novels.

"Convinced?" he asked.

She was convinced. It was only logical.

"Someone framed me for this murder. Someone who knew you, me, and Clara. Only you could possibly know who," he added.

"I don't know anyone who...fuck. I have to tell Nick!" She went to stand up, but was so shaky with rage she bumped the table, rattling John's chains. He kept smirking. Vivienne didn't pay him anymore mind. He was on the way to his death. Right then, they had a real, mortal killer out there who already had a taste for blood. In her haste, her hair began to come loose from its braid, and she hurriedly shook it out, not bothering to fix it again. She had bigger things on her mind.

She hailed a taxi and said the cliché "step on it" for her to get to the gallery as quick as possible. In Manhattan, however, it got a bit difficult to drive speedily. She got out of the cab three blocks away and ran the rest of the distance. Before she went into the gallery, she reached into her purse and checked her weapon. She had learned to shoot and got her carry concealed license as soon as she was able to, knowing that working in law enforcement, even as a doctor, could get dangerous. She had never had to use it before, and she prayed she wouldn't have to now, either.

She knocked on the gallery door. It looked like the two investigators from the PID were about to leave, when one of them passed her by. "I think there was a mistake with the arrest. Clara wasn't killed by a vampire."

"We know. Detective Falcon agreed to help us find out who would frame a vampire," the man said.

She dashed ahead of him and called, "Nick!"

He turned. "Hey. Did they come to extradite the vamp yet?"

"Not as of when I left. Nick, he didn't kill Clara," she said. "I want to help find the killer."

Nick had an odd look on his fair face. "Clara was...collateral damage."

"What?" Vivienne gasped. "What do you mean?"

"I had to make sure you knew what monsters vampires can be. I had to convince you that it was your beloved John who was doing the killing. I couldn't catch him without you, and you needed to be shocked back into reality. I'm sorry. I know there's no way I can make it up to you—"

He did not see the punch coming, connecting with his nose. Vivienne had one Hell of a right hook!

"*You*? How could you? Are you mad?" she cried, wondering if she was going to faint, cry, or kill.

"Vivienne, listen," he said, as blood gushed from his broken nose. "I needed you to see John for what he really was. A monster."

"Right now the only monster I see is standing in front of me," she said.

The two PID agents came back in, saw Nick's bloody nose and asked what was happening. Unfortunately, both men were mortal, so when Nick pulled his .38 and shot them both in the head, they dropped like potato sacks, spouting blood like unicorn horns from their foreheads.

She screamed, but didn't completely lose her cool. Nick had no idea she was armed. She didn't know when Nick had gone darkside and she didn't give a damn. He was a true monster, worse than John or her father had ever been. Her training had taught her to keep crazy people talking.

"Why, Nick?"

"Because you were falling for him, and it was all Clara's fault for introducing you!" he spat.

"What is this? A Lifetime movie? Nick, you killed a girl because you were jealous of John? And you think, after all this, I'll want to be with you?"

"Doesn't matter," he said. "We'll be together in Hell."

He raised his gun, but before he could fire, she beat him to it. Her 9mm was out and her shot was fired into his chest before he could pull his trigger. The impact made the gun fly from his hand and he fell against one of John's "paintings", decorating it with even more blood. He was still alive, and he tried to go after his gun, despite the amazing amount of blood he was losing.

She stilled her shaking hand and fired again, three times in a row. His chest nearly exploded from impact, sending blood and flesh flying in great gobs, narrowly missing her. He fell to the floor at her feet, dead. His blood was soaking into her boots.

While she knew this would damage her psyche and she'd need to deal with that in the near future, common sense and medical training kicked in. She called the PID, who promptly ordered her to come back to the facilities. Upon arrival, she saw a flurry of activity around the door that led to John's holding cell.

The two werewolves were lying dead on the floor, strangled by the chains that had once held the most wanted vampire on Earth. Eyeballs were bulging and tongues were protruding. They looked as if they had been ready to transform before they died.

A female voice was shouting so many obscenities, Viv was pretty sure the woman was making some of them up on the spot.

"*You*!" Between the bodies of agents came a beautiful young woman with long black hair, fair skin, and the frightening eyes of a vampire. Those eyes were set on Vivienne.

Vivienne had never been so scared in her life.

"You ignorant mortal!" the girl cried. "Do you realize what you've done? Ugh. Why am I asking? Of course you don't!" A delicate hand roughly yanked on Vivienne's hair. "Your fucking bobby pin fell out! Because of your vanity the biggest threat to humanity just escaped after being pursued for centuries!"

"I-I'm sorry, but please let me go!" she cried.

The girl let her go, running her hands through her hair. "I apologize. It isn't your fault. There wasn't nearly enough security around him."

"Miss, what can I do?" she asked.

"You're the one who helped catch him?" Vivienne nodded. "Then the best thing you can do is pray he doesn't come for you. If he does and you actually manage to live, here." The girl handed her a black business card for the PID. "Let me know."

"Angelica Cross," Vivienne read aloud. "Director/Founder. Since *1881*?"

Angelica smirked, looking eerily like John had. "Founded specially to catch this son of a bitch."

"He's more evil than I realized. But you should know something, Angelica: mortals can be just as cruel as vampires," Vivienne said.

Angelica turned, getting ready to leave. "Of course I know. Vincent used to be one."

"Who?"

She turned back. "Vincent Cross. My father. The vampire you just let escape."

DIARY OF A DEAD BIMBO

BY PETRONELA UNGUREANU

I'VE GROWN ACCUSTOMED TO MY casket. It has a white velvet interior and a fetching pillow supporting my decomposing head. All this comfort has sweetened my transition into the world of the dead. Not even the ever-growing worms, some fat and short, others long, ringed and slimy, have managed to spoil my disposition with their small beady little heads making their way into my flesh. I am determined to stay positive. Something MUST happen. I am still waiting for the freaking angels blowing their trumpets and some odd white tunnel, where I am supposed to dive into eternal life. If I can reminisce well, it's been almost two bloody weeks since my departure, so you must understand my frustration. But I must keep my cool and enjoy the silence. As if I had another fucking choice.

Oh, how I wish I could raise from the fucking dead and haunt the hell out of the moron who ran me over with his shit of a car!

Haunting could be so cool, I could stretch my legs and feel the air on my face. Or what's left of it. I could visit my boyfriend and watch him fuck some big-breasted bimbo. I am quite certain he wasted no time putting his dick into someone else, he was already desirous to explore other vaginas when I was still alive. So why should he stop now? To mourn me? I wonder what would he say, should he actually see me, as I am now, rather bloated and swollen with lots of fluids oozing out of my cavities and maggots feeding up my ass.

Oh, if only someone could end me for good! I am so tired and bored and clueless. I could die of boredom. Again.

Instead of putting velvet inside the freaking casket, they should have decorated it with pages of popular magazines or, even better, a TV, a phone and a tablet with Internet access. Oh, how I yearn for a season of Walking Dead, a strong coffee, a steak, and a good fuck. The kind when you knock your head against the headboard. Wow, I shall never be fucked like that again! That's even more depressing. Almost as depressing as the steps I, sometimes, hear trotting around. What the fuck are they doing up there? Dancing on my friggin' grave? That shit's bothering me. So are my neighbors. My grave neighbors. The constant wailing and mourning and weeping is mind-fucking me.

You are dead! Get over it!

I am also frustrated because I haven't managed to produce a single peep ever since I kicked the bucket. How the hell can they howl like fucking wolves, I have no idea. They must be some evolved dead ass people. Crap! I sucked as a living human, I suck eggs as a dead one, too. I sometimes wonder if there was something good about me, at all. Maybe my body. Men did pay a lot to fuck me, but other than that? I must be honest and admit that I was a fucking loser.

I sometimes wonder if my self-awareness as a dead human has something to do with the Walking Dead premise. Such an awesome movie! Fuck, that would be amazing! That meant that ultimately I would be able to move and maybe even get out of this hellhole. Yes, but it also meant that I must feed on other people too. That's fucking disgusting. Although, if I think well, I might feel inclined to bite the head off some people.

Shhh! I can hear them howl again! Fucktards! What the hell are they doing up there? How the hell can they get out of the ground? Fuckkkk! I want to get out too! It must be fun to scare the shit out of people. I would literally crap myself, considering the fact that I, no longer, have an ass-hole, I would crap maggots from all the laughter. Sometimes, when I am too tired from all the thinking, I space out somehow and I am able to rise above my body. For a brief moment I can actually see myself from above, which is also amazing and horrifying, since I look like shit, hollow orbits and all...I have one more eye hanging down my left socket, it somehow escaped the wrath of those little fuckers who munch on me. They probably dislike myopic eyes. Also the shithead who embalmed me was kind of stingy with the chemicals. I heard of corpses lasting decades, so why do I look like a fucking rag doll after only two weeks? My gorgeous skin is all blistered and it suppurates all sorts of disgusting liquids and foams. My front teeth fell inside my mouth and I look like a hillbilly, a zombie hillbilly. Only my tits, my perfect silicone tits are untouched, still looking gorgeous in spite of them being smeared with all that disgusting goo produced when my chest exploded from the accumulated gas.

Shit! Fuck! Motherfucking shit! I can't believe I am dead. Fuck this shit! I want out! I hate this coffin, and all the darkness. I want out. Where is my fucking tunnel? I want my tunnel. Please, God, take me already, don't let me die with boredom here.

* * *

Yeah, I got my tunnel. Nevertheless, there was nothing luminous and angelic about it. There was some sort of illumination, from the overwhelming flames. Yet, nobody blew any trumpet for me. The sounds were somehow...different.

There was some drumming, some yelling, moaning and screaming, and also, the never-ending snakes that outflanked me, were constantly hissing and rattling their tails.

Yes, I am probably in hell, the traditional one.

It was somehow expected, if you know what I mean. When you blow other women's husbands' dicks for a living, you cannot expect to end up in heaven, playing the freaking harp. I am satisfied with the outcome, it could have been worse, I could have ended up in that fucking grave for eternity, doing nothing. At least here I can...float. There is a lot to discover down here. If you manage to escape the nagging presence of some very pushy three-headed midgets chasing you and sticking their claws in your back, you can actually find some interesting spots. Let's make it clear, this is a huge fucking pit. I find myself at the bottom of this pit that seems to be formed as a multi-level abysmal shit. I can only reach up to level two, which is incredibly annoying. But I realized that the higher you float, the shittier the monsters are. I now realize that my few, brief interactions with the church, when I was a child and grandma would forcibly take me there, somehow paid off, because now I can actually identify the famous lake of boiling sulfur that Father McDonalds would frighten us with. It is la piece de resistance. If you notice the way it's been placed in the middle of the pit, strategically positioned to get your attention and validate your suspicions. Yes, you are in hell, there is no doubt about that, you moron! And yes, there is blazing fire everywhere you look and it's hot like hell, if you know what I mean, but you somehow get used to it. I got used to the fire, to the stench of sulfur and putrid flesh– it could be my own B.O –but I could never get used so far to the ugly fucks roaming around all over the place.

Short, bald, black as coal or greyish, two or three headed, they spit fire and dance in the flames like it's their greatest merriment. When they meet a damned soul like myself, they stick their tongues down your throat and blow fire inside you. I know how it sounds. I don't have a chest cavity anymore and you can actually see the contents of my throat, but somehow this shit is incredibly disturbing and painful in a way that I cannot explain. But who can explain hell, really?

I've learned to avoid them. Don't get me wrong, there is never a dull moment here, if you manage to get rid of the short mongrels, there come the moths that penetrate your nostrils and your ears and you can actually feel their fucking flutter inside you. That's sick. There are also spiders and worms the size of a human arm, they get inside your mouth and exit through the ass. Yes, hell is a constant torment and there is an obsession with the ass. All the snakes, worms, insects and all the other freaking demons want to enter my ass. What the fuck, what's with this anal obsession? Is hell some sort of BDSM under cover? Because if it is, I'll pass.

I'd rather let a mongrel ride me, and I don't mean fuck me, but literally carry it on my shoulders. I noticed a lot of poor damned bastards, like myself, being ridden by these horned fucks. I suppose it's a form of torment and here it's all about tormenting us poor morons.

It's not a pretty picture. But I still prefer it to my solitary coffin. At least here I can see other people. I can witness their suffering and actually understand that I am not alone. Loneliness is a fucking bitch and she's been riding my ass ever since I was a child. With a drunken mom and a suspicious uncle, every other week, you can imagine my childhood or my life as a teenager. Anyway, it's too late to complain or to motivate why I've turned into an asshole. This is who I am and there is nothing I can do about it. I've ruined so many marriages, I've lied so much and, in doing so, I've ruined more lives. Looking back, I suppose I realize I've always acted out of grudge and despair and some sort of fury. I wanted everyone to feel just as crappy as me.

Who cares anyway? Those I've wronged are happy and alive, I am here with insects up my ass and gremlins tongue-fucking me. The world is right again. The evil one is punished.

I have no sense of time and that is kind of frustrating. It's not like I am in a hurry to go anywhere, but I'd love to have a glimpse of time. To really see the world out there and observe what has changed lately. I must confess I miss it. I did not have a nice life. That is a fact. I was a hooker, a woman of pleasure for most of my life. Men, and some women, paid to touch me and do all sorts of sexual things to my body. It wasn't always disgusting. Yet, every touch took a bite out of my soul. I was aware of that.

I am getting sentimental here. Maybe it's from all these clouds of sulfur. And there is so much shit everywhere, demon shit. But who the fuck am I to complain. My putrid flesh is probably fouler than all the demon shit in hell.

While floating over a lake of blood (they use it to drown us in it) I couldn't help but notice my figure. What a slender silhouette I have now, I've never been thinner. Yes, I must confess I smiled a bit realizing the idiocy of the concept.

* * *

No more exploring Inferno. I ran into *someone* with authority, if you know what I mean. Yeah, who would expect to meet the boss in such a short time? Although it appears that it's not such a short time, after all. Seemingly it's been more than a decade since I left the land of the living. Anyway, I've reached a few conclusions and I am quite certain they are well founded.

> Hell is boring and I suspect that dullness and monotony is one of its torments. I've mentioned other tribulations we must go through, but, for me, they are somehow bearable. I tried connecting with other damned souls, but most of them are scared shitless and barely manage to keep themselves in one piece, literally. And besides, I am not very good at this wordless communication thing. So, aside from floating around and running away from all sort of insects and shit, that are constantly trying to fuck you in the ass, it's eternal apathy.
>
> My life on Earth, that I've squandered so carelessly and mindlessly, is a very precious stage in one's evolution as a spirit. I know, I sound too affected for a hooker who has performed fellatio on over 900 men, nevertheless, since I have nothing else to lose I don't give a shit how I sound. It's the conclusion of a damned soul who has experienced a significant slice of hell.
>
> I have a very feeble feeling that we all might have a last chance to get out of here. I long for some light. I suppose that,

> however black our souls might be, we all yearn for some light in the end...There is a possibility for ascension, but these cases are rare and they involve very particular damned souls. I don't dare to believe that I might be one of them. A hooker in Heaven...come on!

These are my conclusions so far, and they've gained some contour after I had the opportunity to meet the boss of hell. I do not want to say its name, it could be perceived as an invitation, and, trust me, one encounter is sufficient. He is a very disturbed individual. My instinct as a hooker who knows men very well, tells me that, it's possible he was a nice guy at first. But only at first. He has no patience, no compassion and he is determined to give you whatever you hate the most. In my case, monotony, loneliness and hopelessness. And please believe me, I would gladly have my ass fucked by all the giant insects in Inferno, if I had a single friend. My ass for a friend. I would flaunt it wide open and even offer a blowjob as a bonus, if I knew there was one single soul, damned or not, who cared for me, or at least, who spent a few decades with me, keeping me company. Yeah, the boss of hell is one mean motherfucker and he represents the sum of all our fucking fears. I know, I sound all intellectual and shit.

* * *

The impossible happened. I got my tunnel of light. Yeah, I know, I am a hooker in Heaven. Apparently the boss of Heaven thought I deserved another chance. I hope I am not going to blow it. Fuck, I hope I am not going to blow anyone!

THE END

INTO OBLIVION
BY KINDRA SOWDER

I WAS DREAMING, BUT HADN'T REMEMBERED falling asleep. Or was I asleep? Was this all a dream? This felt too real to be a dream, but what I saw couldn't be real. Could it?

My name was Sophie. I was a student in the undergraduate Physics program at MIT and things like this just didn't happen. At least, not in what we knew as our reality.

My feet hit the concrete with heavy thuds as I ran through the empty campus, not another student or even faculty member in sight. Everyone and everything was gone, leaving me to fend off the hideousness that now followed me. It had been following me for a while, barely making any noise as I walked, which had turned into a run as the sensation of being trailed continued to creep up my spine. I had never seen it. I only heard the scraping of claws on concrete as I moved to keep as much distance between me and it as possible; even if I didn't in fact, know what *it* was.

My heart raced as it threatened to erupt from my chest and spill out of my mouth, a nice sheen of sweat covered my entire body in an icy chill as the air sped past me. I couldn't stop. Wouldn't stop. It was winter in Massachusetts and snow littered the ground, leaving small icy patches that I nearly slipped on a couple dozen times, but I wore no coat to protect me from the chill. Nothing to bring the warmth of my dorm room into my bones.

It was nighttime, but I couldn't remember when the dark had descended on me. I was scared of the dark, a small fact that I kept hidden from those around me. Only children were afraid of the opaque blackness of night. Adults were supposed to be impervious to its effects, but not me. My muscles burned as I ran. They weren't used to this much physical strain. As a student in physics, you didn't find yourself running a lot of 5ks.

My head spun as I continued to run as if my life depended on it and, as far as I knew, it did. I hadn't turned to see what was perusing me— not even once, for fear of what would be there in the darkness, prowling and sleuthing through the velvet thickness of it.

When I had fallen asleep, I was in my pajamas, tucked into the cocoon of warmth my blankets provided. I woke up not too long after slumped against the outside wall of the Koch Biology Building, facing the North Court, fully dressed in jeans, t-shirt, and boots. My breath came in short gasps and sent a cloud into the atmosphere, and was even more so now that I was trying to make my getaway. But I knew I couldn't, no matter how hard or how fast I ran. Then a voice moved through my mind, slinking through the inky blackness to greet me like we were old friends. We were nothing of the sort, and I tried to block it out as its words filtered through gray matter.

"Yes. Oh yes, you can run. Run as fast as you can, but I will always find you." It was a woman's voice, deep and sultry and inviting.

I stopped in my tracks, shaking my head, trying to get rid of the words and the voice that spun them. I couldn't stop, but it was ringing in my ears, and my head began to pound as my lungs burned with the effort of my escape. Looking around, I found myself between the start of the East Campus and the Wiesner Building. I could've sworn I had gone farther, but time and space seemed skewed here. Panic set in, and the voice came back, my ears resonating with its sound yet again.

"The dark will always follow you," the voice whispered, catering to my worst fear. Not only was I terrified of the dark, but I was even more afraid of what lingered in it. The fear crept up inside of me then, getting caught in my throat and forming a pit in my stomach, my heart racing even faster now.

Closing my eyes, I counted to ten. It was a trick that had worked in the past when the anxiety settled inside me and had caught me in its sticky web and refused to free me. It only crept in further, gripping me like a vice that tightened with each number counted instead of alleviated. The presence that I felt creeping up on me grew even stronger as I stood there, frozen to the spot not only by the intense cold, but also because of the extreme dread that took up residence in my chest. The urge to run was there again, but I couldn't make my legs move. My eyes refused to open in fear of what I would see. Then a scraping noise started in front of me like a sharp talon raked along the concrete sidewalk with the full intention of bringing me to my knees with terror.

I squeezed my eyes shut even tighter, not willing to see what I knew with certainty was now in front of me. Its hot, sour breath took the place of the cold on my face. The air blew my hair slightly as I suppressed a yelp and froze even further into a stone statue. At least that was how I felt. From the sound of it, the creature was large and menacing. That was if the low and breathy growl were an indication.

That was when the realization hit me. This wasn't a dream. It felt too real, and the terror was too stark to be a dream.

I felt a cold, wet talon graze my cheek. My eyes shot open, and a scream ripped from my throat, only to find nothing there. But stark, frigid horror ran through my bones once I saw the scene before me. I was exactly where I had started, and the campus was still as empty as it had been when this all began. The light of the streetlamps bounced off of the glass. A few empty offices I could see from the ground had lights on, but bore no inhabitants. Everything was just as quiet and deserted as I had feared. The only things here were me, the dark, and the presence of something beyond my waking world. My logical mind said it wasn't possible, but the irrational side that wanted to believe in things beyond myself and the world I lived in knew this was a reality. I sank to my knees. The snow melted beneath me and soaked into my jeans. Not only fear, but hopelessness flooded through me like a tidal wave to wash me out to sea.

Hot tears stung my eyes and cascaded down my cheeks. I was never going to get out of this alive. That much was clear now, and there was nothing left for me. Nothing but the darkness surrounding me and absolute death. I began to shiver, the cold finally coming to affect me once I had stopped moving just long enough for it to seep into my flesh, muscle, and down into bones. My teeth chattered. The voice was silent. It was one thing I could be thankful for, but I knew it wouldn't be for long. Its silence solidified the fact that the point of this was to render me hopeless, ready to give up just enough for them to take me.

But who were they? What I knew was this, they were terrifying and powerful beyond anything I had ever known. Not even the advanced physics courses could've prepared me for anything like this. String theory and Schrödinger's Cat couldn't have prepared me. They were all just the tip of the iceberg as far as I was concerned.

Laughter with a high, feminine, trilling quality came from behind me, then surrounded me within seconds. I turned slightly, trying to find the source of the sound, but found nothing. I knew I wouldn't, but instinct compelled me just enough to try. If I could find it, I could find my way out. A renewed hope bloomed in my chest, causing my heart to skip a beat as I rose to my feet and began a brisk walk into the Koch Biology Building. The outside light flickered as I swung the door open and stepped inside. The cold from outside had followed me in, continuing to nip at me like a yippy dog begging for attention. It was like someone had left the air conditioner on instead of switching to heat once the summer was over. There was no transition. Just the cold and the silence that had returned once the laughter faded away into nothingness.

The light outside flickered again and then went out, thrusting shadows into the doorway I was standing in. Looking down at them sent another pang of anxiety through me. I felt like they could grab me at any moment and as I watched them, they began to writhe around my feet, reaching to touch me even if just once. I skipped around them, nearly falling, but catching my balance in just enough time to avoid colliding with the bench to the right of the door. I fell to the ground in my quest to avoid it. Pain seared from my tailbone and up my spine, sending a shriek spilling from me and into the silence, bouncing off of the walls and back toward me. The shadows continued to reach for me as I sat. I tried to compose myself and work through the pain of what I was confident was a broken tail bone.

Looking up into the stillness of the hushed building, I let the tension and the fear bubble up and yelled, "What do you want from me?"

I began to cry again, the hopelessness of my situation building up inside of me, despite the resolve I thought I had in the wake of a sliver of hope. It easily crumbled under the weight of my own existence in this solitary space, surrounded by nothing and everything all at the same time. Using the bench beside me for balance, I stood for what felt like the millionth time in one night. I wasn't sure if it was truly night, or how long I had actually been there. Time didn't seem to exist. Of course, neither did anything else.

Silence. That was all there was to greet me, and not even crickets made a sound. I wasn't even sure if crickets existed wherever I was. I wasn't even sure where I was. Yes, I was at MIT, but this obviously wasn't the same place I had left when I closed my eyes. My tailbone throbbed and made it so I could barely stand up straight because, once I did, the pain shot through me once again. And it was nearly crippling. Yes, it was definitely broken.

I straightened myself, a low hiss through gritted teeth escaped my parted lips, but I uncurled my back regardless. I wouldn't make it through whatever this was if I couldn't stand, so I would force myself to do so. My father had always told me that giving into your pain was a sign of weakness, and I took that to heart. So I practiced that when it came to it, but he wasn't here. No one was here, and the pain was excruciating. The terror flooding through me was all there was beside the creature that was teasing me into hopelessness. It worked, and my fear of the dark was nearly debilitating, the curiosity of that emotion compelling me to even face the creature at all. Curiosity is the impediment of horror, and it was the downfall of the human race.

Then, out of the corner of my eye, a dark figure was there. It began to run in the opposite direction of where I stood. I turned, my breaths coming out in irregular gasps because of the fear, to find no one there. My eyes had barely locked on him, but I had seen where it took off to, and I would be following it. Anything to answer the millions of questions I had about where I was and why I was here. The inquisitiveness and the horror were taking over.

Taking off in a sprint, I headed in the direction I had seen the dark figure go. Before long, I realized I had reached the Koch Biology Center's gallery where large pictures of cells and other microscopic images hung in a beautiful display. Pain ran from my injured tailbone, up my spine, and down my legs as I ran, but I didn't stop. Nothing was going to keep me from my answers now. Not the fear, not the hopelessness, and not the agony. My father had raised me to be a strong woman, but I wasn't as strong as he had hoped I would be. If I were, the curious nature of people wouldn't be driving me to seek out the answers. My first instinct once I got to the gallery was to scream and curse and throw a tantrum like a child because the figure was gone, but I resisted it. Then it appeared again, right at the edge of my peripheral vision and, as soon as I turned to try to catch a glimpse, it was gone. It was toying with me, whatever it was. Why else would it continue this charade?

I yelled out as I gazed down the gallery, the photos reflecting off of the windows and the light causing a glare that made me nearly have to squint.

"Hey!" I screamed at the top of my lungs, into the cold and empty night air. The single word echoed off of the walls, photos, and glass, bouncing back toward me to sound like at least a dozen syllables. "Where are you?"

This time, it was more of a whimper instead of a scream. My question remained unanswered as the silence crept onto me yet again, causing goose bumps to become more prominent than they had been before. The fine hairs on the back of my neck stood at attention. I could feel it all around me, but there was nothing in sight. The only time I had seen anything was in my peripheral vision. Nothing head-on, like it wanted to be seen, but didn't all at the same time. What did it want?

"If you want me, I'm right here!"

Then a voice from the darkness. I recognized it instantly as the one that had been playing in my head from the moment I woke up outside in the cold dark. I was being swallowed whole by it until that voice had pulled me only neck deep out of it.

"Oh, don't mind him," the voice sounded through the gallery, coming from everywhere and nowhere just like the laughter I had heard outside.

A slight woman came from around the corner at the end of the hall, dressed in a white floor-length sundress and tracing a finger down the very edge of a canvas. "He doesn't like strangers."

The lights went out completely, leaving us in almost near darkness if it weren't for the streetlamps outside. My breath caught in my throat, and I fought to stifle a startled scream. Her raven hair twinkled in the twilight as she made her way closer, not even once removing her fingertip from any canvas she passed.

"Oh?"

The word came out in more of a gasp than anything, and I watched her warily. She was the first person I had actually seen if she was a person at all. Normally, I would say if it looked like a duck and quacked like a duck, but this wasn't the normal circumstance, was it? My eyes never left her face as she made her way toward me, literally putting one foot in front of the other as she moved barefoot across the cold tile floor. A shiver ran up my spine, but it wasn't from the cold or the pain that still pulsated at my tailbone. She scared me, and I wasn't sure why.

Out of the corner of my eye, the figure was there, but didn't shrink away this time. He was small and hunched over on himself, hands folded together like he was pleading for something with red eyes that could penetrate any soul. His black skin mirrored the darkness around me, making me surprised I could see him at all. I stared at him as the woman moved closer, not daring to take my eyes away from him. He seemed like the larger threat, but my mind screamed at me to look at the woman before me. He seemed as decrepit as any old man, but I knew better. I had seen him, granted it was barely, out of the corner of my eye as agile and stealthy, moving through the dark like he was meant to. I felt it creeping up my spine again, threatening to cover me like a blanket just like the terror turning my blood hot.

"Yes," she sighed as if she was already bored with the conversation. "People make him nervous."

Her eyes met mine then, and I could only see darkness in them. Her pale skin reflected the lights from outside just so, making her look translucent and glowing. She seemed like a light in the dark, but why didn't I believe it? My gaze moved to her, shifting back and forth between her and the huddled creature. Even he seemed to be afraid of her, which made the alarm bells ring inside my mind and the anxiety spill from my gut to my throat.

"Why is that?" I asked. The words came out at so low of a pitch that I was surprised she was able to hear me, but she responded just as if I was standing directly in front of her.

She shrugged and answered, "I'm not sure. Maybe it's the light. Who knows?"

The light? Now I could add confusion to the kaleidoscope of emotions I was feeling. I had no idea what in the world she was talking about, and I was confused about who he was exactly. Now I could see him, and I knew he had led me here. He had drawn me here with his quick appearance and disappearance. But why? Was it to draw me to this woman? A feeling of knowing slithered over my skin and I knew I had been right in my conclusion. She smiled then, sinister intention leaking from between her curved lips and her dark eyes. My heart began to beat frantically in my chest, the alarm bells ringing even louder than before.

"I am drawn to the light, but it only drives him further into the shadows."

She paused for a moment, taking a few brazen steps in my direction as the creature folded himself further into the darkness surrounding us.

"He finds the light for me." Within an instant, she was in front of me. I hadn't seen her move—just saw her flash from point A to point B with a flicker. Her voice changed and sounded as if a million voices were coming from her vocal cords and cried, "And I take it."

A scream ripped from me as her onyx eyes turned white and her teeth sharpened as I watched; turning her from the beautiful woman I had just seen into a monster straight from my nightmares. In my instinct to get away, I tripped over my own feet, landing on the hard floor and cried out as my already broken tailbone made contact. Hot tears sprang to my eyes as the pain ricocheted from that area all the way up my spine and down my legs, back and forth, until I was terrified to move. She was on me like a cat, hovering over me with only an inch of empty space separating us when she began to open her mouth, her jaw elongating like it had dislocated.

I screamed out again, paralyzed in absolute horror at the sight before me. She held down my hands and moved her face closer to mine, breathing in with a gulp of air that I didn't understand. I struggled beneath her, but as I did, I couldn't tear my eyes away, and then something happened. A light gathered in the space between us at the apex of my chest, and it was moving upwards, making me feel like I was choking. I tried to cry out again through choking gasps, but nothing ever came out. I could hear my boots squeaking on the floor as I tried to get away. I wasn't making a difference, and she acted as if I wasn't moving at all. The strength she possessed was a surprise, considering how small she was. But nothing was as it seemed here. The dark and frightening creature was harmless, and the beautiful woman was the actual threat.

She was still gasping in gulps of air as the light inside of me continued to move up until I felt warmth in my mouth that could only mean one thing. She was about to take it from me, and I still wasn't even sure what it was. A garbled shriek filtered out around the warmth and the light, sounding more like a gurgling sound instead. I felt it flow from my mouth and saw the blue, crystalline light of whatever she had been drawing to flow out of me and into her, imbuing her skin with an even brighter glow than she had had before, from the inside out. My vision flickered for all of a moment, going black at first until I was on the other side of the debacle.

I met my own eyes, looking deep into their depths as my body wheezed and then went flaccid like all the life in me had gone the very moment the light was gone. For an instant, all I could see were my own dead eyes, and then everything went black.

POVEGLIA

The Island of the Dead

A SHORT STORY BY A. GIACOMI

Preface

WE ALL KNOW ABOUT THE rich history of Venice, Italy and its relationship with Napoleon Bonaparte. The French leader was famously greedy for territory and antiquities. Two centuries have passed since his invasion of Venice, the looting of its art and destruction of its buildings. What few people know about his dealings in Venice has to do with an island nearby to what tourists know as Venice today. In 1805 Napoleon made Poveglia a permanent Island of the Dead, with the plague running rampant during this time, the only solution was quarantine. The dead along with the infected were sent to the island to rot.

The gruesome history of Poveglia doesn't end there. Predating Napoleon, the island was rumored to be infested with demons and lost souls who were tormented by Hades. In 1527, the Doge of Venice offered the island to a group of monks who refused the land, which was considered a huge offense, but perhaps they had known then what the island truly was.

In the 1920s the island was transformed from quarantine zone to an asylum for the mentally ill. This was a long term care facility. People who arrived were never meant to leave, but when strange disappearances began to occur, including one of the doctors jumping from one of its towers, the asylum was forced to shut down in 1968. The legends remained intact, that ghosts had haunted the halls, demons had possessed patients, Doctors became mad as well, and a bitter Lord Hades was the culprit for all.

If you've never heard of Poveglia it's most likely because the locals dare not mention it. The superstitious Venetians never venture near the island. It is now abandoned and forgotten, until today. A recent document was found floating in an abandoned boat near the islands edge. A local discovered it, hoping to restore the abandoned boat and keep it for himself. Inside he discovered the papers and passed them to the authorities. The document you are about to read is a story, and although it can't be proven true, the Venetian authorities did verify that a tourist by the name of Anna did go missing about five years ago, and the mystery was never solved. I have translated it and edited the best of my ability for your reading pleasure, whether it's true or not is for you, the reader, to decide.

PART ONE: THE TOURIST

THE TOUR GUIDE SCREAMS OVER the hoard of people who stream through the palace. His Italian accent is so thick that it's hard to understand any explanation about the history or architecture of this place. I tune out, and decide to create my own inner commentary as I glance around. It's not hard to ditch the crowd, I don't know anyone in it and I don't plan on making any new friends. I begin to move away from them toward the second level.

The Doge's Palace, or Palazzo Ducale, is one of the most beautiful places I have ever seen. I wander across the courtyard toward the stairs, admiring its Venetian gothic style and taking in the rays of sunlight that poke through the elaborate archways. This building had to be reconstructed three times, due to three different fires, what terrible luck. Three fires in a building that rests on water, talk about irony!

As I tiptoe up the stairs looking at the golden ceilings, I hear a faint cry. Standing very still, I try to seek out where the sound is coming from.

A few seconds pass and there it is again, a much heavier wail. I want to turn back and avoid this person, but my curiosity gets the best of me and I move ahead. I continue to tip toe up the stairs and place my camera back in my purse.

When I reach the top floor, the sound seems to be coming from every direction. I don't see anyone. I decide to walk toward the balcony facing out to the water, I am at least going to enjoy the sights until I find out where the cries were coming from.

The water sparkles like dark sapphires. I watch the gondolas and speed boats arrive with smiling passengers. Yes, this is a beautiful place, my first vacation, glad I picked Venice. I feel this overwhelming urge to wave at the people below, so I do. I smile as some wave back. As I am waving, I feel the hairs on the back of my neck stand up. It's a warm day and I can't explain the chill I feel. It's as though someone was watching me, or following me. I glance around quickly to discover a dark figure coming toward me. I scream and it vanishes into thin air before I can react.

I take a moment to catch my breath. "What the hell was that?" I pant loudly. I'm starting to regret my decision to wander off and start for the stairs. Before I reach the banister, I see the dark image at the end of the hallway. It is simply standing there in wait. I catch my breath in my throat, and blink hoping that the dark figure will disappear again, but it doesn't.

The figure looks womanly, the dark mist around her looks like a flowing garment. She has a dark hood on and I can't see her eyes, but her lips are saying something that I can't hear. The garments flow to point in my direction, then point back to the hallway around the corner. She is waving me forward? My body is telling me to stay put, but my mind is wildly curious. If she is a ghost, she can't hurt me anyway.

I decide to follow her around the corner and down the next hallway. She takes a quick right and I continue to follow her. Where was she taking me? What did she want? As I continue walking it seems to get darker and darker. I start to sweat; my curiosity seems to be running out. Perhaps I should just turn back now? Before I can turn to run back, the woman stops. She looks back at me and then points to a balcony. I'm a bit hesitant at first, but since I've come all this way I might as well see what she's brought me here to look at. As I approach the balcony, she steps back, giving me some space. How courteous. I would be thankful, but I am still too skeptical.

As I hold the marble railing and look below, I can see a canal. I can't imagine why that would be interesting, but as I begin to look up, I understand. Above me is the Bridge of Sighs. I smile with delight, it's one of the most gorgeous bridges in the world! Lord Byron had given it its name, and it was a good choice, because that's precisely what I do when I see it. I forgot all about the ghost woman and stood in stunned admiration. Who would even know that such a pretty bridge meant something so awful? The bridge is supposed to lead to a prison. This bridge connects the palace to the execution quarters. I shiver at the thought; I had even read that the bridge was the last thing that criminals saw before their imprisonment.

That final thought woke me out of my daze. I can sense that the woman in black is still watching me. I turn to stare at her smirking. I don't like that look. It isn't the kind of smile that seems inviting. She glides closer to me and a cold breeze surrounds me. "Why did you want to show me this?" I had to ask.

Her grin grows larger and she mouths something that looks like "die" except no sound comes out. She begins her approach again.

I should leave, I should run, but my feet don't seem to listen. In one quick movement she has me by my pink cardigan and is holding me over the canal. I didn't think ghost could do that, and she is incredibly strong. I try to wriggle free, but her grasp is firm. As I glace below, I have no idea how deep the water will be, I sure hope I remembered some of my swimming lessons from first grade.

I glance at her again, and simply ask, "Why?"

She grins and releases me into the watery abyss. I sink fast, almost as if I had been thrown in instead of dropped. I try to grab at the surface, but I seem to be getting nowhere. Holding my breath is something foreign to me and I'm not sure how long I can do it for. I kick my arms and legs furiously, hoping to make some headway, but I just seem to be sinking deeper.

Bubbles start to escape my mouth and nose. My body is aching for air, and I take in a little water. I want to sob, but fear of taking in more water stops me. I look up and I can see the surface, but it is so far away. I guess I will have to accept my fate. I have no choice, no one is coming for me, and there is no escape. I close my eyes, and I might have shed a tear, but I would never know for sure. I release all the air from my lungs and let the water take me.

PART TWO: THE BOOK KEEPER

"ANNA...ANNA" A VOICE WHISPERS IN the distance. The voice is not a familiar one. I open my eyes and blades of grass brush my lashes. The sun is setting, there is barely any light left, and I can't quite see what's in front of me. I lay there on my stomach for a while, where am I? I remember the water surrounding me. I don't remember anyone coming to my rescue. Perhaps I should get up and get some answers, but my body aches and I feel very weak.

The whispering returns louder this time, "Anna...Anna."

Who is calling my name? I open one eye and quickly scan the area ahead of me. There is no one there, not a soul.

After a few more moments of moaning and groaning I decide to get to my feet. This is no easy task, I feel as though I had just gotten new legs. Beneath my feet, the grass is lush and dewy, and up ahead, all I can see is water. I look to my right, water. I look to my left, more water. Is this some kind of island? How did I get here? Did I wash up on shore?

As I look around I notice a building, it looks a little worse for wear, but perhaps there is someone inside who can help. The looming darkness is making things cooler, and I am still soaking wet. I think I better get warm soon or I will be sick as a dog.

For a building that seemed so close, the walk seems a bit too extensive. My body doesn't have much left to give. I collapse in front of the door to the disheveled building. I close my eyes for a moment and when I open them, there stands the woman in black. I press my back against the door, making as much space between us as possible. I thought I had dreamed her up, I think I might be dreaming even now. She glides closer like a dark fog. I cover my mouth before I can scream. Instead a whisper seeps through my fingers, "What do you want?"

She comes so close that I shiver. "It's not about what I want," the eerie woman says. She speaks.

The fact that we can communicate peaks my curiosity and I forget my fear for a moment. "Where are we?" I ask as boldly as I can muster.

She slithers out the word, "Poveglia."

"What?" I ask, I couldn't quite hear her.

She repeats, "Poveglia."

And when I still look confused she points to a sign just behind her. I try to read it, but most of it is in Italian. It said 'Poveglia' in large letters and then below it, it said, 'L'isola della morte.' I knew that last word too well. *Morte* meant death. At that point I began to ponder the idea that I may actually be dead, I might have drowned, and this may just be my new place of residence.

With pleading eyes I ask the dark lady, "Why me? Why am I here?"

She smirks at me in that evil way that sends prickles through my skin. "Sei qui perche hai avuto una mallevita," she says in a playful way.

"Well what does that mean? I don't know any Italian, sorry."

Her smile fades and she drifts toward me with a scowl. "You are on the island of death, Poveglia. You are here for your sins. You have led a bad life, and you are here to pay your penance to the Lord of the Underworld."

My eyes grow wide at her explanation, and I begin to realize that Poveglia sounds familiar, I remember now, I had read about this place in my tourist book for Venice. Poveglia is a haunted island that was abandoned many years ago. The last family to live here fled when their daughter suffered a strange injury. There was not much reported on that story, but ever since, no one had dared venture here. In the Roman era, Poveglia had been a dumping ground for bodies that had contracted the Black Plague. They burnt the bodies once they died, to try and rid the island of infection, but the land was still infected, I could feel it. Something was not right about this place.

The woman in black gestures toward the doorway. She wants me to go inside, but the idea terrifies me and I run in the opposite direction. The dark figure watches as I sprint away, but she does not follow me. I run as fast as my legs will allow, I will find a way out of here, I must! As I run, the ground seems to quake beneath me. The soil rumbles and a sink hole appears. The dirt beneath me begins to slide away. I lose my footing, and fall in with only my hands clawing onto clumps of dirt and grass above. I scream out for help, but no one comes.

The woman in black appears above me with a grin. I wish she would stop doing that. She looks at my hands and they struggle to hold on, and she shakes her head.

"Wait, please don't, please..." I beg as I begin to understand her gesture.

She doesn't pity me, I'm not sure she has pity for anyone, with one final smirk she pries both my hands free from the ground and drops me into the sink hole without a hint of remorse.

As I fall for what seems like hours, I hear moaning beneath me. Wailing and screaming voices below give me the impression that wherever I'm going won't be pleasant.

I hit the ground so hard I fear I may have broken my jaw. Not the greatest landing, but I seem to be alright. I try to stand up slowly assessing my injuries, but there aren't any. I just spit out a bit of dirt, which I ate upon impact. When I look up I can see the full moon over head, something about that moment felt familiar. I search my thoughts, and it all rushes back to me.

That lady in black, the water, the drowning? Was I dead? Really dead?

This all seemed like a strange dream that I would wake up from soon.

My heart races as I look around. The area is dark, all except for a giant spotlight on me, courtesy of the moon above. The moaning is getting louder; a few screams are thrown in the mix as I shiver waiting in the moonlight. I feel breathing behind me, and turn to look. A pair of green eyes peer at me without expression, and then the rest follows. Attached to the eyes is a face, or what's left of the face. The man's nose is missing, and his teeth are exposed. His flesh seems as though it has rotted away. He hisses through his exposed teeth and stumbles closer to me. There is a strange look of desire in his eyes that frightens me.

"Stay back," I say, hoping that he will retreat, but of course this does nothing, I didn't think it would, but it was worth a shot. Instead what I find is that I've attracted more moaning, more creatures with a similar look of decay appear behind him. I back away from them slowly and slam against something cold and slimy. As I turn to look, another pair of green eyes greet me. He opens his mouth and lunges at me. His mouth is inches away from my face, and I try to keep him at a distance with my arms. I can feel the others closing in on me, and my hands begin to shake. With my arms occupied, I am unable to fight off the first bite. The first zombie chomps into my shoulder and I scream feeling the sharp pain as he digs into the flesh. They all moan with delight, as if the scream was a dinner bell sounding. As the warm blood rushes down my arm, I can see another zombie licking it.

Another stabbing pain in my thigh tells me that another one has bitten me. I'm screaming frantically now. How am I going to get out of here? My arms are still busy holding one of them away from my face, my legs kick at whatever they can find, but my energy is fading fast. There are too many of them and they are too strong. I begin to sob loudly; none of my prayers would be answered tonight, would they?

As I close my eyes, I imagine my house, my cat, and the comforting feeling of sipping hot tea. How beautiful that all seemed to me now. It's amazing how we appreciate things so much more when they are out of reach. With my eyes clenched shut, I drop to the floor and crouch into a ball with my arms overhead in a protective manner. The biting continues alongside my sobbing.

"Stop please, stop please," is all I can utter through my sobs, and then it all stops.

The biting had stopped and so had all the moaning. I am afraid to peek out of my crouched position, but after a minute or so I decide to look around. They are gone, all of them. It is a miracle. I laugh so hard I must have seemed mad. I look ahead to see a doorway, there is a faint glow beneath the door and I decide to make my approach. Before I turn the handle, I hear my name again.

"Anna, Anna, come on in," the voice says in an eerie whisper.

When I open the door a man greets me. He is seated at a large desk made of solid oak. He motions to a seat in from of him. I am hesitant to approach, but his smile seems kind enough. As I head toward the chair I glance around to see that this is much like an office. There are bookshelves, a fireplace, and a few eye-catching arm chairs that looked more like thrones.

The man himself seems very old. His long hair is grey and he wears thick glasses that make his eyes seem gigantic. His smile and demeanor seem pleasant as he watches me take a seat. Once in the chair he opens a book and grabs a magnifying glass, as if his glasses weren't enough. I cough to get his attention away from this book, but he continues to pursue a few pages.

I cough again, "Excuse me, sir, but can you tell me what I'm doing here?"

He looks up at me grinning, not in a sarcastic way, or vicious way, it was more the smile of a very simple man. He didn't seem very concerned with anything. He was too calm for my liking, and that put me on edge. He waited a few seconds before answering me, "No one has told you why you're here?"

I shake my head feverishly. "No."

He looks a bit distraught and starts mumbling words like, "Idiots... all the work to me...lazy bones...good for nothing," and then the rest seemed like a foreign language. After his little rant, he put the magnifying glass down, folds his arms and leans his head toward me like we are about to have a heart to heart. I instinctively lean closer too.

He clears his throat. "You are here because you have led a horrible life."

My heart catches in my throat. "I...I..." is all I can mutter.

"Yes, you, you. You're a horrible person," he says flatly. Then he returns to reading his book.

I sit in stunned silence for a few minutes waiting for the information to register. When I feel more composed I ask, "Am I dead?"

He looks up at me with a confused look on his face. "The living don't come to Poveglia, do you understand?"

I nod as his words pierce my stomach. I feel like throwing up, but I'm not sure dead people do that. My next question scares me more, "Am I in hell?" I ask with tear filled eyes. I cannot look at him while I await his reply.

He reaches across the desk and pats my hand. "Yes darling, this is hell, and I'm afraid you deserve to be here. From what I see in this book, you're not exactly a decent human being. I should use the past tense actually, because, you're not exactly human now."

Another lump forms in my throat. "Oh god, what am I?"

He points toward the doorway.

I sob a little as I blurt out my next question, "I'm going to turn into one of them? Those things out there? But why? Why..." My voice trails off and he removes his hand from mine.

"Well I'm going to tell you why, dear, part of this process is revisiting all of your demons. I rehash everything, and you must listen."

I nod. He was abnormally kind for someone working in the underworld; it was a very odd fit.

"Okay where do we start? Do you start by telling me where we are?" I ask through chattering teeth.

"Yes of course, where are my manners, dear? So sorry! You are in Poveglia, this is the Island of the Dead. It's been here for centuries undisturbed, well mostly undisturbed. There is the rare human that decides to travel here by boat and explore, but I assure you they immediately regret their visit. Like I said before, this is no place for the living, and the dead don't really appreciate the living visiting and flaunting their beating hearts all over the place."

I place my hand over my heart as he says this and realize that there is a cold silence.

He continues, "Many visitors end up dead themselves, if they deserve it. Others are horribly disfigured by a freak accident so that they have a reminder of why they should never return. I would say most people don't even venture out this way, the island has a bit of a reputation of being haunted, and the Italians know better than to mess with spirits. It's the tourists that never learn." He chuckles to himself. He seems to be enjoying his little history lesson, because he grins with each piece of new information. I can tell he has been doing this for a long time.

He turns a few pages in his book and shouts, "A-ha!" when he finds something he had been looking for. "Here is your first incident. They record everything in this book."

I wanted to ask who "they" were, but I thought it better not to know. I was already scared enough, I didn't want to know what else awaited me, I figured I would find out soon enough.

He clears his throat in preparation. "Your first incident on my list: You were twelve-years-old and decided to pick on Berta Kempfleur. Oh my! That is a silly name, I agree with you, Anna, but you didn't stop there. Apparently you commented on her weight as well as her lack of intelligence. It says in my book that you would push her around at recess until she cried and you and all your friends would laugh at her when she did."

I nod as tears stream down my face, I hadn't thought about Berta in years, I don't know how I managed to push her out of my memory, but I had managed to forget her and my guilt until right now.

"Anna, Anna, Anna," the old man says shaking his head. "Do you know what happened to Berta? What you made Berta do?"

My eyes are burning and I look away from him. I don't answer; I can't answer, so he does it for me.

"Well she killed herself Anna, yup, a twelve-year-old threw herself in front of a subway car because of you. She didn't want to have to face you again, so she decided death was the only way out. How horrible. Oh and you know what else? Her mother had been standing next to her before she decided to jump. Her mother watched her daughter die. Now that can damage a person. It also says right here that Berta's mother committed suicide a year later, drug overdose. Did you know that, Anna?" He looks at me inquisitively.

I had known about Berta, but I had not heard about her mother. I hang my head and let the guilt eat away at my insides. I did deserve to be here. I did that to her, and then I was allowed to forget it all? I was allowed to forget about Berta, and what I had done. That wasn't fair, I'm sure Berta's family would never forget.

The old man watches me curiously, but doesn't ask again. I think he knows his answer. He gets up from his desk and walks toward the fireplace. I watch as he grabs a hot poker and places it in the fire. As he does this I feel something tighten around my ankles. When I look down I see vines creeping up my legs and holding me in place. I try to wriggle free and I'm screaming so loud I think I might bust a vocal cord. The wriggling makes the vines hold tighter to my flesh, making it bleed. When the vines strap my wrists down, I stop fighting altogether, what is the point?

"What are you doing?" I ask the old man.

He stares blankly at me, and his eyes seem black now, not the ancient blue they were a moment ago. He doesn't answer, but he approaches with the poker that he extracted from the fire and is now pointing it in my direction. I can see the warmth of it. The red glow reveals the letter 'X'.

"Those who sin must wear the mark," he says in a demonic tone.

He is not the man of five minutes ago, and I'm so frightened I start to lose consciousness. The room seems to be going dark. The old man rips the sleeve of my shirt and presses the hot iron into my arm. I scream as the stench of burning flesh fills the room.

"Stop, stop, no, no, no!" I scream through clenched teeth.

When he is done, he places the hot iron away and returns to the book on his desk. He licks his fingers so that it is easier to turn the pages. How is he suddenly calm again?

It may not have been wise, but I blurt out, "Is this some kind of joke?"

He looks up from his book with a scowl that could melt away your soul, but does not answer my question. "Incident number two," he continues.

I try to stay alert, but the searing pain in my arm is making it difficult to concentrate.

"You now have your driver's license. How wonderful! One of the many new responsibilities you had as you began your journey to adulthood." He sighs and reminisces as if he had had a similar experience back in his day.

It was hard to imagine him outside of this place, but perhaps he had been human once, and maybe, just maybe if I could appeal to that he might just let me go. I held onto that hope as I listened further.

"It says here that shortly after getting your driver's license you decided to have a night out with friends. Sounds lovely, but here is where it goes downhill, dear. While at Jeff Parson's house with a few friends, you decide to partake in some illegal activities such as drinking under age, and drug use." He wags his finger at me in a very parental manner. "It seems as though Jeff provided the alcohol and drugs, and oh quick fun fact, Jeff will be joining us next week." He meets my eyes and smiles when he says this, and his smile has lost all of its appeal.

"Poor Jeff," I mutter under my breath, but he hears me.

"Poor Jeff? Poor Jeff, you say? Do you even know what he's done?" He's raising his voice for the first time, as if I wasn't frightened enough, my body jerks with terror filling it's every vein. "Your buddy Jeff is a murderer and a coward! He killed his wife and two children in their sleep! In their fucking sleep! What kind of man does that? I will tell you what kind.

The cowardly kind! He didn't want his wife to leave him, so he thought 'better dead than gone'. He was afraid to be lonely, but that's exactly what he is now, and when he gets down here, I will have a perfect surprise for him. I can't wait for Jeff's arrival actually. But enough about Jeff..." He ignores my wide eyes, and trembling state. He acts as though he's telling me a bedtime story, not a glimpse into the future of a former friend. Jeff had seemed like a nice guy, I guess most monsters seem nice at first glance.

The old man pats down his hair and regains his composure. "Now let's get on with the story shall we? ...It says that after a night of binge drinking and drugs, you decided to drive home with a friend. Her name was Keri or Kristi, the name is not important. On your way home it's difficult to see. It's dark; you're intoxicated, so naturally you had some difficultly." The word difficulty slithers off his tongue with such arrogance that I spit at him.

I didn't think it through, but I am starting to get pissed off, this woman he is describing isn't me anymore. I had changed, doesn't that count for something?

He takes of his large glasses and wipes the spit away with the back of his sleeve. Then he walks over to the fireplace again.

"No please, I'm sorry, no more. I can't do this anymore!" I sob, but he ignores me.

He's eyes burn like the fire before him. With the hot poker in hand he comes toward me at great speed and presses the 'X' to my cheek without so much as a warning. I'm screaming as he speaks, but it's as if it has no effect on him, it's as if he's used to the screams, and I'm sure he is.

As he presses the poker harder into my cheek I hear him screaming at the top of his lungs, "You killed her! You killed her and dumped her body in the woods!"

He releases the hot poker and I feel the steam coming off my cheek. I find it hard to speak, so I just continue to sob. I wish I could press my hand to my cheek, because the pain is just so excruciating, I guess that is the point.

"How could you do it, Anna? You knew she was suffering from an overdose, why didn't you take her to the hospital? Wouldn't a good friend do that? But no you were too scared, another coward. Too scared to have your parents find out what you'd been up to. So you let her die in the woods. That was your solution? You're disgusting!" And now he's the one spitting in my face. His saliva stings my new wound, I can feel it throbbing, but I know this isn't over yet.

"She was already dead," I mumble through the pain, "I was scared, ok? I was just a kid. I was scared." I sob so hard that my entire body aches.

He comes closer to me and runs his slender fingers up and down my bloody arm. I cringe as he passes over one of my bites. He reaches my head and begins to run his fingers through my hair in a loving way.

I shiver and whisper, "Don't touch me."

He retracts his hand, which is more frightening because I'm sure whatever comes next will be worse.

I can't see what he's doing behind me. I hear him shuffling through...a drawer? And loud clangs of metal. I freeze. Not seeing what's coming makes my stomach twist into a knot. I purse my lips and try not to cry anymore. My tears only seem to give him more malice.

In a moment there is a blade in front of my eye. The tip of the knife is almost touching my pupil. I have to say something now, something that will distract him, or I may lose an eye this very second. I ask about him. "Why are you here? Who are you?"

He does not remove the knife from its precarious position, but he does seem intrigued. "Me? Why thank you for asking," he says after taking a dramatic bow. "I have many names. Demon, Devil, Hades, Pluto, Satan...although that's my least favorite. I'm here because I've killed many. I enjoy killing, but I only kill those who kill. I thought I was doing a service to man-kind. Superheroes don't exist, so I thought I would be the next best thing. When it came my time to die, I ascended into Heaven, but God didn't know what to do with me. He admired the fact that I had saved so many lives that would have otherwise been taken, but there were no murderers in Heaven, so he was unsure of where to place me. After some time, he decided to make me the Book Keeper of the Underworld, and Poveglia has been running smoothing ever since."

"Wow," I say in a half interested way. "So you're a good guy and a bad guy? Well what about me? I didn't mean to do any of the things I've done, I was young and stupid! I am sorry for my actions; surely there must be some way I can be forgiven?" I can hear him grinding his teeth at my remark, and the knife remains in place. "Please let me go, I promise I will change, I promise to help others more. I won't run from my past, I will help those I hurt. I will turn myself in for my crime. Whatever you want!" I didn't notice at first, but I am pleading with him, I am begging for salvation, would he free me? Could he free me?

His voice feels like frost against my ear when he speaks again, "I'm afraid my hands are as tied as yours are, my dear. You see here in Poveglia we have a three strike system. If you commit three sins, your fate is sealed."

A chill runs through me, but I have to speak, this was my only chance. "But I didn't commit three, that's only two! And both were accidents. If I could take them back I would!"

The Book Keeper lowers the knife and I utter a sigh of relief. "That can't be, you wouldn't be here unless you have three incidents or more." He looks at me curiously, almost as if he's trying to see into my thoughts. "Are you lying, Anna?"

I shake my head. "No, no, of course not!"

He walks back over to his book before speaking again. "Well then, let's make a little wager, shall we? If my records are wrong, you can go free, simple as that. But if you're lying to me and there is a third strike in this book, then you will suffer unimaginable torture. Worse than the fate of a zombie. Understand?"

At this point I'm sweating profusely; I can't think of anything else that I've done. I search my thoughts for any other possible scenario where I might have done something awful, but I can't! So I agree to the Book Keeper's terms with a quick nod.

Without a word he stabs the knife into his desk, leaving it gleaming in plain sight, a reminder that I will suffer if I am lying. He sits down at his desk, adjusts his glasses, and picks up the magnifying glass. He reads silently for five minutes, leaving me drenched in sweat. I'm fairly sure there is a puddle of sweat beneath me.

"I'm sorry, dear." Those words were painful. "You have another sin on the list."

I glare at him. "You're making that up! I haven't done anything else!" I pause for a moment, "You were never going to let me go either way were you?"

His seemingly kind eyes go dark again, and he picks up the knife with vile intention. He races toward me and plunges the knife into my left eye before I can protest. He twists it in deeper as he pulls my head back by the roots of my hair. I can't even scream I just moan like the other zombies that live down here. I feel the blood trickle down my face; it's odd that it is slightly refreshing after the burn mark and all the sweating. When he removes the knife, I hear an odd 'pop' and the lights go off on my left side. I continue to moan as my head flops from side to side, trying to cope with the pain.

It feels as though hours go by, as I sit there moaning and bleeding. I don't hear the Book Keeper, and I can't really see well enough to search him out. So I just slump in my chair and wait, for what, I don't know.

Eventually he speaks again. His voice seems to be everywhere. "You lied, Anna."

I shake my head. "No, no I didn't! Tell me what you read! What could it possibly be?" I am so sure that he had nothing.

"Anna you may not remember this, because you were very young, but it doesn't make you any less innocent."

My heart races, what could he possibly be talking about? I couldn't think of a damn thing and I was too exhausted to argue, so I listen.

"You had a brother once…" he pauses.

I nod, I was four or five years old, and I remember my mother taking him home from the hospital, but not two weeks later he had passed away from some mysterious illness. I look at the Book Keeper. "He died before I had a chance to know him." I couldn't even really remember his name at the moment; our time together had been so short. Is it something with a 'T', perhaps Trevor or Trent? I couldn't be sure.

The Book Keeper continues, I think I hear pity in his voice. "Anna, you killed him. You murdered your baby brother."

I don't know what to say, so I stay silent for a moment. This wasn't true, it couldn't be! My mother would have said something; it is not something that can be forgiven or forgotten.

"You're lying!" I yell at him. "You're lying!" I sob.

"Anna, I'm not lying. It's in the book. It says here that you were jealous of all the attention that your baby brother had garnered. One night you slipped into his nursery and placed a blanket over his head until he stopped breathing. You left the room and went to bed, and awoke to your mother's screams the next morning. You're mother never knew that you were the one who did it, thank God for that, she might have killed you herself."

I'm not sure if I'm crying. My one remaining eye seems raw from tears. I couldn't take anymore. How could this be true? The Book Keeper had been right about the other two incidents, what if this actually happened? I had no recollection, but I could have blocked it from memory, I was young enough to forget it.

I sob in agony. The physical and emotional torture was taking its toll. I felt myself giving up. I deserved to die. I deserved whatever the Book Keeper had designed for me. I hear him walking toward the fireplace, no doubt he is ready to add the final strike on my quivering flesh. The hot iron sizzles as the 'X' is pressed into my chest where my heart should be, but it's gone I'm sure of it, I feel nothing, I am numb.

In the moments ahead I feel weightlessness, a feeling that I am floating. I can't see anything or hear anything, but I know that I'm moving. I'm too weak to ask where we're going, or care for that matter. Wherever it is, it smells like rotten food. My nose brings me out of my stupor for a moment, and I try to look around with my remaining eye. I can see the ground moving under me and there is something solid holding me. Perhaps a man is carrying me? But I hear his grunting and realize that he is just a rather large zombie, probably following the Book Keeper's orders. The zombies were his minions, but they also used to be people. I didn't want to be one of them. Perhaps it is too late to wish for a better fate.

When the zombie stops moving, I know we have reached our destination. He dumps me on the cool, hard ground. It winds me, but I rise through my gasps, trying to assess my new surroundings. The area looks like a small cave. The floor and walls are solid rock, and the only exit is now blocked by a zombie guard the size of a football player. The only sound is my fearful panting and drops of water dripping from above. The silence is unbearable; luckily it is soon broken by the arrival of a guest.

The large zombie moves out of the way to reveal my visitor. The Book Keeper. I am not thrilled to say the least. "Ahh, you're awake, dear, wonderful!"

The sweetness in his voice leaves a sour taste in my mouth. I try to scowl at him, unsure if I succeeded. "Why are you torturing me? Just get it over with. I'm ready to join your little army."

He chuckles. "Anna, it's not that simple. This is not an initiation into an exclusive club. It's more like revenge. You see down here the souls you injured in your human life have an opportunity to acquire some payback for what you've done."

I think my mouth hangs open as he says this, the torture wasn't over yet. I nervously ask, "What will they do?"

He shrugs. "They have very specific requests unbeknownst to me." He stops grinning as he ponders that last bit, and then turns to leave. My bodyguard returns to his post, and I hear the Book Keeper's last words as an echo, "Good luck."

Why would I need luck? It's not like it would do any good, he said my fate is sealed, that I was sought out for my three sins, and am to remain here in Poveglia eternally.

PART THREE: THE AFFLICTED

MY FACE IS PRESSED TO the cold stone floor. When I rise, I feel the chill of frozen water all around me. I don't remember falling asleep, and I'm not sure how I managed it in such conditions. Sitting up is difficult. My body is stiff and aching.

I forget for a moment where I am, but then the memories flood back. Drowning in Venice, arriving here, the Book Keeper, and this strange cave that I now wait in. Instead of self-loathing, I opt for self-pity, yes I had done a few things wrong, but did I really deserve this?

"I'm a good person," I utter softly. Pulling my knees into my chest, I think of my mother, she will wonder what has happened to me. I will never see her again and she is all I had left in this world. My father had passed away a few years ago, I had no boyfriend, and not many friends that I would call 'close'. I am a bit of an introvert these days, but I was hoping to change all that with a trip to Venice, maybe try and make a new friend? Which I was never any good at, so I mostly just turn my nose up at the whole ordeal.

Lost in my thoughts, I don't hear the arrival of my next visitor. I look up, startled to find a dark image in the doorway. Where was the Hulk-like Zombie, and how had I missed his departure? The figure steps into the thin stream of light running through the tiny cave. As she approaches, I gasp. I am face to face with Berta Kempfleur.

"How?" is all I can utter.

She smiles at me in a very innocent way. She looks like the same twelve-year-old Berta that I remember, but she's different, she's more confident somehow. She doesn't glance away from me like before, or try to hide. She doesn't fear me now, but it dawns on me that I should be very much afraid of her.

I start the only way I see fit, with an apology. "Berta, I'm so sorry, if I could take it all back, I would. I never meant for you and your mother to get hurt. I was a stupid kid, and you deserved so much better."

She holds her hand up signaling that I should be silent, and I oblige.

"You don't get to be sorry, Anna. It's much too late for that. Do you know how long I've waited for you?" Her voice seems so much more adult than that of a twelve-year-old, but I suppose she had had many years to mature in the afterlife.

She tilts her head sideways almost as if she was examining me, and then speaks, "What I want you to do now is follow me. You can do it willingly, or I can call upon a few zombie guards to persuade you."

I see two guards arrive behind her anyway. They are growling like dogs, their eyes pale and their skin flaking and oozing. I almost throw up at the sight of them. Berta turns to leave and I cautiously follow behind her. We enter a stone hallway, it looks like an underground mine. There are zombie guards at each doorway we pass. I hear people screaming inside of their small caves or prisons and it makes my legs weak.

I try to ask Berta, "Where are we going?" but she ignores me as if I hadn't said anything at all.

When we arrive at the end of the long hallway there is light. It is very bright and I find it hard to see what's in front of me.

Berta stands to my side and says, "Jump."

I don't quite understand. "Jump?" I look up and notice a large hole leading up to daylight, how I longed to climb up and be free of this place. When I glanced down it was a different story. I was on a ledge and the hole beneath me was not only large, it seemed infinite.

Berta shoves me a bit and repeats, "Jump," more adamantly.

I give her a pleading look. "Berta I've already suffered more than you know, please don't make me jump." My words only seem to make her furious.

"Anna, if you don't jump, the alternative is much worse, trust me!"

I look into her eyes and see that she is very serious, but how could it be worse? "What's down there, Berta? Why do I have to do this? This isn't you, you were a nice girl. I should have never treated you that way. I know that now. Can't you just forgive me?"

She looks at me and laughs, and then she places her hands on my shoulders and shoves me off the ledge.

I can hear her laughter as my body plunges down the opening. I try to fall toward the wall, maybe I could grab onto it and climb down rather than splatter at the bottom? I try to reach for anything. My hands slide against sharp pieces of rock that tear at my skin and stain my hands red. My hands can't seem to find anything large enough to hang onto. I close my eye and continue to fall. I can only hope that the landing only breaks a few bones.

I can see torches below me. There are people standing around in a circle. I see the bottom now and brace for impact. My arms cover my face and I wait for the blow, but it doesn't come. I slowly peel away my arms and find that I am hovering only a few inches from the ground. I breathe a sigh of relief. As I glance up I see many figures in dark robes carrying torches. They surround me, but do not approach me.

Berta reappears, pushing her way between two of the robed individuals.

"Berta, how come I have to fall down a well and you get to casually arrive down here? Doesn't seem the least bit fair!" My comment is too bold; I know it as soon as I blurt it out.

Berta begins to walk around me, her silence makes me anxious. "I'm not sure you get it yet, Anna, none of this is about fair. What you did to me wasn't fair, and what I'm about to do to you isn't either."

I sob. "Is this what you really want, Berta?"

She hesitates for a moment and simply says, "Yes."

In the next moment I am flipped over in mid-air. I am now facing the opening of the hole. I can see a small opening above, and the light falls upon me. Suspended in mid-air, I can see the robed figures clearly, but I lost sight of Berta. I move my head from side to side trying to locate her. Instead, I can only hear her voice echoing around me.

"Anna, you are here today to pay for your sins. As one of your afflicted, I have chosen a suitable form of punishment for your crime. Your crime is cruelty; your punishment is the removal of one vital organ. Your heart."

I swallow hard. "Is that really necessary? I'm already dead!"

Berta appears now above me. "You may be dead, but I assure you, you will feel every bit of agony that a living person would. Just imagine if you were having open heart surgery while you were awake, that wouldn't feel very nice would it? No anesthetic, no form of pain relief at all! That's what you can expect."

My fists clench into balls while I try to steady my nerves. "What happens to me without a heart? What will I be then?"

Berta smirks above me. "It really shouldn't make much of a difference for you, you never seemed to need that heart of yours while you were living, so you won't miss it much, I think. It will however leave a rather large and painful scar that I hope will remind you of me every time it aches." With that last remark, Berta is gone.

A large hooded man takes her place, he has a small circular saw in hand, and that's when I begin screaming. It hasn't even begun and I am thrashing around in mid-air screaming without a hope of escape.

The pain is so unbearable, that I pass out as soon as the saw touches flesh. I can feel sweat on every inch of my body, but it's as if all this is happening to someone else and I am just a witness to it.

The blade continues to make its grinding sound, and although it's lights out for me, I am still able to feel everything as Berta had promised. When the saw stops, I feel a crunch in my chest that winds me. My ribs! Oh god, my ribs!

My eye opens slowly and I see the robed man holding my bloody, motionless heart in mid-air for the others to see. They all clap as if he has completed a life-saving surgery, I wish that was the case. The next thing I see is a silver plate. He places the heart on it and then it is taken away by someone else.

"Where will it go?" I say lifelessly.

He does not answer, instead he signals to another, as if he needed something brought to him. The tray that is brought to him, holds a needle and thread. He picks up the needle and mimics stitching across his chest.

I nod, very glad that they wouldn't leave me open like this. Every stitch burns like the hot poker the Book Keeper had used earlier. I grind my teeth and try not to scream. I am so tired of screaming.

The bastards in dark robes bow, and one by one they leave the circle. Once they are gone so are my invisible restraints. I fall to the ground with a thud, it feels as though I cracked my head open. It was definitely enough force to knock me out. Everything goes dark, and I think about nothing for a long while.

I am eventually awoken by someone kicking me in the ribs. I groan and tense up as my right eye shoots open in alarm. I squint my right eye hoping to see who it is clearly. The blonde hair flows across her face with each violent kick, making it hard to know who my visitor is.

"Stop, stop it hurts so much!" I cry out.

She mimics me in a mocking way and then laughs to herself. She does quit kicking me, which I am most grateful for. "Get up, bitch!" she rudely replies as she kicks sand into my open mouth.

I spit it out and attempt to rise to my feet. It takes me some time, but I'm not finished yet. I would fight until the end. When I look up, I see a young lady of eighteen or nineteen years old. "Keri?"

She nods. "That's right, bitch, I'm back and you have some explaining to do! I thought we were besties?"

"Well we were, Keri, I was different back then and I guess trash like you was good enough to call friend." I am getting mighty cheeky now, but my anger has been boiling since they put me in that cave and it was only a matter of time before I started biting back. It wasn't wise, but it couldn't get much worse could it? Why not put up a good fight before they make me into one of those god awful zombies? My whole body is hot with rage and I charge at Keri. She is unprepared for my attack and I have her to the ground in seconds ignoring my pain.

I take her gorgeous blonde hair into my hands and start smashing her face into the ground, over and over again. I must be going out of my mind, but I don't care, and I don't stop. "You're the stupid bitch, Keri. You took all those drugs and drank three bottles of Vodka straight! What did you think was going to happen to you? I wasn't gonna go to jail for you! I'm sure you would have done the same thing if you were me!"

When I calm down from my fit of rage, I release her hair and her head falls limply to the ground. Her body is motionless. I back away from her body. Oh god, what have I done? Before I can inspect the body, two zombie guards arrive and pull me to my feet. They hold me in place so firmly that I feel my arms may detach.

I stand there and all I can do is watch Keri's still body in shock. How could I do that? I had never been so violent in my entire life, but there was much that had happened to me since my life ended. This place was changing me, turning me into something vial, slowly eating away at my soul like an acid.

As I watch Keri, I almost think I see her chest rise and fall. Maybe I wanted to see it. I wanted to believe this never happened. I look closer and realize I'm not wrong, she seems to be breathing, or at least moving. Her fingers twitch, and she slowly places her arms under her torso and tries to push off of the ground. When she is finally upright, I notice a large dent in her head and she looks ravenous, she would be much hungrier for her revenge now.

"Anna, I can't believe you did that!" She shakes her finger at me in a disapproving manner. "I'm really going to enjoy informing you about your punishment now. This dent in my head is going to be difficult to fix, but I will feel much better about it knowing you will be suffering a great deal." She smiles so venomously that I almost feel her burning a hole right through me.

Then Keri begins to talk about my punishment, much like Berta did. "Anna, you are here today to pay for your sins. As one of your afflicted, I have chosen a suitable form of punishment for your crime. Your crime is selfishness; your punishment shall reflect the crime. You are sentenced to watch your mother die. I know you would help her if you could, but today I will not allow you to use your selflessness. You are unworthy of partaking in any act of kindness. You are selfish, you are worthless." She spits on me through my screams of protest.

"You can't do this! It's my fault, not hers! She's innocent! That makes you a murderer!"

Keri is about to walk away, but she turns to glare at me with that demonic look in her eyes, "You're right, Anna, it is all your fault. She has to die for your sins. You are the monster. You are the murderer. Everything you touch turns to shit. I should have known that about you." She gives me a look of disgust and then leaves me with the zombie bodyguards.

A robed gentleman brings in a large mirror and places it in front of me. It does not show my reflection so it must serve some other purpose. I cannot stop shaking. I want to run and help her, my uselessness is more excruciating than any punishment I had suffered so far.

The mirror shows my mother driving. She looks relatively content. It breaks me. This mirror is a view into the world of the living, and it may be the last time I ever see my mother. I sob looking at her beautiful face. I love her so, and all I ever did is hurt her, I don't want to hurt her.

She is driving and hears her cell phone ring. I see her furrow her brows contemplating if she should answer it or not while on the road. She decides to pick up. I can't hear what the other end is saying, but my mother is distraught. "That can't be! Are you sure?" she blurts out. Tears start to stream down her face. "My baby is gone? Are you sure? How did this happen?"

They must have told her about my death, they must have found my body and had to inform her.

"When will they bring her home? ...ok," and that was the last thing she said. She hangs up the phone and begins beating it into the steering wheel sobbing hysterically.

I myself am in hysterics watching her. I see a car approaching, I scream, "Mom look out!" but of course she can't hear me.

She sees the vehicle, but it's too late. It T-bone's her car and I see my mother's head whip around violently. Her car spins out of control and heads directly for a lamp post. The impact causes my mother's head to fly into the windshield. She's not moving and her eyes remain open, lifeless, her body mangled.

It's too much to bear, I have to look away. "I'm so sorry, Mom," I sob.

I stand there for what seems like hours. I don't move or speak. I don't know what else to do or say. It is as if I am no one now, the only person I really loved is gone.

The zombie bodyguards drag me to another room. I don't bother to walk, or struggle to free myself. I just want to be a mindless zombie right now, it would be better than having memories that cause you pain.

The room they take me to looks like a large library. It is wall to wall books. The zombies throw me into the middle of the room. I look around at all the books; they must belong to the Book Keeper, records upon records of sinners and their dark deeds. He kept them all.

Soon a door opens in front of me. Two figures stand in the doorway. As they approach I see that one of them is the Book Keeper and the other is a woman with a bag over her head. When they are close enough I stand to greet them. "Book Keeper, please save my mother. This isn't right and you know it. She did nothing..." I choke on the rest of my words, they are much too painful to utter.

He places his finger to his lips to shush me. "Sweetie, it's too late. What's done is done. I don't choose the afflicted, and I don't choose their punishments, it's out of my hands. However, I have brought you the next afflicted, you may be glad to see her."

He removes the bag from her head and reveals my mother. She looks a bit torn. She seems glad to see me, but disturbed by me as well. I must not look myself. I must look pretty gruesome. I try to say something, "Mom, I..." but she grabs me and holds me to her before I can say anything more.

The Book Keeper pulls her off of me. "Now, now, Mrs. Sablo, we had a deal. I would let you see your daughter, but we have some business to take care of now."

My mother nods and backs away from me. She looks at the Book Keeper. "You understand she is still my daughter no matter what?"

To which he simply rolls his eyes.

"Anna, he told me the truth."

I know what my mother is talking about immediately.

"I know about your brother. I know what you did."

None of my sins feel as heavy as this one. I had broken my mother's heart and there is no way to repair it. I couldn't give her her son back. I crawl toward her pitifully and beg for her forgiveness. She seems moved, but firm in her resolve.

She looks to the Book Keeper who simply says, "Now."

Which cue's my mother to begin reciting my punishment. She is my final visitor, the next afflicted to select my rightful punishment. Her voice cracks as she begins, "Anna, you are here today to pay for your sins. As one of your afflicted, I have chosen a suitable punishment for your crime. Your crime is envy; you envied your brother's place in our family and took him from us. Your punishment shall reflect the crime. A life for a life. You will remain here for eternity. Your soul will rot away as you become one of the zombies in their army of undead. It will be painful, since your soul will..." She stops.

The Book Keeper nudges her, signaling her to continue, but her words are caught in her throat.

"It's okay, Mom. I deserve this. I hurt you. You're here because of me. I didn't mean to kill my brother, I would take it back if I could, but that doesn't count for much, it's too late. So go ahead recite the rest. I will be fine. I just want to know one thing...will you...can you...forgive me?"

My mother sobs into her hands. The sound tears at my insides. When she looks up, she gives a slight grin, and says, "I forgive you, my child. I forgive you."

The Book Keeper screams at the top of his lungs. "No! You can't do that! That is not how this works!"

She stares at him and retorts, "I just did!" She walks toward me and embraces me.

For the first time since arriving in Poveglia, I feel safe. A light opens up overhead and surrounds us. It's as warm as my mother's embrace.

LA FINE...

I AWAKE IN A WHITE ROOM. Moving is not an option. As I look around, I notice that I am covered in wires and tubes. As the haziness recedes, I am able to pull off the different medical equipment. The most horrible part is removing the breathing tube. I only realize how extensive it is when I try to slide it slowly out of my throat. How long have I been kept here?

What sort of horror awaited me now? I stand in my hospital gown prepared for anything. Whatever it is, I will fight it. I am tired of being tortured. I grab whatever weapon-like object I can find. There is a syringe on one of the medical trolleys next to my bed. As I hold the syringe up, I notice something different about my body, there is no pain. I check my arms, no blood, no scratches, nothing. I carefully reach my hand up toward my left eye, and find it perfectly intact, that's probably why I can see so much better.

"Where am I?" I whisper to myself.

I hear someone's footsteps in the hall. They enter the room and I hold the syringe up silently, ready to take action. A stranger with a kind face enters, "Okay Anna, how are we feeling today?" she says with a hint of an Italian accent. She is holding a clipboard, but drops it when she looks up and finds me crouched on top of my bed ready to attack. She holds her hands up and looks frightened. "Anna, calm down, I'm not going to hurt you. I'm a nurse at Ospedale San Giovanni e Paolo. This hospital. That is where you are."

I am too afraid to believe her. "Tell me how I got here," I screech.

At this point, a doctor enters the room; he stops in his tracks next to the nurse. "Anna, you are awake! That's fantastico! I am Dottore Rossi. You have been my patient for the past three weeks. Now, I know you are scared, you have been in a coma since you almost drowned in one of the canals in Venice. Do you remember anything?"

I stand there stunned. Could I be back in the world of the living? Did my mother save me?

"But how?" I say out loud without thinking.

"I am sorry, but I was hoping you could tell us how you got in the canal."

I shake my head. "I don't know." I feel safe enough to drop the syringe. If they were going to hurt me they would have done so already. "I've been asleep here for three weeks?"

The Doctor nods in reply.

My next question startles Doctor Rossi. "Did I die?"

He takes a moment to think about his reply, "Well yes, it took a lot of effort to resuscitate you. You had taken in a lot of water and could not breathe. The important part is that we were able to bring you back. You are here now, and you have a visitor if you are ready for one."

I give him a confused look. "Who is it?"

My mother walks in with a bouquet of flowers and a huge smile on her face. "Oh my god, you're awake! Thank you! Thank goodness!" She hugs me and I accept her arms with my desperate embrace.

I sob immediately, "Mom I was so scared."

She runs her fingers through my hair. "Shh honey, you're fine now, it's all over. You did scare us there for a while. Don't you ever do that to me again!"

I shake my head. "I won't, I promise, I love you." I hug her so tight and don't let go until Doctor Rossi interrupts, suggesting that I needed to rest.

My mother kisses my forehead, fluffs up my pillow, and tucks the blankets around me. "See you tomorrow, darling, get some good sleep."

I nod and she exits the room.

Doctor Rossi and the nurse ask if I need anything else, when I assure them that I'm fine, they take their leave as well. I lay back in my hospital bed with an incredible sense of relief. It had all been a horrible, horrible dream. I feel so blessed to be alive. I even say a quick prayer thanking God for my mother and my second chance at life. I shut my eyes and feel total and utter peace.

As I rest, I hear something. It's like a faint drumming in the distance. I hear it again and again until I realize that I hear a heartbeat. My eyes spring open, and the room feels different to me now. Something in the air has changed.

I slowly turn to look at the right corner of the room and there in one of the chairs sits the woman in black. Her flowing mist-like hand is stained red, and she is holding something. I see it pulsing in her hand, 'buh boom, buh boom' it was a beating heart. I shiver as I look down to find my bed sheets stained red. I am too frightened to scream. When I look back at the ghostly woman, she has that same twisted smile on her face, I know her now. She is me.

SARAH, ARE YOU THERE?

HORROR SHORT BY T. M. SCOTT

DETECTIVE ROBERT ANDERSON SAT SILENTLY at the end of the interrogation table, his eyes flicking quickly across the pages of the report in front of him. He had been on the force for well over thirty years, had seen his share of violent crimes during his time as a police officer on the beat as well as a short term as Police Chief, but, while he wasn't one to be easily unnerved, everything about his new case had him completely uneasy. He knew what he needed to do, what he needed to ask the young woman sitting across from him, but every fiber of his being fought against even looking in her direction. Every time he managed to force his gaze up he would find himself locked in her dark stare, every hair on his body standing on end as she just observed him unmoving. It wasn't just her eyes that threw him off kilter.

The girl was young, a college student, about twenty-years-old with great grades and a nearly unblemished record before her recent troubles. He stared at her school picture pinned to the front of the folder in front of him. She was gorgeous, with smooth mocha skin, bright, hazel green eyes and wild black curls that tumbled around her in a glossy mass. Her smile was big, showing off perfect teeth and two big dimples in her cheeks. His eyes flicked up at the figure sitting in front of him and he winced. No. She looked completely different. He looked into her eyes again, blazing green pits that seemed to look into his soul in that instant. Her brown skin was caked with mud and who knows what else. Her once glossy curls clinging to her skin with sweat and gore, streaks of blood trailed down her face dark and sticky with pieces flaking off here and there. Her hands rested on the table in front of her, nails packed with so much dirt and grime that one couldn't tell which ones were even there. The room seemed dimmer around her almost like darkness hovered protectively over her shoulder, whispering dark secrets in her ear.

Anderson managed to break eye contact and glanced down at his folder, quickly reading her name before addressing her for the first time since he entered the room. He knew the other officers would be watching the exchange through the two way mirror to their right, no one else wanted to deal with the girl so he pulled up his pants and walked right in. He still regretted it.

"Hailey," he muttered low as he leaned forward and switched on the recording device in the middle of the shiny wood table. Her eyes were still on him, her body unnaturally still as she seemed to study all his movements. "Hailey, we know you've been through a lot in the past few hours, but we need to know what happened."

She blinked at him, her eyes suddenly shining with unshed tears as she balled her grimy fists up. They remained silent for a moment and Anderson could practically feel the men behind the glass leaning forward in anticipation, waiting to hear her voice for the first time since she strolled into the precinct, dripping blood and leaving thick mud foot prints on the white tile floors. She swallowed, blinking rapidly as tears seeped from her eyes.

"She..." she started, pausing to clear her throat before looking back up into Anderson's eyes.

He quickly looked down at his folder, not wanting to get distracted just as he finally got the nerve to address her.

"She said she just wanted help. To get out. That she wasn't supposed to be there!" Hailey continued, her grimy hands spreading across the table as if to ground herself.

"Who, Hailey?" he muttered, looking back up at her again as he scribbled down notes. "Slow down and tell me. Who are you talking about?"

Tears poured down her blood coated face, dripping big red droplets on the brown table surface. She closed her eyes, taking a long shuddering breath before looking back up at him, her hazel eyes blazing green once more.

"Sarah..."

Twelve Hours Earlier

Hailey sat with her legs folded in the middle of her dorm room floor, a bright pink Ouija board sitting in front of her, covered with glimmering rhinestones and an irritating amount of purple glitter. She had been talking to her friend Bryana about the strange occurrences going on in her room, things moving on their own and even the occasional darting shadows against the walls. When the whispers started, however, Bryana apparently decided Hailey needed to figure out what the ghost wanted, hence the sparkling atrocity sitting in the middle of the floor.

"Surprise Bitch!" The card started and Hailey laughed, picturing Bryana sitting at her room desk writing the message out with a sparkly purple pen. "Get those ghosties a-talkin! Have a great Christmas! – Bry" Nervousness prickled at her arms as she looked down at the board, the little heart shaped planchette sat innocently in the middle adorned with little heart shaped jewels. She felt strange. Sitting alone with a Ouija board, sun blazing through the windows making the room unusually warm with the sounds of her dorm neighbors arguing over who stole who's favorite shirt as they packed for their winter break. Everything else in the world felt so normal except the board which, despite all its new adornments, seemed forbidden and out of place. She swatted away a bead of sweat as it trailed down her forehead and placed her hands on the little wooden heart piece.

"H-Hello?" she called out louder than she meant to.

The arguing next door stopped for a moment before she heard a door open and one of them yelled, "What?"

She sighed, glancing over at her own closed bedroom door covered with winter coats and scarves. "Not you guys!"

"Sorry!" the voice called out once more, their door slamming hard enough to knock down her blue and black checkered scarf before going back to their arguing. Hailey shook her head and placed her fingers on the heart again, speaking in a lower tone this time.

"Hello?" Strange electricity spread through her fingertips making her gasp loud as the marker was moved to HELLO. She gasped, her entire body shook, but her fingers seemed to be locked on the small heart piece.

"W-What is your name?" she whispered this time, the words barely audible even to her own ears. The electricity spread again, her fingers vibrating hard as the marker was moved swiftly around the board.

"S... A ... R... A ... H? Sarah?" The marker went still, the electricity gone once again, but Hailey kept her fingers attached. Her heart still pounded in her chest, her arms shook, but at this point she didn't know if it was fear or adrenaline. She licked her lips, glancing quickly around the room to try and catch a glimpse of Sarah, but the room still seemed the same as it had a minute ago. The sun still blazed through the open window, the black curls that framed her face now clung damp to her sweaty forehead. The neighbors still argued, this time about a pair of pants that one of the pair seemed to lose at their last party. Seemed all too familiar when everything felt so different with her hands on the board.

"Sarah?" she whispered again. "Are you there?" The piece jolted beneath her fingers, violently jerking her forward to land on YES. The prickling in her fingers started to grow painful this time, goosebumps trailed up her arms from the sudden jolt of electricity causing a fresh spike of fear to spread through her.

"Why are you here? What do you want?" Hailey called out trying to sound less afraid than she felt, but her voice shook slightly, ruining the bold effect. The planchette jerked forward again, dragging Hailey's arms back and forth across the board.

"O... U... T." The piece went still again and Hailey's mouth grew dry as she whispered the letters over and over again. Out. She wants out. The room felt different. Heavier and somehow over crowded. Her lungs tightened, the rising sense of terror grew inside her as her fingers remained locked on the smooth wood of the marker. Moments ticked by and nothing happened.

"S-Sarah?" She waited, peering around the room for a few minutes. The air still hung heavy around her, still pressing in on her and sucking the oxygen from her lungs. "Sarah, Are you there?" In an instant, the world around her changed. Silence engulfed the room with such violence that her ears gave a slight ringing noise for a few seconds. Darkness seemed to bubble from the ceiling, tendrils of inky blackness oozing along the floor and walls until all sunlight was blocked from the room. Her heart thundered in her ears and seemed to echo in the silence of the room. The sound of shattering glass tore through the room as a thin, pale hand appeared from the board, pointed fingertips creeping upwards covered in what looked like coal dust. A scream ripped from Hailey's throat and the hand lurched forward, snatching at her ankle with an icy cold claw.

"Help!" she called out as the claw gripped her ankle tight; yanking her hard closer to the board that now seemed to be emanating a sinister red glow. "PLEASE!" Her struggles became more frantic, her nails now digging into the wooden floor in an attempt to get away from the razor sharp hand. Sweat poured down her face, her breath coming in short cloud bursts in the freezing room as she scrambled with all her might toward the door. The claws bit down harder into her flesh, yanking her sharply back across the floor as another blackened hand materialized from the depths of the 'talking board'.

"NO!" she yelled, kicking out hard and managing to break the hold on her legs. Blood leaked from the deep gashes as she scrambled to her feet, her heart thundering in her chest as she raced through the darkness toward the door. A low growl rumbled behind her, vibrating harshly beneath her feet as she ran; the sound of sharp nails digging into wood sent chills down her spine, but she refused to look back. It wasn't until her hand wrapped around the icy metal of the doorknob that she chanced a look back, a sharp spike of fear sliced into her heart at the scene behind her. A young woman climbed up from the board, her long white blonde hair hung heavy with blood and grime around her pale face. Her elongated black claws gripped the floor as she pulled the rest of her small frame from the board. She grinned wide, her teeth blackened from rot and decay made her mouth look like a hallow pit. Her eyes were pure white, blazing bright against the background of her filthy flesh and dirt packed hair. There was a faint silhouette of someone sitting behind her, arms extended toward the board and legs folded, but she couldn't quite make out the figure. The girl gave another low growl, the sound rumbling beneath Hailey's feet and snapping her from her momentary revere. She yanked the door open hard, not meeting the girl's eyes again as she threw herself into the hallway.

As the door slammed shut behind her, Hailey remained frozen with wide eyes as she took in the scene of the hall. Her hand was raised over her mouth, her breath coming in quick bursts as she slowly started moving forward. There were dark figures lined up along the hall, facing the wall as they drug their nails slowly up and down the brick surface. Blood trailed down the walls as their nails ripped free from their fingertips, the sound of the thick crimson liquid plopped to the ground with audible thunks that made her flinch as she made her way quietly down the hall. The figures whispered softly, their focus entirely on the wall in front of them, but she still made her steps as silent as possible.

Hailey crept her way down the hall, her eyes locked on the backs of the men and women lined up in the halls as she neared the exit. Suddenly her heart froze, her eyes locked on the scene ahead, but her attention focused on the sound of a door opening behind her. It slowly creaked open, the faint grinding of the hinges caused the hair on her arms to stand on end and she threw herself into the first door she could reach.

She slammed the door behind her, pressing her ear against a familiar draping of scarves and coats, the scent of lavender oil filling her nose. Shock caused her throat to tighten, her fingers running along the familiar lines of her own blue and black scarf that she'd left hanging behind her door. She turned slowly, her heart hammering hard in her chest as she found herself standing in the room she had just run from.

The Ouija board sat in its same place, the little wooden planchette sitting in the middle with the dark figure still sitting behind it, legs folded and arms still extended over the board. Hailey remained still, her eyes trying to focus in the darkness to make out the features of the girl sitting there. A cold breeze blew through the room, the hair on Hailey's arms stood on end as the scent of blood and rot filled the room. She quickly turned back toward the door, fear pumping through her as she yanked open the door only to freeze. The people in the hall now faced her, their faces clawed and bleeding as they stared at her with black eyes. Their whispers now audible.

"Sarah..." they muttered in unison, repeating the name over and over as they watched her with unseeing black orbs. "Sarah.... Sarah... Sarah..." The muttering started to become louder, echoing through the room behind her until her eardrums pounded violently. She slammed the door, wheeling around to find herself staring into the face of a young woman, waist length white blonde hair caked with blood and dirt. Her face was torn, thick dark blood dripped down her cheeks and onto her dress that used to be white, but was now covered with inches of dirt and mold. She grinned, her teeth rotted away leaving a gaping black pit with the putrid smell of death so strong that it stung Hailey's eyes.

"S-Sarah?" she choked and the girl just looked at her for a moment, not moving, just staring and smiling that toothless grin. Hailey tried to step away, but Sarah was on her in an instant, knocking her hard to the ground and sending the air rushing out of the girl's lungs. She blinked dazed, her green eyes trying to focus on Sarah's sightless white ones, but her gaze kept returning to the gaping maw of her mouth. The smell of dead flesh and sulfur burned her nose, causing her to gag as the dead girl leaned closer. Horror struck Hailey as she could see small pieces of white squirming in the black abyss of Sarah's mouth, maggots creeping and crawling in ever increasing numbers until they dribbled from the girl's lips and onto Hailey's terrified face.

"N—" was all she could get out before Sarah's mouth connected with hers. Maggots poured into Hailey's mouth, the feeling of wiggling, rotten meat rushed down her mouth as the girl held her down to the ground. She screamed, fighting to get away, even kicking hard at the girl until her weight just suddenly disappeared. Hailey rolled over; retching hard onto the dorm room carpet, but nothing came up. Tears streamed from her eyes, her stomach convulsed violently to remove the putrid substance from her body, but nothing happened. She was closer to the figure sitting at the board now, through streaming eyes Hailey could easily make out the girl's face. Her face was slim, her once smooth brown skin was covered with deep scratches and her wild curly hair hung heavy with blood and dirt. Hailey crawled weakly toward the board, her body shaking hard with tears pouring down her face as her thoughts all came crashing down. She lay there, staring into her own face, her expression blank except for her green eyes which started to glow a blinding white. Sarah said she wanted out and Hailey just understood how.

Twelve Hours Later...

"She said she just wanted help," Hailey whispered as she gripped the table as if grounding herself. "To get out. That she wasn't supposed to be there!"

"Who, Hailey?" Detective Anderson muttered, looking back up at her again as he scribbled down notes. "Slow down and tell me. Who are you talking about?"

Tears poured down her blood coated face, dripping big red droplets on the brown table surface. She closed her eyes, taking a long shuddering breath before looking back up at him, her hazel eyes blazing green as the tension started to rise in the room.

The hair on Anderson's neck stood on end; his eyes were captured in Hailey's dark gaze once again. The green lightened to an eerie white as a grin started to spread across her face. The deep scratches across her brown skin started to ooze once more, blood trickling down her chin and plopping onto the wooden surface of the interrogation desk. His body was frozen, his hands spread in front of him as he was stuck in her white hot gaze. Fear thundered through his chest, his entire body shook, but he couldn't make himself move away from the table. Hailey leaned forward, the fresh scent of blood and death filled the room as she pursed her lips, sliding a piece of balled up newspaper toward him. His eyes trailed down, a sense of foreboding crept along his spine as he saw the all too familiar headline.

SON OF POLICE CHIEF CLEARED OF CHARGES

Anderson glanced back up at Hailey who watched him, silently waiting for him to finish reading the paper.

"Jan. 13, 1983— Eric Anderson, Son of Police Chief Robert Anderson, has been cleared of all charges regarding the rape and murder of College Sophomore Sarah Mitchell. Mitchell, who disappeared after a date with Eric, was found lying naked at the bottom of Robert's Hill on the morning of Dec. 12, 1982. It was quickly determined she had been sexually assaulted before being left to die days prior to discovery. With all evidence pointing to Eric being the culprit, the charges were quickly dropped amidst rumors of witnesses being threatened as well as evidence disappearing from the police station.

Despite all charges being dropped, however, suspicion seems to grow with regards to Robert Anderson who quickly resigned as Police Chief after his son was cleared of the allegations to return to the detective desk. His hasty departure leads people to believe the former police chief had a big hand in covering up the brutal crimes of his son and leaving Ms. Mitchell's family heartbroken, desperately in need of justice for young Sarah. We will continue to follow this story as it progresses—"

Anderson's blood ran cold as he looked back up into Hailey's knowing eyes, his hands balling into tight fists to keep them from shaking. She knew what he had done. He couldn't be sure how she knew, but everything in that white-hot glare told him. Swallowing hard, he turned to glance at the two way mirror and wondered what they we're now discussing. He licked his lips, looking back to Hailey and taking a deep breath before speaking.

"W-What do you want?"

She tilted her head and eyed him, the dark blood from her cuts trickled down her shirt and onto the floor. "She wants out," Hailey whispered harshly, her voice taking on a deep grumble that vibrated around this room.

"Who wants out? Tell me. Who?" he knew the answer before she spoke, but everything denied the possibility.

She leaned forward once more, her mouth spreading into a wide grin and the scent of death and decay filled the air around them. "Sarah..." The room went silent, a thick icy chill rolled into the room followed by a low chuckled that seemed to resonate everywhere at once.

Anderson staggered to his feet, stumbling away from the table and moved quickly to the two way mirror, knocking hard on the glass. He could see figures standing there, but no one moved, just stood stock still as if frozen.

"Sarah..." Hailey whispered again behind him, but he refused to turn, still knocking on the glass hoping to get someone's attention. "Sarah, are you there?"

He paused, the reflection of a familiar girl appeared in the glass. Her long blonde hair caked and dirty, her face clawed and bleeding. She stood in the glass, staring at him a moment before her mouth spread into a dark grin. He couldn't move as he stared into those white eyes, didn't flinch when the sound of shattering glass tore through the room and Sarah dug her long black claws into his throat. He gasped for air as she wrapped her hands around his trachea, gripping tightly before ripping the bloody flesh from his body. Anderson dropped to his knees, his eyes still staring into hers as she held up the mass of blood and tissue before his eyes.

He knew his past would come back to haunt him.

SEVERED

TANIA HAGAN

I WINCED AS I SAWED THROUGH the last remaining tendon attaching his head to his neck. The fingernail I had snapped during the struggle was really starting to sting and I paused to suck on the tip of my throbbing forefinger.

I hated men. That much was a given. But, more than that, I hated the thought of being alone. My collection was almost complete and the poor handsome devil on my operating table was going to make a pretty topping for my recipe.

I met him in a nightclub. It was always easier to drag the fools out of a nightclub than it was to simply entice them in off the street.

Of course, being a physical therapist helped me in my mission. My current visitor was easy prey. I simply handed him my card the night we met. After a few sessions at my clinic, it was a no-brainer getting him to come back in for a promised private appointment after hours.

"Bingo," I said out loud as I heard the final rip of the skin along the back of his neck.

I couldn't remember this one's name, I mused as I grabbed my prize by its thick, blond locks. I dropped it in the fabric shopping bag I'd brought along for this very occasion.

I always dreaded the cleanup, though.

I shoved the useless bulk of the rest of his body to the ground, where it hit my intended target in the middle of the tarp. I made my way to the small bathroom at the rear of the clinic where I rinsed the finger with the hangnail and applied a bandage.

Afterwards, I slowly dragged the heavy tarp out into the alley behind the building where I hoisted it into the back of my minivan. The heavy thud it made was like music to my ears. It was always a sign of a job well-done.

I grabbed my bleach bottle, sponges, and paper towels from the backseat before I returned to the treatment room to clean up the mess. I carefully laid my shopping bag in the corner of the room. I didn't want to splash any cleaning solution on it.

With the room looking just like it did at closing time, I snapped off the lights, gathered my bag, and retreated to my van.

On the way home, I was nearly giddy. I knew this last piece would complete my work, and I couldn't have been more elated.

He was the final chapter in my seemingly-endless quest to create the perfect specimen. He was number seven.

His blond hair and blue eyes had drawn me to him. For reasons I didn't understand, the face had to look like his. It was chiseled and handsome, with just the right amount of wrinkles revealing his forty-to-fifty years of life. With men, it was always hard to tell. Some of the bastards seemed to grow more attractive as they aged.

He wouldn't age one more day, though. I had seen to that.

Sorry, Charlie, or whoever you were, I thought, laughing to myself.

I was acutely aware I was collecting the Seven Deadly Sins with my work. It was kind of a private joke with myself. Years ago, I saw a movie where a male serial killer followed the same pattern and I was mesmerized with the possibilities.

I took the right arm from some poor sap named Wayne, in order to represent Greed. He was a wealthy creep who thought he could buy a night with me by taking me to a fancy dinner and a play in his Ferrari.

Gluttony came in the form of Aaron. He had too much of everything. The foolish young actor had been visiting New York during a run of his best friend's Broadway play. He had rented a penthouse which was fully stocked with enough food, drugs, liquor, video equipment, and various other excessive luxuries to satisfy ten men. At least.

Aaron had graciously donated his left leg to me.

I almost felt sorry for Richard. I had relentlessly flirted with his buddy one night at a club, just to make sure Richard was the right choice. The moron made a play for me the second his pal stood up to go to the bathroom. I knew I had found my Envy, and the right leg for my project.

Randy had been pure Lust. He oozed the crap. When I took the needed part from him, he made it easy for me, exposing that repulsive area thirty seconds after I had closed the door to the treatment room. With it dancing proudly in front of me, I decided it would be so much more fun to just lop it off before I had actually killed him. He didn't deserve to die before I appropriated his favorite body part.

Seeing the look in Randy's eye was almost as rewarding as adding his donation to my collection.

Wrath came from Eric, the high-powered attorney. He had handled more famous divorces than just about anyone in all of New York. He tended to enjoy socking it to unsuspecting women who had been unlucky in love. Somehow, he and his predominately-male clients seemed to leave the wives writhing in the dust, with very little alimony or child support as rewards for standing by their cheating husbands for years on end. As much as I hated men, he appeared to hate women. In the end, I took his heartless torso for payment.

Nicholas was one of my favorite finds. He was a brooding painter living on his dad's money. In his thirties, the scumbag simply laid around his Manhattan flat, pretending to everyone he was working on his next masterpiece. Nick was the very epitome of Sloth, and he made my skin crawl. Since the phony artist had been left-handed, I took the entire arm.

This last guy was the icing on the proverbial cake. Mister-no-name was Vanity all the way. He was blindingly handsome, and he knew it. At home, he had a wife and young son, and he proudly told me all about them that evening in the nightclub. He also had bragged about his ability to entice women with just a sideways glance of his gloriously-blue eyes.

I made a mental note to sew those eyes open as soon as I stitched his head to the rest of my piecemeal body.

I drove the van into my two-car garage when I arrived home. I had already planned to leave his sorry body in the rear of the vehicle overnight. I was far too excited about extracting his head from the bag, and sewing it onto its final resting place. I knew no one would be dropping by over the weekend. And even if they did, no one would need to look in my garage for any reason.

I would dispose of him in the basement, behind the cinderblocks with the rest of them, whenever I felt up to the task.

I practically skipped down the stairs to the basement where I kept my workroom separate from all the other subdivided space down there. I unbolted the lock I always attached to the door when I left.

As I flipped on the florescent lights above my head, my work of art seemed to glisten in front of me. I had propped it up in a high-back chair I bought at a garage sale last summer. To me, it looked like a throne suitable for a king.

"Hi, handsome." I winked at the collection as I laid the ten-pound bag on the table. "Did you miss me?"

He didn't answer. He never did. Of course, I knew he might be more vocal once he had a proper head attached. I certainly knew he would be a lot better company than he was now.

I pulled my sewing kit out of the drawer in the ancient hutch I kept down there. I removed the head from the bag and rinsed the dirty, red part in the utility sink. Patting it dry with a paper towel, I was excited to line it up on top of its new neck.

It was a perfect fit. More or less.

Maybe the neck and torso were a little too hairy. They came together, after all, and they had no idea they'd be joined with such a clean-shaven, golden head as this one.

"Oh well." I squinted as I sized up the problem. "I can fix that with my razor."

Over the next hour, I painstakingly completed the project. I stopped only to go make myself a ham sandwich and to grab my shaver from the shower.

When he was finally done, I stood back and looked at my work. The moment was bittersweet. I had so enjoyed working on this project, and I was going to miss the action. But, I was also very proud of what I had created.

I pulled on the clothes I had collected and washed for him. Every piece came from a different one of my conquests. Together, they made a stylish ensemble.

I leaned over and kissed his cheek before I shut off the lights and left the room.

Leaving the padlock off the door was my only mistake.

I scooted around the house, trying to decide what to do with the rest of my night. The two-story, four-bedroom home had always been too big for me. I often wondered why I had made such a choice in the first place, especially since I was aware of my newfound aversion to loneliness.

I gathered the mail the postal carrier had dropped through my slot. Bills. All bills and ads. I had to laugh every time I read my name. It was as amusing to me now as it had been when I chose it.

I had named myself after Willa Cather, the strong, brilliant author who also probably carried a solid distaste for men.

When I was a foster child during the first sixteen years of my life, my name had been Karen. It was a simple and boring name, given to me by parents who were unfit drug addicts.

When I was finally adopted by a kindly old woman, she allowed me to change my first and last names in front of the judge on my adoption day. I didn't hesitate to tell the clerk to type "Willa" on the paperwork.

My adoptive mother died when I was just twenty. I immediately packed up and moved to New York, where I spent more than twenty-five years being used and abused by almost every man who crossed my path.

Not anymore, I smiled to myself as I took a seat on my sofa.

I flipped through the channels until I settled on an old black-and-white film. In it, the male lead had just rescued the platinum-blonde woman from the clutches of a couple of gangsters.

I laughed out loud. No such chivalrous men existed in the real world. If they did anything for a woman, they expected something in return.

All I had ever wanted was someone to keep me company with no expectations. I finally had him in my basement.

I had just settled back and drew a blanket over my middle when I heard the clunk. Or, maybe it was more of a clang.

The noise sounded like it was coming from the backyard, so I ran to the kitchen to get a good look. I flipped on the floodlight on my back porch, but I saw nothing.

Then, I heard it again. This time, I was sure it was coming from inside the house.

As I heard the sound twice more, it was clearly emanating from the other side of the basement door.

A cat? A raccoon maybe had hidden out in the basement? My mind first traveled to plausible explanations.

But, I knew I would have heard something while I was down there if it had been an animal.

When I didn't hear it again for more than a minute, I walked into the living room and sat back down on the sofa.

It happened again. Now, the noise sounded more like shuffling, as if someone was trying to amble along with an injured leg.

I sprinted back to the kitchen and pressed my ear to the basement door. There was clearly someone moving around down there.

My first thought was that someone had discovered my hobby and was currently investigating what I had done. Still, I was sure there would be no way anyone could have gotten into my basement. Even though it was a maze of rooms down there, I had no doubt I would have been aware of somebody hiding there while I was working.

I was suddenly hit with the overwhelming fear that maybe someone wanted to steal my creation. Maybe they wanted to take my work and claim it as their own. The thought was more frightening than my worries about the authorities honing in on my activity.

I heard the sound of a closing door below me. There were so many doors in the basement, it could have been coming from anywhere.

I picked up the baseball bat I normally kept tucked between the wall and the refrigerator. I had left all my dissection tools in the van and I didn't want to have to go back out there to get a weapon. Slowly, I opened the basement door.

As I crept down the stairs, I paused every couple of steps to listen. Everything was silent.

I moved past my washer and dryer and peered around the corner to the ancient stack of cinderblocks where I had discarded all of my extra parts. I peeked over the wall and saw little more than darkness. The lye I had always used definitely accomplished the task I had intended, and there was no sign of anything other than slimy-looking stones in the shadows.

After I had opened and closed every door in the place, but didn't find any intruders, something at the back of my mind told me to go have a look at my newly-finished companion.

Surely he wouldn't be moving around down here. He has no life until I tell him to. That's what makes him different than the division of his parts.

I opened the door to my work room and switched on the overhead lights. As they buzzed to life, I could already see the chair. It was empty except for a few dark, dried stains.

No! I screamed in my head. *Someone took him!*

What sounded like a kick of a pebble made me spin around on my heel. I approached the door cautiously, certain to find intruders hauling away my prized possession. Instead, I saw nothing but the empty space leading to the rest of the basement.

Out in the dark hall between my basement rooms, I looked left and right. I dismissed the area to my left, since I could clearly see to the end of the row of doors. I turned back in the direction of my washer and dryer and the stairs. I had laid my foot on the bottom step, when a sound behind me caught my attention. I moved back around the corner.

He was standing there, leaning against the wall. My creation had come to life and he was smiling wickedly at me.

"No!" I shouted to him. "You aren't supposed to do this! You don't walk unless I tell you to."

He nodded as if he was poking fun at my statements. He took a few wobbly steps in my direction before he started walking more normally.

But, it wasn't a normal gait. His feet turned slightly inward and the familiarity of his movements made me cringe even more than the sight of him standing upright. It was a walking pattern no one would have noticed if he was a normal man, in an everyday setting. I noticed it because I recognized it.

"What do you want from me?" I pleaded, backing away from him.

I silently cursed myself for sewing those brilliant blue eyes open. They were staring at me grotesquely.

"I didn't mean it, Willa," he said in a voice that I didn't want to hear.

"What?" I found the stairs with the back of my heel. "What didn't you mean?"

He only moved closer. I could see a line of blood starting to drip slowly from his neck.

"I was just so mad at him, don't you see? You can't blame me, can you?"

As my foot landed flatly on the stair behind me, I spun around and bolted to the kitchen. I locked the door behind me.

Still, I heard the heavy thump of his footsteps coming up the stairs.

I didn't waste any time jogging through the living room on my way to the second floor. I scurried into a guest room and pressed my back to the far wall. Somewhere below me, I heard what sounded like wood splintering.

I squinted around the room. To my left, I spotted an old armoire I had picked up at a thrift store. I threw my body between the piece of furniture and the wall.

Someone was shuffling up the stairs as they noisily creaked in their usual way. I dared to peek out of my hiding place, just as he stepped into view in the doorway. He was still smiling.

"I only talk to her because she's your friend, Willa," he said in a sing-song voice. "You believe me, don't you?"

He moved closer. In the moonlight streaming through the window, I could see his whole body. Somehow, it had morphed into one solid man, as if he had been born that way. There was no awkwardness to the way his limbs hung from his torso. All of the remnants of blood were also gone and he seemed to blink his eyes freely.

"Please, what do you want from me?" I begged.

"I need you to see it my way, Willa." He was so close now, I knew he could touch me if he wanted to.

Bastard. Even dead and chopped up, this sonofabitch is going to try to touch me.

I realized I would just have to kill him again. And, even again if that's what it would take. My mind started running through all possible weapons in the room. I was sure I had some metal coat hangers in the armoire and maybe even a letter-opener in the desk in the corner.

I stifled a smile. I had done it with less on at least one occasion. There was no reason I couldn't have done it now.

I reached around the side of the cabinet. I had just pried open the door nearest me when I felt a brisk, chilly wind blow through the room.

As I glanced again in his direction, he was gone.

In his place was a small boy, who looked to be about six-years-old.

He had the same eyes, hair, and facial structure of the man.

"No," he said simply as he closed in on me.

* * *

The weary fifty-year-old man raked his hand through his dark-blond hair as he leaned over his wife's hospital bed. She had been in the psychiatric facility for nearly three years, and this morning was the first time she'd spoken a word since her incident.

"Please, Willa. Speak to me again." He grabbed her hand and pressed the back of it to his lips. "I heard you say Peter's name. Just...try it one more time."

Warren had been sitting there next to his wife of twenty-eight years since seven that morning. It was nearly noon by then and she hadn't spoken again since she uttered the name of their only son three hours before.

"Why don't you come out into the hall and have some coffee, Mr. Hadley?"

Warren looked up at the unfamiliar face behind him. He realized immediately the older woman must have been a new nurse on duty in Willa's ward. He flinched as the woman touched his shoulder.

"Has Doctor Marsden been called?" He craned his neck to look at the glass window separating his wife's room from the nurses' station. "He really needs to know she said our son's name earlier."

"I've paged him." The woman nodded her head as she turned toward the door. "He promised he'd be here this afternoon." She stopped and looked at Warren again. She smiled warmly at him. "Come with me. I make the best pot of coffee this side of the Mississippi."

"Okay. Thank you." He nodded and kissed Willa's hand again. She was snoring softly. He knew she'd be awake soon, as her naps were rarely long ones. But, for Willa, being awake was just a time to eat and take her meds. Her state of consciousness was just as catatonic as her sleeping state. "I think I'll take you up on that offer, Miss...?"

"Jackson. It's Rebecca Jackson."

"Are you new here?"

"I sure am." She smiled again. "I'm the new head nurse working the day shift. I'm replacing Marybeth Wheaton. She retires on Friday."

"Oh. Okay."

Warren had gotten used to old Mrs. Wheaton over the past few years.

But, to him, one nurse was just about as good as any other. None of them had truly been able to help his wife or her condition.

Sighing, he stood up from the stool he had been using at Willa's bedside. He slowly walked out into the hallway, feeling his bones creaking all the way there. Since everything happened a few years back, Warren had been working exclusively from home. His editor at the magazine had been understanding of his situation and had offered to allow him to turn in his articles remotely. He assured Warren he knew he was one of his best reporters and he trusted him to still stick to his deadlines, despite the disastrous nature of Warren's personal life.

But, one of the problems with working from home was the lack of exercise. He had realized lately he used to be so much more active when he actually went into an office every day. The arthritis he had inherited from his mother screamed at him for it.

But, if his mom was still kicking at seventy-nine, he figured he could handle the pain at barely fifty. Besides, his extra-curricular activities managed to keep him feeling young enough. He smiled in his mind, making sure not to do it on the outside.

In the hall, Mrs. Jackson patted the back of the dingy, but comfortable sofa. Warren took the hint and had a seat at the end of the couch, nearest the end table.

"Here you go, honey." The kindly nurse handed him a cup of steamy black liquid. She placed a small basket of creamers and sugar on the table next to him before she took a seat on the opposite end of the sofa. She sipped her own coffee once before she spoke. "I've been going through the records of our long-timers all morning. I glanced at Willa's only briefly though."

"Okay. Thank you." He didn't know what else to say. His wife's case was so unusual and tragic, it would probably take her a whole year to get through the file. But, he was grateful this woman was trying to familiarize herself with everything so quickly. "I'm sure our file makes for interesting reading material."

"I understand she's been like this for a while." The nurse pursed her lips. "I'm so sorry about all your troubles, Mr. Hadley."

"Please, call me Warren."

This woman seemed genuinely kind and motherly, even though she clearly only had about ten years on him. While Mrs. Wheaton was always very cordial, she had never sat down and actually talked to him like this.

"And, I want you to call me Rebecca." She settled back in her seat and took another drink from her cup. "If you feel up to it, Warren, I'd like to hear your wife's story from your point of view, especially since Doctor Marsden is on his way in." She paused as if she was giving him a chance to think about her request. "You don't have to discuss it, if you're not comfortable."

Warren thought about it for a second. He'd relived the events so many times in his mind that telling it to someone else almost felt like reading a book out loud. He'd gone over the whole thing, again and again, with countless doctors and therapists throughout the years. Reciting the nightmare once again couldn't hurt.

"My son," Warren started, clearing his throat. "He's our only son. He's our only child. It was difficult for Willa to get pregnant, so we went through three cycles of in-vitro fertilization before an embryo actually attached. The fertility treatment was still a fairly new and expensive one at the time. Of course, our insurance barely touched the costs. Thankfully, we had some very generous relatives supporting our venture."

"That experience alone takes a lot out of a woman." Rebecca leaned forward and put her elbows on her knees. "My eldest niece had her twins through that procedure. It was rough for the whole family every time an attempt failed."

"Yes. Willa was pretty exhausted by the time the pregnancy was confirmed. But, we were both so elated, we overlooked the discomfort."

Warren gulped the last of his coffee and discarded the paper cup in the basket under the table.

"And, was the pregnancy an easy one for her?" The nurse followed Warren's lead and tossed her cup into the trashcan.

"It wasn't that bad, as far as first pregnancies go. I mean, she was in her early twenties at the time, so she was in perfect health."

"That always helps."

"And, she had a natural birth." Warren leaned back and closed his eyes. "Peter was a dream child...such a good kid." He thought about Peter as a toddler. "He was the apple of our eye. He looked just like me, and Willa couldn't have been more thrilled. We didn't really have any trouble with him at all until he reached seventeen."

"He hit a rebellious stage?" Rebecca raised an eyebrow and gave him a knowing look.

"I suppose you could call it that." Warren swallowed hard and looked at the woman. "Peter came out to us right after high school. We had no idea he was gay."

"I see." She nodded slowly. "How did you and your wife take the news?"

"Not as well as I wish we would have. Willa always said it was me who drove him to his self-destructive behavior. I mean, I tried to be supportive, but... I was just being a jerk."

No, being a jerk would have meant not speaking to him for a day or so. What I did went beyond that pedestrian title. So far beyond, he thought.

Warren leaned over and laid his head in his hands. All of the old guilt rose up in his throat and he was unable to control the choking feeling.

"So, you carry that blame by yourself, since Willa has been in her current state?"

Damn, this woman's good. She should have been a doctor herself, Warren observed.

"Yes. All of it." He wiped at a tear.

"What happened to your son?"

"After we failed to accept him fully, he fell into a deep depression. He started running with a bad crowd, drinking, drugging. You name it, my son did it."

"I'm so sorry."

"Yes. So were we." Warren took a deep breath as he looked at his wife through the glass. "After a few years, we ran through several rehab programs and plenty of therapists. He didn't start to come around until he was nearly twenty-one."

"What happened then?"

"He woke up one day and he finally decided what he wanted to do with his life. When he was much younger, he had planned to become a physical therapist. He broke his arm pretty badly falling off his skateboard when he was twelve. It was so bad he required physical therapy to learn to use it properly after the accident.

"I didn't know about his internal struggle at the time. I'm not even sure he knew. But, one of the therapists helping Peter was a young man in his late twenties, maybe. His mother was a friend of my mom's, so we sort of knew the kid outside of the office. In any case, the man was openly gay and in a relationship with a man who worked with me."

"Small world, isn't it?" Rebecca smiled at Warren as if she was attempting to lighten the moment.

"Yes. Truthfully, we lived in a very small town up until recently when I sold the old place and moved to an apartment here in the city. If you didn't know everyone in our old town, you at least had common connections.

"In any case, Peter really took to this young man. The therapist had a way with kids and really made Peter feel special, even when the session was particularly tough. Maybe he saw a little bit of himself in our son, and he felt a bond with Peter. He did everything right and our son even looked forward to attending therapy because of this kind man.

"Peter took away from the experience a desire to help people through physical therapy. During his early teen years, he was excited about taking up the profession when he grew up, and his mother and I were delighted at the possibility."

"Then came the destructive behavior to stomp out that dream?" Rebecca glanced down the hall as another nurse entered a different room. "He failed to pursue his career because of the addictions?"

"At first, yes. It was difficult, as you can imagine. We had to get used to a whole new set of expectations for our son. During the dark days, seeing his car drive up with him in one piece was victory enough for Willa and me.

"Then, after a drunken night with his questionable group of friends, he woke up rejuvenated, somehow. He ran downstairs to tell us he was considering physical therapy again."

"I'll bet the two of you had your doubts still."

"We did. Of course we did. Willa didn't even want to even talk about putting up the money for him to go through training. I rallied for him, and Peter and I together finally convinced her. When he dumped the thugs he was running with and really buckled down with his studies, she finally agreed we may have made the right decision with trusting him once more.

"Everything went well for about three years. He got a job right out of school working at a therapy office literally in the same parking lot as our local hospital."

"It sounds like he was on the right track." The nurse genuinely seemed interested in his story.

"He *was* on the right track," Warren repeated Rebecca's words. "My wife and I were also recovering from all the misery our family had gone through during his self-abusive days. Peter had introduced us to a nice young man he had been dating from his school. He and Josh were planning to get an apartment together as soon as his boyfriend finished his clinical work. We couldn't have been happier with our son for all of his accomplishments and choices."

At least, Willa couldn't have been happier, he thought, miserably. *Keep it steady and the old woman will believe the bullshit.*

"But, it is true there's always a calm before a storm." Warren wiped his whole face with his hand. "And, we were in for a tsunami."

"Oh no. Did he fall back into his old ways?" Rebecca scooted closer to him and laid a reassuring hand on his shoulder. 'Did he go back to using?"

"No." Warren shook his head wearily. "He became dedicated to maintaining his good health, both mentally and physically."

"Then, what happened to him? What caused Willa's breakdown?"

"Peter had always been kind-hearted. There was nothing he wouldn't do to help someone out." Warren sighed. "There was a man who walked into the clinic about a week before. He claimed to be in his fifties. He also said he had sciatica and he was suffering a flare-up."

"Yes. I'm very well-acquainted with that malady." She briefly touched her own back. "I've been through a few bouts with it myself over the years."

"Well, this man probably didn't have sciatica at all. He was a cash patient. He didn't come with a referral. Of course, he asked to be billed instead of paying up front. Someone in the office should have followed up on his name and address.

"But, the clinic was very trusting. They had no reason not to be. Like I said, this guy pretended to be a few years older than me."

"You say, 'pretended'. What was he pretending?"

"Looking back on the events, everyone who saw him agreed he was probably wearing a disguise. His gray hair and beard were fake. His illness was made up. Whoever he was, he only had one thing in mind."

"What was that?"

"He wanted my son dead."

* * *

I blinked a few times, but the child still stood there, staring at me.

He took a few steps closer to me and I could see his features more clearly. I had no doubt he was a tiny version of my creation. The way he held his hands, the way his feet turned slightly inward, the golden shock of hair was all the same.

No. This boy was different. The look in his eye was pure innocence. Although they were the same shape and color of the demon I had built, there was a sadness to them. In this small boy, I saw a purity that was normally lacking in the male species.

"Please stop," he said suddenly. "Please."

"Stop what?" I asked.

Of all the frightening events I had witnessed that night, I knew his answer would be far more terrifying than any of it.

"Stop, Mommy."

"*What?*"

I was so stunned by his response, I moved backwards, forcing myself farther behind the giant cabinet. I was not a mother. I certainly wasn't *his* mother.

"You can't fix it from here." He continued to approach me, even though I had backed away. "You have to wake up and we'll take care of things the *right* way."

* * *

"What?" The old nurse's eyes grew wide. "Why would anyone want to harm your boy?"

Why indeed? Warren thought, feeling the guilt hit him in the stomach, as it always did. *As it always should.*

"The men were never caught." He tented his hands and pressed his nose to them. "The cops are pretty sure it was a gay bashing."

"Men? I thought you said it was one man."

"On the night he was attacked, there were two. The first one, the guy who pretended to be the patient, brought along a buddy that evening. I guess he called in shortly before his scheduled appointment with my son. That was close to seven-o'clock, and the clinic closed at eight. He said he was running late, but really needed to come in because he was in pain."

"And, your boy, being a kind and understanding soul, offered to stay late?"

"Yes. He did. The woman working with Peter said later she was suspicious when the two guys showed up as she was closing down the clinic. She had offered to stay with Peter, but he assured her everything would be fine."

"And, it wasn't?"

"No. It was far from fine." Warren stood up and walked over to the glass window to Willa's room. She was still sleeping. "The security cameras caught both of the criminals, but the footage was useless. The older man was probably heavily disguised and the younger man also wore glasses and a hat over what looked like an auburn wig. Neither man's features were distinct enough to offer any help to the cops."

But, Warren was sure he knew who they were. He had brought them there, in an indirect sort of way.

It happened one night when Warren was seeking solace at the bottom of a few bottles of beer. He had wandered into a bar, feeling sorry for himself. His only son had come through years of addiction, and was on the road to a healthy lifestyle. But, the boy was still gay and Warren couldn't handle it, no matter how hard he'd tried.

He had been sitting there when two men saddled up to the bar next to him. They were laughing and chattering homophobic remarks back and forth among themselves. These were the type of guys who waved the flag in one hand and a beer bottle in the other, daydreaming about beating the wife and kids over the weekend.

Warren didn't care. He was sure they'd turn a sympathetic ear when he told them about how miserable he had been with a gay son.

By the end of the conversation, these men knew everything they needed to know about Peter, including where he worked and what his schedule looked like. Warren wasn't sure why the information was important to the pair, but he was too drunk to analyze the possibilities.

Later, when the police showed him the video of the suspects, he recognized one of them immediately. He was sure the older man was the second guy, decked out in a clever disguise.

He said nothing to the cops.

"What did these men do?" Rebecca asked in a soft voice.

Warren swallowed hard before he continued, in an attempt to wash away the memory along with the guilt.

"The back alley was dimly-lit. The clinic was in the hospital's parking lot, but no one really strayed into the alley behind both facilities." He took his seat back on the sofa. "They lured him out there and they beat him." He sucked in a long breath before he continued. "They carved the word, 'fag' into his stomach."

"Oh, my goodness. I'm so sorry. How can people be so cruel in this world?"

"If that would have been the end of it, maybe things would have been different."

"It went further than that?"

"Much further." If beating up his son would have been the extent of it, then Warren would have been no better than those monsters. He brushed away the thought and took a deep breath. "They ... um ... they severed his left arm."

"What?"

"Yes." Warren cleared his throat and tried not to break down. "They severed his arm and they were working on cutting off his legs and his other arm as well." He gasped, despite himself. He bit on his knuckles to stop himself from losing control. "When Peter was found, they had been attempting to ... *decapitate* him. Dear Lord. They had been trying to cut his *head* off!"

At that point, he lost it. Warren leaned back and stifled a wail with his hands over his mouth. He couldn't stop the tears, which were as much for himself as they were for his son. Rebecca moved closer to him and touched his shoulder.

"Oh, you poor thing. I *am* so terribly sorry." She paused and her voice quivered. "I can't imagine losing a child in *any* way, let alone at the hands of such demons."

"We didn't lose him," Warren managed weakly.

"So, you mean he...?"

"Survived." He nodded. "Yes, my son somehow survived the attack."

"He did? That's amazing."

"He survived." Warren repeated the words, as if they would make him more comfortable with the whole thing. "There was a homeless man, in the alley. He heard Peter's screams. He said, at first, he wasn't going to do anything because he thought it was just a fight among a bunch of young hooligans, and he didn't want to be discovered."

"But, he *did* step forward? In time to help?"

"The man hid behind a trash bin. He said curiosity got the better of him. Thank God it did. He said, from where he was crouching, he saw the blood...he saw the pool of blood in the snow around my son. He saw Peter become motionless as the men continued to hack away at his poor body."

"My Lord." Rebecca bowed her head and almost looked like she was praying.

"When he realized Peter might really be in trouble, the homeless guy started banging on the trashcan. The two attackers jumped up and ran away immediately and he didn't get a good look at them. The man hurried into the clinic and called 911. Help was there within a few minutes."

"And, they were close to the hospital anyway. Right?"

"Yes. They rushed him into surgery." He paused. "Peter was unconscious and had lost so much blood. This happened in January, and it was about twenty below zero that evening. His doctors said later the air temperature had a lot to do with his survival, but the limited time from injury to treatment also helped, of course."

"Were they able to...help with his...arm?"

"No. He lost it for good. Those bastards chopped it off crudely, so there was no way to save it. He nearly lost his right leg too, since one of them was clearly working on removing it as the other asshole started sawing at his neck."

"I don't even know what to say." Rebecca sounded truly sympathetic. "I'm relieved they saved his life, but I'm so sorry Peter had to go through such a horrible ordeal. I can't imagine he'd ever be the same afterwards."

"He's not." Warren shook his head slowly. "Willa doesn't even know he survived."

"So, you mean she was like this before it happened?"

"No. She had her breakdown the *night* it happened...shortly after we got the call."

"Oh, dear. She doesn't even know he lived? What a miserable outcome." She glanced at Willa's room before she continued. "Of course, there is the very real possibility she *does* know. When people are in psychological states like your wife, they sometimes are able to take in information. We just never know...unless they recover."

"Which she might," Warren said, feeling mildly encouraged by the thought. "She did say his name today, after all."

"The doctor will assess her as soon as he gets here."

"I hope that's sooner, rather than later." Warren glanced at his watch and stood up again.

* * *

"Please, Mom." The boy held his hand out to me.

"What do you want?" I sunk farther into the space behind the armoire and the wall. "Who are you?"

Somehow, I knew this boy would be the end for me. He knew things about me no one should know. He knew *everything*.

"I just want you to stop pretending, Mommy."

"Don't call me that!" I spat.

I was no one's parent. He must have been mistaken.

"Wake up now and we'll take care of it." He still approached me, sounding much older than his appearance indicated. "He hurt me, Mommy. He's the one you need to deal with. The *only* one."

"He hurt you?" I felt tears rolling down my cheeks even though I hadn't cried in years. "He *hurt* you?" I repeated.

The boy nodded.

"He hurt me more than the strangers did."

I slipped forward, out of my hiding place. I reached my arms out to him and he fell into them.

* * *

Warren excused himself from the conversation and stepped into the bathroom nearest to the waiting area.

As he was washing his hands, he looked in the mirror. The blue in his eyes had definitely dulled over the last few years, but they still had a distinct sparkle. He smoothed his blond hair with a little bit of water. At least, he was still handsome enough to keep Margo's interest.

Margo had been Willa's best friend since college. Their affair had started about a year before Peter came out to his parents.

The state of his relationship with Margo had been the catalyst for his anger toward his son that weekend. Margo and Willa had gone to New Jersey to visit Margo's daughter for a couple of days. Peter had only just admitted his homosexuality the week before.

Willa had second thoughts about the trip, but Warren had encouraged her to go. After all, Margo would be gone no matter what, so he didn't care where the hell his wife stayed for the weekend. He had planned to spend the whole time drinking with his buddies and watching whatever game might be on at the sports bar.

He had just come home that Saturday night. He tried to text Margo, but she wasn't answering. When he walked through the front door, Peter was sitting on the couch next to another young man. Warren blew a gasket. He stormed off to the kitchen and opened another beer.

A few minutes later, the front door closed and he heard a car drive away. Peter found Warren in the kitchen.

"Dad, I know what you're thinking, but Steve's just a guy from school who's trying to sell me this killer skateboard." He smiled at his father. "I actually think I might buy it."

Warren didn't think. His blood was boiling. He didn't care about whatever line his gay son was trying to pull on him. He just wanted to shut him up. Without batting an eye, Warren swung around and bashed Peter in the nose with his nearly-full beer bottle.

At that moment, he despised his son and everything he represented.

As the boy fell to the floor, Warren's contempt for him grew. He kicked Peter in the ribs several times. Then, he picked up a chair and brought it down on his boy's chest.

"Disgusting faggot!" Warren shouted, unable to control himself. "Bringing your lovers in to *my* house!"

"Dad, no!" Peter cried from his position on the ceramic tiles. "Daddy, *please*, no."

Warren steadied himself by hanging onto the kitchen counter. The boy cried wretchedly for a few seconds before he stood up and left the room. Ten minutes later, Peter returned to the kitchen where Warren was sitting at the table, clutching a sugary soda.

"Dad," he said softly, holding a washrag to his face. "I think I broke my nose."

Warren felt pity for him at that moment, and the father and son spent the next few hours in the emergency room, under the pretense Peter had been testing a new skateboard and took a nasty spill at the skate park. The story stuck when Willa returned home. She bought every word of the lie and Peter and Warren never uttered another sentence about the incident. At least, they never talked about the truth of the matter.

After that horrible night, Warren tried to genuinely accept Peter for who he was. During the years Peter was an addict, Warren convinced himself anything would be better than seeing his son living such a destructive life.

He always had Margo to fall back on whenever he was worried or tense about anything. She was his rock.

Margo, what will we do when she gets better? Warren asked the image in the mirror.

He pulled out his cellphone to see if she had texted him.

"Hey, babe," she had written. "Getting ready to have breakfast with two young studs. Don't worry, though. I'll explain later. Lol!"

He checked the time stamp. Margo had texted him about an hour after Willa had uttered Peter's name.

He typed out an answer. "Young studs, huh? I'll bet they've got nothing on me."

Warren smiled and tucked the phone back into his rear pocket.

Working from home had definitely given him much more time to be with Margo. But, it also caused him to feel obligated to visit Willa every day. She was, after all, the reason he had requested to work away from the office.

When he exited the bathroom, Rebecca was just coming out of his wife's room. She smiled at him and shut the door. When she sat back down in the same spot she had previously occupied on the couch, Warren did the same.

"So, where is Peter now?" she asked.

"In Jersey, as far as I know."

"You don't keep in contact with him?"

"No. It's more like he doesn't keep in contact with me. He and Josh were married last year and he didn't invite me." Warren sighed as he thought about the son he'd estranged. "I'm not sure why."

"And, has he been to visit his mother?" Rebecca raised an eyebrow.

"No. He only calls. From what they tell me, he calls fairly regularly to check on her status."

He couldn't really blame Peter much, though. Warren would rather do anything than to be stuck here, day after day, with a zombie.

He looked at his watch.

Soon, he thought. *Only a few more hours until I can excuse myself and get on over to Margo's.*

* * *

"Peter?" I said the name aloud as I hugged the mysterious little boy.

He didn't answer me. Instead, he seemed to shrink in my arms until there was nothing left but fabric. I pulled the material closer to me and I shut my eyes.

When I opened them, I realized I was not in my guestroom at all. In fact, I wasn't even in my home. I looked at my chest to see I had my arms wrapped tightly around a stark white sheet.

"Peter," I said again as I became aware of the bed beneath me. I struggled to kick off the sheet and blanket covering my body. An unfamiliar panic rose up in my throat and I screamed. "Peter! Oh God, Peter!"

Within seconds, my husband and an older woman burst into the room with me.

"Willa. Can you hear me?" Warren sat at my bedside and touched my forehead as he spoke.

"Where's Peter?" It was the only question I cared about.

"He's fine, sweetheart." Warren smiled at me with the grin of a used car salesman. "He did fine. He recovered nicely from his injuries."

"His injuries?" All at once, the memory flooded my senses. My poor little boy. Someone hurt him and he was nearly dead when they found him. But, Warren said he had recovered. Was that even possible? "Can I see him?"

"We'll certainly give him a call, Mrs. Hadley." An older man with salt-and-pepper hair and an honest-looking face entered the room. He turned to the woman who had come in with Warren. "Rebecca, go call the son, please. I think he'll be happy to hear about this development."

"Right away, Doctor Marsden." She turned around and dutifully scurried out of the room.

"How are you feeling, Willa?" The man leaned over my bed before he took a seat in a chair next to me.

"Okay, I guess." I pushed myself upward in the bed until I was sitting. I looked around the room for the first time. "What happened to me? Why am I in a hospital?"

"You're in a psychiatric facility, Willa." the man answered, still maintaining his reassuring smile. "I'm your doctor." He paused and looked at Warren before he addressed me again. "About three years ago, you suffered a major breakdown as the result of a traumatic event. Since that time, you've been experiencing a sort of catatonic schizophrenia."

"A what?" I blinked at him trying to wrap my mind around whatever he just said. "You mean, I'm crazy?"

"We don't use that word, Willa." The doctor chuckled a little. "Although I've never personally seen a case like yours, I do know your conscious mind was buried fairly deeply in the disorder. To tell you the truth, I was fearful you'd never recover entirely."

"So, I *am* crazy?" I tried to match the doctor's smile with my own.

"Not at all." He patted my knee before he stood up. "I'd like to run some tests, Willa, to make sure your body— specifically, your brain —is functioning how it should be. If everything looks good, we'll consider letting you go home in a few days." The doctor looked at Warren again. "Of course, we'll need you to attend outpatient therapy indefinitely, and there are a few medications I want to try. I need to have a promise from your husband that he'll help you maintain whatever regimen we lay out for you before you leave."

"Absolutely." Warren nodded, but I could see a trace of dread in his facial expression. "Just write it down for us and we'll follow it to the letter."

"Very well." Dr. Marsden scowled a little for the first time since he'd entered my room. "I'll check up on you tomorrow morning, Willa. Make sure to get plenty of rest and plenty of food. And, I'd like to see you moving around a little before the end of the day."

When we were alone, Warren took my hand.

"This is a miracle, honey." He looked at me, but seemed to avoid my eyes. "Everyone will be so thrilled. I'll get Margo in here if I can track her down."

Margo? Her name passing through his lips made my blood boil.

"Okay. Fine." I gave him a half smile instead of strangling him. "What about Peter? Do you think that nurse will get him to come in? I really need to see him right now. I don't think I can go through a day without him."

I didn't cry, even though I wanted to. I noticed Warren pursing his lips and looking downward.

"He doesn't speak to me, Willa," he said finally.

"What?"

"He, um...I think he blames me for a lot of things." Warren let go of my hand and leaned back a little. "I haven't talked to him in more than two years."

I nodded, settled onto the pillow, and closed my eyes. I didn't know for sure why Peter had distanced himself from his father, but I had a pretty good idea. He probably secretly hated Warren as much as I did. Neither of us ever came right out and said it, but both my son and I were fed up with the lies and the pain.

When I looked at my husband again, he had pulled his phone out of his pocket. He was gazing at the screen with a worried look on his face.

As the older woman returned to my room, my husband stood up, still looking at his phone.

"Is it work?" I raised my eyebrow suspiciously at him. I knew he wouldn't look so concerned if he was worried about something at the office.

"Hmm?" he asked as he moved towards the door. "No. I mean, yes. I'm waiting on a call from work. The guy's late in calling me."

"Okay." I nodded.

Warren wandered out into the hallway. I saw him look left and right before he finally disappeared through a door to the left of my room.

"Hi, honey." The nurse smiled at me before she sat on my bed. "This is such a miracle, from what I hear."

"Rebecca, is it?" I asked her.

"I sure am." Her smile broadened. "I'm the new head nurse on this unit. It looks like I got here just in time to see you come around."

"I can't remember any of it," I confessed.

"It's been a long time since you've been able to communicate with anyone."

"How long had I been like that?"

"I'm not sure." She clicked her tongue. "I think it's been around three years."

"Wow." I thought about my son and my throat filled with a painful lump. "Are they sure he's okay? My boy, I mean."

"He's just fine." She touched my arm. "I just spoke to him, as a matter of fact."

"You did?"

"I sure did. He's on his way here from Jersey. I expect you'll see him shortly, dear."

I reached up and touched my head. My straggly hair caught in my fingers.

"I'd like to get fixed up a little before Peter gets here. Do you think I can get a mirror, some face powder, a hairbrush, and maybe trim my bangs?"

"I think I can arrange all that for you." She stood up. "Let me hunt around the nurses' station. I'll be back in a jiffy."

"Thank you."

A few minutes later, Rebecca returned, followed by Warren.

"Let's get you over to the chair, Willa." Rebecca laid down the small zip-lock plastic bag she had been carrying, along with a mirror. She draped a sheet over an ancient-looking recliner by the window. "Warren, can you help me get her over here?"

"What?" He scratched his head. "Oh. Yeah. Sure."

Rebecca helped me stand up. My legs felt a little weak, but I wasn't terribly unstable on my feet. Warren and the nurse stood on either side of me as we walked to the chair.

She pulled up a small, rolling table and locked it into place in front of me before she dumped the contents of the baggie on top. There was a comb, a pair of scissors, and a small, brown compact inside.

"Do you want to comb through your hair, or should I?" She picked up the comb and the scissors.

"Oh, I'll do it." I raked the comb through my hair. I was surprised my hair had grown past my shoulders.

"The ladies here have been tending to your grooming for you, Willa." Rebecca stood up with the scissors in her hand. "I'm sure their work wasn't perfect, but I hear they've kept you cleaned up rather nicely over the years."

"It's fine." I smiled at her. My thin hair had always been unruly and difficult to keep free of tangles. As I combed, I noticed it was not as bad as I thought it would be. I only had to pull through a few tiny knots at the back of my head. I looked at the instrument in her hands. "Do you mind if I cut my bangs?"

"Of course not." She handed me the scissors and looked at Warren who was, once again, checking out his phone. "Just be careful."

I turned the mirror toward me. My reflection looked a little scary. My eyes appeared to be more sunken than they were before and they had noticeable dark circles beneath them.

What did you expect? I asked myself, shrugging.

When I had the long hairs at the front of my face combed out neatly, I easily cut a straight path through them in front of my forehead.

"There," I said as I looked again at my image. I opened the powder and patted some under my eyes and around my nose. "I look much better."

"You look lovely," Rebecca scooped up the fallen hairs in her hand and threw them in a wastebasket.

A younger woman, who was also wearing scrubs, peeked her head in the door.

"Ms. Jackson," she said. "You're needed in four-B. The patient is a little belligerent and demanding to talk to management."

"Oh, my goodness." Rebecca moved to the door. On her way out, she placed her hand on Warren's arm. "See to it that she gets back into bed safely when she's ready. I'll be back as soon as I can."

As she slipped out the door, I looked at my husband. He appeared to be getting frazzled about something, and I knew whatever it was didn't involve me.

At that moment, I made a decision. Every time I thought about going home with him and his cheating heart, I felt like I was kicked in the stomach. After all the years we had spent together, I would have thought fidelity was a given fact. I knew Warren didn't share my beliefs.

He didn't share anything with me, including an unconditional love of our son. He personified every single sin known to man and he was disgusting to me.

I curled my fingers around the scissors. I knew it would be so easy, if I caught him off-guard. After all, who would have convicted a crazy woman following an act of passion? At worst, I'd end up exactly where I was now, with a few extra years added to my sentence.

"I want to go back to my bed," I said to him. "I'm getting tired."

I stood up and carefully tucked the scissors into my left hand. I pressed them up to my hospital gown and twisted the fabric once so they were concealed.

Warren supported me with my right arm until I could sit on the bed. I swung my legs up on the bed and quickly pulled the sheet up over me, and over my weapon.

Warren took his seat on the stool next to my bed again.

"Did you contact that guy?" I asked him, hoping the contempt wouldn't be evident in my voice.

"What guy?" He looked at me, but it felt like he was looking through me. "Oh. Yeah. I found him."

"Good."

I knew one swift movement would do the trick. I tightened my fingers around the small instrument and started to pull back the sheet with my other hand.

Warren was leaning over, looking at the ground, as if he was praying.

Pray for your own soul, I thought as I slipped the scissors closer to the end of the sheet.

I drew back my elbow, readying it to take the plunge. I shifted in my bed so I could be in the best position to lunge forward and shove the weapon into his cold, cheating heart.

"Mom?"

I was distracted by the voice in the doorway. I tugged at the sheet until I was sure the scissors were hidden before I turned my attention to the front of the room. Two handsome young men were staring at me, one of them wearing an ascot around his neck.

The blond man approached my bedside and I had to blink a few times before I recognized him.

"Mama?" He smiled at me. I noticed immediately that his front teeth were not his own. "You're better."

He slipped his arms around my neck and I felt the mechanical stiffness of one of them. It was clearly a prosthetic.

Tears flowed freely from my eyes as I tightened my grip on my only son.

"Peter. My sweet, beautiful boy." I didn't want to let him go.

"How nice of you to stop by to see your mother." Warren's voice was stiff and emotionless.

Peter stood up and looked at him.

"Yes, it is." Peter's tone matched his father's. "I called this morning and that new nurse told me Mom was coming around. When she called me back a little while ago, Josh and I dropped what we were doing to get over here."

"Sit down, honey." I waved to a chair on the opposite side of the bed from where Warren was sitting. "I want to be able to get a good look at you."

Warren jumped up and wandered out into the hallway, as if he was disgusted by the whole scene.

Peter took my hand and looked me in the eye. His blue eyes were so much like his father's, yet they were absent the anger and the deceit.

"I've missed you so much, Mom." He hung his head and wept silently as his companion stepped forward and laid his hand on his back. Peter looked over his shoulder and then back at me. "Mom, do you remember Josh?"

I smiled at the dark-haired young man behind him.

"Yes. I do." I released Peter's hand to shake Josh's. "Thank you for coming with him. It's so nice to see you again."

The scissors slipped from my lap and laid between my legs, with the sharp end turned upward, poking through the thin sheet.

Peter must have noticed, and somehow *understood*. He reached forward and shook my sheet before he pulled it up to my chest.

"Stay warm, Mom." He bent over to whisper in my ear. "And, don't worry one bit about Margo."

He tilted his head back and looked me in the eye again. His eyes were nearly twinkling with something I had never noticed before. It was ominous, but comforting and familiar at the same time.

"Margo?" I asked, not sure if he knew about the affair his father had tried so hard to conceal.

I looked beyond my son's shoulder at Josh. The young man nodded to me with a closed-lip smile right before he winked.

"I'm really sorry, Mom," Peter continued quietly, with his lips close to my ear again. "It looks like your best friend won't be stopping in for a visit." Now, Peter looked at Josh for a second before he turned back to me. "You see, when I called over here and found out you were talking again, Josh and I just *had* to pay her a visit, to fill her in on the good news."

"Paid her a visit?" I felt my heart lurch. "Do you mean you...?"

"Yes." Peter beamed at me and kissed my cheek, clearly proud of himself. "She won't be a problem anymore...for any of us."

"Oh, sweetheart." I scooted farther up in my bed. "You *didn't*."

"Of course we did, Mom. We did it for *you*." He paused for a moment. "And, those assholes who chopped me up are *long* gone." He let out a soft chuckle before he whispered again. "They were common drunken thugs, and no one's even noticed them missing."

My Lord, I thought. *Peter may look exactly like his father, but his heart and soul are Willa all the way.*

As I stared at him and patted his cheek, I noticed a splatter of what looked like dried blood on his pale yellow, button-down shirt, near his scarf. I straightened out the ascot and draped it so it was covering the stain more efficiently.

"You're my good boy." I pulled him to me for another hug. "I love you so much."

I grinned widely as I fantasized about good old Margo's final moments.

"No more working on your own. Okay, Mom?" Peter reached behind him and took Josh's hand. He clasped it to his heart as he leaned in to me again. "We will take care of the final situation...*together*."

END

THE LEGEND OF OLD JACK

OCTOBER WEEKS

WHEN OLD JACK WAS A wee young lad, his mother passed. Her love was the first and last he'd know. His father was strict and fast with a switch, and he taught young Jack to rely only on himself.

"Don't let yourself love, don't let yourself give," his father would say with a scowl. "All that will follow is sorrow and pain. Others will take what you give and treat you as if you owe them more than what you have."

"But Da," Jack would start with a curious glint, "what of mum and the love she shared?"

His father's eyebrows would lower and knit in anger, and his gaze would bore into his son's unflinching. "Your mother was special and gave us two what she could, but others used her without thought. They're constant need to take her love and kindness drained her strength until she could no longer breathe."

Jack didn't budge under his father's stare, because he knew if he did he'd be considered weak. His father did not allow for that. So he held his father's dark gaze, knowing that would make his him proud. "She died because they took too much?"

"That's right, Jack," his father would reply, then he would lean back in the rocking chair and light his pipe. "So you don't give them one breath or one inch."

Jack believed his father with all his soul, and as he grew he pushed all away—they wouldn't take his money, his heart, or his life. He turned away the poor, the wealthy, charities of every kind. Even the thought of a wife. He became mean, even cruel, to those who but wished him good. When he was aged fifty-eight, he died alone on his father's farm, on a rainy day in his barren thatch hut.

After what seemed just a short time, Old Jack opened his eyes to see a light as bright as the sun, which dimmed a bit after he blinked several times. A large gold gate stood several feet ahead, atop white fluffy clouds with soft hymns in the background. "Is this Heaven?" he wondered aloud, curious as to why he'd be dreaming when he was dead.

"This is no dream," a calm, male voice replied. Then, in a blink, a man appeared in front of the gate, dressed in white robes with shades of green.

"And who are you?" Jack asked with gruff.

The man bowed ever-so-slightly. "I greet the departed with warmth and care, and God tells me when to open the gate and allow souls in."

Jack's gaze moved from the man to the gate, several times until the words sunk in. "Will you not let me in? Surely my mother wants me near?"

"I'm afraid you are unwelcome here," the man said with sorrow in his tone. "Therefore you are not allowed to see her, or your father, and others who have gone."

Jack's eyes narrowed and his temper grew. "How dare you keep me from the only love I knew!"

"You chose your path of cruelty and hate." The man stepped back, then disappeared. "You are unwelcome here."

Before Old Jack could reply, the bottom dropped out and he began to fall. Light faded into dark, and the fall was long, giving Jack time to realize what would come.

He landed on wet sand and rock, though he did not feel the impact as he would have thought. No pain came, no bones broke. He simply landed on his front side as if falling on a cloud.

"Stand Old Jack," a deep male voice bade, "for we must speak of your soul's place."

Jack stood, then turned around. Torches lit as if on command, and a man stepped forth from the water's edge. This man was tall with shoulders broad, and eyes so black Jack could see his reflection in them. "I am to be in Hell, as God declared," he said, bitterness ripping the air.

The man smiled and shook his head. "Afraid not, old man. I do not want you here."

"Then why was I sent to this place at all?"

"I am doing what God would not, and sending you where your soul won't rot."

Jack stared at the man in confusion. "And where is that?"

"You are to roam the living realm, unable to be seen, with this—" a lantern appeared in the man's left hand "—your only light." The man held out the lantern.

Jack took the offered light, as if his hand had a mind of its own. "But I see them?"

"That's right, Old Jack. You are to walk amongst the living, unseen and unheard, but they will speak of you and your plight so as not to repeat your mistakes and wind up with the same fate."

Anger lit within him, sharp and loud. Jack growled, and his hand tightened on the handle of the lantern. "You and God will regret this, oh King of Hell. The day will come when you both will look back and wish you'd chosen far more wisely. I will see to it, be certain of that."

The man—the Devil for sure—laughed heartily. Once he stopped he clapped his hands, and Jack found himself in the living realm.

Over the years it was as the Devil said—people hollowed out turnips and set a candle inside, and set his tale as a warning to the all."

"Be like Jack, and this will be your only light. Unseen by the living and roaming without peace or home," they'd say.

Jack's anger grew year after year, festering eternally as he searched for his revenge. And one night he found it, quite by mistake, when a child blew out the candle before the midnight bell rang. His soul, it vibrated as smoke rose from the wick, and the child looked at him with eyes so wide Jack had to laugh.

"You see me, boy?" Jack asked with hesitant glee.

"I do," the boy whispered, frozen in place, unable to flee.

Jack jumped up and down like a child with excitement, happiness he hadn't known for countless decades rushing through him. "But can I touch you?" Jack wondered aloud, stepping close to the boy who couldn't even blink.

Reaching a finger out towards the boy, he slowly moved it forward, to the center of his chest. And sure enough the boy felt real. Jack picked the lad up and swung him around, hooting and hollering as if he'd found a pot of gold. Then he set the boy down and said, "Thank you, young lad, you've given me the greatest gift I've ever known."

And so glad was Jack for the gift the boy gave, he left him alone outside of the house. The following year he thought and he thought, until it dawned on him how to spite Heaven and Hell. When the night of All Hallow's Eve came once more, Jack waited for an impatient sot to snuff the candle out. And when that moment came he attacked, leaving his victim bloody and slashed. But Jack didn't realize his hate had grown so deep, for when the victim's family returned to the house, he killed them all with the blood covered ax. When they were all dead Jack realized with pleasure that not only could he kill the one who'd snuffed out the light, but also those who dwelled in the home with that person.

From that night on, the legend of Old Jack grew:

"Keep the wick lit until midnight comes, else you wish Old Jack to appear with revenge in his eyes."

Jack couldn't be more pleased as the legend spread, especially when the New World joined in. Pumpkins instead of turnips as time went on, and more treats instead of tricks, but the young...oh the young! They foolishly tempted fate year after year, and some of them met their fates at his hand. With every death he could feel Heaven shake, and after midnight he heard the bells ring as souls ascended before their time. And the King of Hell, oh He shook with rage, and Jack would grin as he walked with his lantern.

"Come get me, old man!" he'd chant as he strolled. "Come get me for cutting those who belong to you before their souls were dirty enough to enter your kingdom!"

"The time will come when your tale will fade to myth," the Devil would reply, "and not enough will believe in you to give you might. When that time comes, I will snatch you back, and burn you in flames for the lifespans of those whose lives you take."

This made Jack happy as can be, for he'd make sure that day would never come. So he walked in the dark of the living realm, with his lantern his only light, until the pumpkins lit and the veil was thin. One night, close to Halloween, he sat down next to a group of the young, and listened to the scary tales they told around a fire in the woods.

"Heaven wouldn't have him," a young man began. "Hell didn't want him. So Jack was sent to wander the world of the living with a lantern as his only light. He was alone for years and years, until a lad snuffed out the fire inside. He crossed into our world then, and has killed hundreds of those who ignored the myth."

Hundreds, Jack mused, a smile on his lips. *Think bigger, laddie!*

"So on Halloween night, just before the darkness falls, light a candle in your pumpkin as tradition holds. Keep the wick lit until midnight takes hold, else Old Jack will come and blood will flow."

Jack stretched out on the ground just then, and took pleasure in the fear he felt. He'd not be joining the Devil anytime soon, and neither would the souls he took.

And Old Jack couldn't be happier because of that.

WALK WITH FIRE

SJ DAVIS

LOOKING BACK, IT'S EASY TO see that my world had changed from what it once was. But what happened, and how it happened, that is the mystery. Some say desire is like a bright sun beating down through holes in an old rusted tin roof, but it isn't like that at all. Not until you feel the blunt force of what you want, or what you think you want, it isn't yours to hold. And soon, I found something that pierced the armor of my heart.

Perhaps it was the smell of his sweat that had my heart beating so fast that I thought it would lodge in my throat, I don't know. The music was loud, so loud that the bass thumped like a metronome in my chest. The smoky haze of lights shone upon his dark hair and eyelashes. There was no talking, but conversation wasn't what I wanted anyway. I went with one purpose— to find someone. Someone who wouldn't text me the next day, making me regret they existed. Lasting relationship? No thank you. Not again. Never again.

Ice was frozen on the outside of the windows, unaffected by the heat of the packed club. On the inside of the windows, steam and condensation oozed from the walls. Staring, I walked past this new man; my red vinyl boots protected my feet from the drunken sway of the hypnotic dancers. My hip grazed his thigh and he turned to look at me. Blue eyes, cold and unblinking. This one wouldn't bother me later, I was certain of it. I smiled. He did not. And that, dear reader was a very good sign.

He placed his pale hand on the front of my shirt and gently slid it down to my waist. I tensed and looked down at the wet floor, slick with drinks and sweat.

"Hello," I muttered. "I'm Sophia." He ignored my words, which was fine with me.

I leaned back against a brass railing to a spiral staircase leading to a darkened bar. He pressed against my body, the smell of him made my eyes close. He stood so close, his feet surrounded mine as he played with my earring— twisting in between his fingers, pulling it almost painfully as my head rested on his chest. I looked up at him, sideways. It was only then that he smiled. Slightly.

His teeth reflected the limited light of the dance floor. So white, they seemed to glow in the dark. I stepped away to go to the bathroom, but he grabbed my wrists to stop me and turned them up to the strobed light of the ceiling. My already short skirt rose way above decent standards when he pulled my right hand to his mouth and I could feel the pressure of his teeth graze my skin.

"What are you doing?" I pulled back, though his hands grabbed mine with a vice like grip. He held my arms against his chest and looked down at me, studying me.

"Whatever," he whispered, almost hissing over his shoulder as he turned away.

I inhaled deeply and smoothed my clothes back to submission.

Shaking my head, I ran up the staircase to find my favorite bartender, a friend of mine since elementary school. He saw my face and handed me a cigarette, smiling through a curtain of blonde dreadlocks. I slowly took a drag and let the smoke roll from my lips. I looked over my shoulder for the strange man with the wrist-sucking fetish, scanning the balustrade to the lower level.

"Avoiding someone?"

"I think the freaks are out tonight," I answered.

"Freaks are usually right up your alley."

"My freak days are over. I want uneventful...satisfaction." I smiled as I French inhaled.

"Well, you're dressed for freaks. Your ass is hanging out and I have a pretty good view of the front too."

"Shut up." I tossed the cigarette on the floor and stomped it out with the heel of my boot.

I looked downstairs and watched two girls dancing together, one platinum blonde and the other a redhead. Both were rubbing against the other and significantly increasing the sex factor on the floor. A damp smell, almost moldy, hit me at once— mixed with the scent of sex and desire. I looked at the DJ and I saw him again, against the wall next to the speakers; his crimson shirt was damp. I could make out his features better from afar as the light hit his face directly. His hair wasn't long, but his bangs were. They were damp too and swept to the side. His hair was dark, almost black— and very shiny.

Suddenly I felt a crushing pain in the back of my neck and pressure from behind as if someone was pushing me. He looked up the stairs toward me as I squinted back, frozen in pain. Still, he gave no expression. I blinked and bent over, reaching around to the back of my neck. My hair stuck to my skin and my breathing staggered.

I felt a hot flash of breath waft into my ear as the pain ran down my spine. He was behind me. *How did he get here so fast?* I turned and tilted my head to question him, but there was nothing to be said. I could make no noise. Everyone and everything around me was frozen in place. No sound, no music, no movement. It was as if I lived in a painting. Cigarette smoke froze in place, white swirls stagnant and still, unmoving in the air. Before I could bring forth a serious scream, my legs buckled and he balanced me with his arm around my waist.

He turned me with a brisk force to face him. I closed my mouth and his palm pressed against my lips to keep me quiet. *Cold, so cold.* He leaned in and slid his hand to my throat and squeezed it slightly as he bent into my neck.

"Enoch. I am Enoch."

That's all I remember until I woke up on the damp cement floor of the bathroom with two blondes snorting coke by the trashcan.

"Nice," I said as I arranged my skirt that was twisted around my hips. My head pounded and my mouth tasted like blood and metal.

"We're not judging," said the blondes in unison and in identical squeaky voices. The white powder dusted on their nostrils matched their hair.

Freaks.

* * *

I walked to my favorite coffee shop the next day, pulling my hair and twisting it into frayed ringlets until I finally gave in and gnawed on the ends. I sat in my favorite spot under the Hemingway portrait while my nervous hands clutched the red cup of my eggnog latte. I sensed the heat of eyes darting around me, as if everyone knew a secret. *Maybe it's just me.*

As the sugary steam from the holiday latte hit my skin, the motions of the customers and baristas slowed as if they existed in super slow motion. Each of them moved like they were weighed down by time and gravity. With each second passing, they slowed further. Some halted completely. Frozen, staring eyes, gaping mouths surrounded me. The music slowed to a monstrously slow sound, low and warped. I stood up quickly to leave.

Should I run? Damn it! My coffee is tipping over. As I grabbed my ridiculously overpriced beverage, the light brown froth stilled to a motionless drip, clinging to the table's edge. Tears stung my eyes. I could still move, as others around me froze.

"What is going on?" My voice cracked above the heads of the crowd as my chest tightened and I began to hyperventilate. No one noticed, most of them still moved in quarter time, as if in a drug-induced waltz. The barista's dark red lips, stained in a cranberry hue, dragged across her teeth slowly, forming words that slowed with each passing syllable. Her crimson-black fingernails gestured slowly up to the menu until they hung still in the air above her head. Still, silent, like a statue. *Just like at the club. What is going on?*

The air in the shop popped with electricity. I felt a sucking feeling pull me back to my chair as I collapsed into the faded wood. Invisible chains held me in place. *I can't move! Get me out of here!* I squirmed to the side, twisting. Then all was still. My heart pounded through my shirt when I saw him. Enoch, the man from last night stood outside the glass wall. He wore a black trench coat, tortoise shell Ray Ban sunglasses, with large droplets of rain beading on his shoulders. His hair hung wet over his forehead as he pressed himself into the glass window. Then, as if the window was made of water, he walked right through it. The glass did not crack nor did it shatter. First his foot and left leg shifted through the glass, then the rest of him pushed through the solid glass pane as if it were a gelatinous liquid. The window was undisturbed in his wake. The sound of a flutter of wings clipped through the air, whispering and blowing.

Watchers! An old crone's voice crackled in my ears for only me to hear. The sound smacked like thunder. *Watchers!*

My mind buzzed and my mouth felt dry. I tried to scream as he held his hand out to quiet me. Even though he wasn't actually touching me, I could feel the icy heat of his hands along my lips. Enoch was pale and seemed tired, but he still exerted a strong force. The shop was filled with the sounds of rushing wind, as if air whistled through a tunnel. I tucked my head down as my scarf flew from off my neck. Next my brown sweater, an oversized warm cable-knit, slid roughly from my shoulders. I felt like I could no longer breathe on my own.

He stared and pointed to the floor at my feet. As soon as I looked where he indicated, he stood in front of me. It was as if he teleported or flew through time. His white face was drained of any color and his blue eyes were dilated in the brightness of the fluorescent ceiling lights. He crouched in front of me and rested his hands on my thighs. My sharp, and pained, intake of breath made him look at me. His nostrils sucked in air like a vacuum. A breeze filled the room, and again I heard the sound of wings.

It's hot, so hot. I feel like I'm on fire. His eyes closed as he kissed my shoulder and neck. *I'm cold ... I can't breathe ... I'm empty.*

I sucked in more air and opened my eyes. The walls of the room bent and warped in rhythm with my pulse. His lips rested against my chest. Then, painlessly, he laid his hands on my heart. I could feel the pressure of the palms, but a numb stillness ran down my body. *It's so quiet. It's so still. But at least there is no pain.*

"Who are you?" I begged. "What are you?"

Watchers. The syllables hung in the air as the room and its occupants swept back in motion. Sounds of coffee brewing and foaming, the sharp laughter of the customers, and the coughing and throat clearing of the bored baristas, all returned as if nothing was amiss. No one was the wiser. But I knew. I knew there was a change. Yet I wouldn't know what it was for many days to come.

* * *

I moaned. Damp sheets of sweat twisted around me. I tossed and turned as my heart fluttered. Flashes of the Enoch kissing my neck burned into my dreams and seared my thoughts.

*I'm sorry...*a deep voice whispered through the curtains. I heard a loud car alarm along the street below, but it didn't even startle me.

Why? I asked the voice in my sleep. *Who are you?* I didn't want to wake up. I finally enjoyed feeling again.

Feeling something, anything instead of the empty anger I'd grown accustomed to. Anger had lived inside me for so long. Ever since, well, ever since awhile. An incredible vibration filled the room and suddenly I felt cold. The window was open, yet I was shimmering with sweat. I sat up, letting the silk sheet slide from me and I walked to the window.

How did this window get opened? It's freezing outside! It's winter for fuck's sake!

The crisp wind kept me tense and alert while I tugged the window closed. The man in the building across from mine stood in his window in a wife beater and holding a Pabst Blue Ribbon; a perfect redneck combination. He put down his beer can and then looked at me again; a cigarette barely clung to his bottom lip as he smiled. *That's right, pervert. I'm naked. Enjoy the show.* I yanked harder on the window. *Yes, my boobs jiggle. It's quite normal.* He closed his curtains behind him as he pushed his hair from his face, staring at me from across the night sky.

He didn't stop staring, which pissed me off, so I decided to give him a little show. I jiggled my breasts in an exaggerated sway, then I squeezed them together, sticking my tongue out. He pointed at his chest and then to me, as if inviting himself over. *No way, buddy.* I jerked the curtains closed behind me. *No way.*

I lit the candles along the edge of my bathtub and ran the water. The surge of water echoed loudly over the cold tile of the floor as I dipped my toes in the water to test the temperature. *Too hot.* The candles flickered for no reason. I slipped as I stood back up. Two strong and slightly rough hands grabbed me from behind— one hand around my waist and the other around my neck. I wasn't afraid; I also had no intention of screaming. I knew who it was. It was Enoch. Part of me wanted this stranger just as he was— unknown and unresponsive. Another part of me wanted to know everything about him, especially who or what the hell he was. I felt his hands on my body. And then I felt nothing at all.

* * *

"Sophia!" a little girl's voice yelled from the back of my mind. Her voice sounded muffled but full of fear. "Sophia!"

Who is that girl?

I jerked awake and looked around, spitting water out of my mouth as the water splashed around me. I had fallen asleep in the bathtub.

"Who's here?" I sat up quickly, completely startled as I woke up from under the water. *And when did I get in the tub? Nothing makes any sense!*

I rubbed my eyes and ran my hands through my wet hair. I splashed from the tub, leaving a river of lukewarm water behind me. I leaned against the door for a moment, and then locked it. Suddenly I heard music. Old music, an orchestra with a big band sound yet with an almost carnival quality, complete with the hiss and pop of vinyl.

The music stopped as soon as I opened the door, wrapped in my pink bathrobe. Water ran down my legs, making wet marks on the carpet. I felt motion in the air. I felt the cool breeze of someone's presence. He must still be here.

I'm everything you wished for. Everything you could want. I'm here to help.

* * *

I rolled on my side with Michael's face still clear in my mind. I turned on my iPod, techno and loud. The beat thudded in my chest and I let it vibrate in all the places I needed it. He's gone, missing, dead. I missed him every day and every night, as I lay paralyzed on my pillow. Sometimes, I never slept at all.

"Michael," I whispered into the darkness. "Michael. Come back to me."

I closed my eyes and his beautiful face appears behind my eyelids. His tanned skin, bright blue eyes, chestnut hair. He wasn't much taller than me; we were often eye-to-eye. He said he loved that the most. As dark and foreboding as his music was, he released me from my boredom. A box I had built, and to which I now returned. It's only been one month. I can't listen to any of his songs anymore. I might never be able to again.

Dead. Like my lover and my heart.

* * *

"You don't remember the Watchers?" asked Georgia. "Mom used to scare us with them when we were little so we'd behave at communion?"

"That old Fallen Angel tale?" I asked. My twin sister was visiting from Ponchatoula, Louisiana, my hometown— a place filled with swamps, voodoo, Catholicism, and catfish. "You came to visit me, not make me crazy. And you're crazy too if you believe that old voodoo hoodoo."

"I'm not saying the Watchers are coming to get you for not following the rules of The Blessed Mother. Even though they should."

Georgia was always the obedient religious one. But she was also the last to be kissed, the last to be with a man, and I am certain the last to touch herself. I'd had almost enough of her self-righteousness in my life. "The Watchers exist only to make children obey the Church," I blurted out. "And I've never been one to adhere to a religion that manipulates people through fear."

"Angels," said Georgia quietly, "Angels are not to be feared."

"Angels? The Watchers are *Fallen* Angels. *Rejected* from a *cruel* God."

"After this time passes," Georgia's eyes seemed to cast a dark glow, "you will see the error of your ways." Georgia's accent thickened and her head tilted awkwardly as she spoke, almost twisting too far. She walked jaggedly to the bathroom. She turned as she closed the door, staring at me with blank, almost yellow eyes. I could have sworn I saw her pull the blade of a knife from her purse.

"There is darkness and there is light," hissed Georgia from behind the bathroom door. "And there are only two kinds of souls, the good and the evil."

"What are you talking about, Georgia?" I shivered. "You're freaking me out."

"You have always been on the wrong side. There is nothing I can do."

"What is wrong with you, Georgia?"

"Your grave was dug before you were born, Sophia." She smiled in the doorway, the light from the sun radiated around her silhouette. "You were born bad."

There is a moment in time for everyone, when you see yourself in a mirror and realize you are exactly who you should be. I glanced at the looking glass next to my galley kitchen. I leaned in and saw blood splattered on my face. Tiny red dots decorated my reflection. I touched the blood and smeared it into my skin, but my hand was clean. My sister laughed. For the first time in my life, I realized my sister hated me.

And so I knew. Everything, as I had always thought it to be, never really was.

* * *

"Don't do that," he said as walked down the front steps of the brownstone.

"Don't do what?" I asked instinctively. "You again? What's going on?" I looked at the passersby; everyone appeared to be normal. "Is everyone going to freeze in place soon? Because that really freaks me out," I whispered up toward Enoch.

"Don't hold your keys like that," he instructed. "Anyone can grab them from you."

"Why do you think you can tell me what to do?" I countered. I looked up at him. His tall body blocked the strong sun from blinding my eyes. Sparks flew in my brain and caused a rush of adrenaline that I felt down to my toenails. I didn't expect it, not in the daytime, but I wanted and needed it. "Are you my new advisor?" I asked sarcastically.

He stood at least six inches taller than me, and I'm not short. Each beat of my heart pulsed in my neck as he stared down at me.

"My eyes are up here."

He looked into them. I saw blood in his eyes. I saw blood dripping down a wall. Next I saw curtains blowing from an open window.

I shook my head to clear my thoughts. *Silly visions, none of it is real.*

"Ready for our date?" he asked.

"Date," I reply in a flat tone. "Date? I'm on my way to work."

"No, you are coming with me." As soon as he finished speaking the world stopped. We walked through a maze of pedestrians, frozen in place on their way to work.

"How do you do that?" I snap with annoyance.

"It's not me doing it. It's you." He leaned into my ear and whispered lightly.

As I look at him, I can't remember who I am. He lowers his eyes to the ground and I reach to him. He takes my hand and I feel a vibration inching into my fingers and up my arm.

"Do you feel that?" he asked.

I say nothing to him. I don't know whether I am mad, scared, or intrigued.

"I'm sorry." He looked genuinely disturbed. He pushed me against the cold metal of the ATM machine. I tried to feel something other than this empty feeling, so I let him push me. Then I let him kiss me. He seemed so hungry with my mouth. His hand touched my face.

"What do you want from me?"

"It's about your sister."

"My sister hates me."

"So you say."

"Why are you bothering me?" I demand. *But is he bothering me?* My bag falls down my arm. "I am just trying to go work."

"You are trying to hurt yourself."

"Really." My eyes roll. "I'm trying to get by."

"Really," he said, mocking my tone. "If you hurt yourself, you think you are protected from other's hurting you." He smoothed my hair away from my eyes. "But you aren't." His hair fell into his eyes, slivers of blue cut through the dark fringe of his hair.

"For someone who knows nothing about me, except in clubs and coffee shops, you think you're pretty smart."

"I know what you need. Michael is gone. But you are still here. Stop wishing yourself away. Hurting yourself won't bring Michael back to you. Ever."

He put my bag strap back on my shoulder and turned to leave. As soon as he turned the corner, the crowds of people walked, cell phones vibrated, and coffee was poured. My world spun on a very strange axis. *How did he know about Michael?*

* * *

Georgia greeted me at the door. Her hair was dry and coarse, sticking it all directions. The fireplace cackled behind her. Her teeth looked strange and her mouth was clenched as if she'd been gnashing at something all day. But it's not her teeth that upset me the most. It's that her eyes were silver with dilated pupils. Her skin looked damp and almost blue.

"Are you sick?" I asked. She retreated to the kitchen and cleaned the table. She dumped the dinner plates into the sink and scraped off the spaghetti from last night. Each scrape of the plate screeched like fingernails across a chalkboard.

"Please, stop it," I said. "Just let them soak."

I stared out the window above the sink into the dark woods. The moon was full and made the room glow with a cool shimmer.

"You brought this on yourself," she hissed. "You had Michael, a nice man, for the first time in your life. Now you are back in the gutter, alone, just like before."

"Shut up, Georgia. You know nothing about Michael. And I don't think you really know me either."

Go look in the mirror. The voice of an old woman, cracking and harsh from years of smoking, whispered to me. *Go now and look. See your secret. She is not who you think. The answer is in front of you.*

Georgia laughed and picked up a glass of wine. She smiled as she turned away from me. Her back was covered in blood.

"Georgia!" I yelled. "You're bleeding."

"Am I?" She looked over her shoulder with a snarl. "Am I, really Sophia? Or is it you?"

"I am *looking* at you, Georgia."

"Look at *your* hands." She walked to the guest room and shut the door. I looked at my fingers, red with dried blood. Flakes of blood coagulated under my fingernails.

Georgia normally stayed close enough to me where I could at least see her, but now she was fading from my eyes.

I stumbled backwards and felt a body behind me. It was Enoch.

"Stay strong," he whispered in my ear. "Face her."

I pulled away from him and grabbed a knife from the table. I raced to the elevator and rushed in, backing up as people ran out the slowly closing doors. The brass doors reflected my insanity back to me. My clothes were splattered with blood and my hand clasped the knife against my thigh, digging at it and making tiny cuts.

"Call the police!" I heard someone yell as the door closed, separating me from everyone else. Enoch rammed a metal rod, a yardstick into the crack and opened the elevator door, following me.

"I'm scared," I whispered. "It's as if I don't live in the right world anymore. Nothing is right. Even the owls are not what they seem."

"You make the world what you want it to be. We are the ones who hurt ourselves."

"And why are you telling me this?"

"When man faces a loss, he can live in a backwards world. Or he can dig his way out."

"Are you talking about Michael?"

"I'm talking about you. You need to let go."

"I'm fine."

"You're killing yourself. You're killing yourself to be with a man that is gone."

* * *

My mobile vibrated in my pocket. My parents.

"Hello, dear!" my mother chirped happily.

"Mom," I yelled into the phone. "Something is going on with Georgia. I can't figure it out though."

"Georgia?" my mom sounded incredulous. "I haven't heard that name in a long time from you."

"What do mean? She's my sister, your daughter. I talk about her all the time."

"Sophia. She's not real. You know that." Click. She hung up.

* * *

I am five years old. My father drives with the windows down and cigarette ashes fly into the back seat, landing on my new dress. He waves his hand recklessly outside of the window, with a death's grip on his cigarette. The Rolling Stones *Tattoo You* album blares into the air.

You wouldn't think the music would still play after the accident, but it did. I sat in the backseat, locked in place by the seatbelt. My father was halfway ejected from the front window, his skin skewered back over whitened bones in his shoulders, glass stuck into his abdomen. His neck was twisted backwards and the whites of his eyes were completely red. His blood seeped through his shirt and made a puddle on the dashboard, mixing with dust and cigarette ash.

I heard a small knock on my window and saw only a small child's fist. Then I saw the rest of her.

"Hi," she said. "Let me in. It's Georgia." And I did. I let her in and we became inseparable, more than I could have ever imagined. "We'll be together forever from now on."

* * *

When I woke up again, it was the afternoon and I was wearing the same clothes that I'd worn the day before. I slept more than twelve hours, but I didn't feel rested. How could I? I missed Michael. I wished I were dead. Nothing was new about that. The air around me felt crushing and I could taste the coldness in my life. The dark feeling of descent settled in my heart. I knew that I was near my end. I even hoped for it.

The memory of Michael hung on me like a heavy wet cloak. I tried to ignore it, but it dripped from me as I walked through my days. I wanted to be free.

The stairs to my apartment felt like they tilted and bent. The carpet moved under my feet. I ran back into my apartment, straight into the bathroom, hoping Georgia wasn't there. It felt like fangs sunk into my skin as a humming fear rung in my ears.

"Let go of me," I cried into the dark room. "Free me!" The mirror twisted and my reflection contorted back at me.

Eyes flashed behind me. *They are my eyes!*

"Georgia," I gasped. She stood behind me. Her profile glowed in the moonlight shooting through the window. She rubbed her arms and neck with her bony hands, her fingers reached into my hair. "What do you want?"

"I want what you want. I want to end your misery. That's why I'm here."

"Don't listen to her." Enoch's voice shouts from the other side of the door. "She has no power over you unless you let her."

"Don't listen to *him*," she countered. "He's a Watcher."

"There is no such thing as a Watcher," I said.

"There is no such thing as Georgia," he said.

"What?" I ask. Tears stung my eyes. "She's right here." I looked at her and I looked at myself in the mirror. She wanted to help me end my pain. I wanted to let her.

"You are the only one here. Look. Look very hard."

"What am I looking for?" I plead, biting my lip and flinching under his gaze.

Blind girl. There will be blood soon. You see me, because you are weak. Give yourself to me. I stared into her eyes and heard a cacophony of howling noises in the wind. I gasp. "It's me or it's you," she hissed. She stared at me through the bluish light coming through the window. Smiling, her mouth was hungry and feral.

"She finds you when you are weak."

"Michael..." I looked into Georgia's eyes and I saw Michael. He was walking backwards, waving at me. His mouth moves, but there is no sound. I am lost inside her eyes, trying to find him. But the more I fought, the smaller he became.

I fumbled for the light. Georgia is gone. I felt like I walked through a pane of shattering glass. Tiny cuts burned my skin.

"What now?" I asked him.

"The rest is up to you. It's all in here." He pointed to my temple and brushed my cheek with the outside of his palm.

"What about you?"

"I come to you with what you want, but I leave you with what you need."

"Are you one of The Watchers?"

"A Fallen Angel?"

I nodded, tears falling from my eyes, dropping like mercury into his upturned hands.

"I am. I am here to keep you from falling further."

"I can't stop. I don't know if I want to."

"You can." He looked at me and tilted his head. "Let go of Georgia, and she'll be gone. She is nothing but a fire... a fire that starts by your own match."

And in a gust of wind, he faded from view. I smiled and looked up to my balcony across the street. Georgia, dressed in white, sat on the patio, wringing her hands. The sun came out and the world began to move around me again. I looked again at Georgia, and she too faded away.

CRY, HAVOC

SKYE KNIZLEY

Dear Diary,

Here's how it is. The world ended. I know, then why am I still here leaving a diary, right? It didn't end the way people thought it would. Thanks to an inexperienced tyro of a President and the itchy trigger fingers of our enemies, a shower of nukes was launched that should have laid waste to everything. Unexpectedly, the defense nets did what they were supposed to and 97.9842% of the missiles were destroyed above the atmosphere, which is what saved us. Still, enough nuclear weapons and residue fell to cook the Earth and change our destinies forever.

I live in the shithole that used to be the United States. Behind the walls of Manhattan and similar sanctuary cities, things are largely as you knew them. Out in the wasteland, it's the apocalypse. Monsters, demons, zombies, everything you ever watched on the vid brought to life in living, gory detail. The nukes cracked the world and brought back the things we thought were only fairytales and legends.

I'm one of the Chosen, I fight the things you still insist aren't real. It's a losing battle, but we were never known for giving up, even when the chips were down.

My name is Angel. Friends call me Havoc.

CHAPTER ONE

ANGEL RAN THROUGH THE BUILDING, her boots pounding on the concrete floor, scarf trailing behind her like a cape of pink wool. At the end of the hall she crashed through a door and vaulted an upturned table without slowing. An entrance at the end of the hallway slammed shut and she heard the crash of breaking glass. Her prey was trying for the window. Angel accelerated, drawing the pair of matched Desert Eagle pistols from the holsters that rode on her hips. When she reached the end of the hall she lashed out with one boot, sending the door crashing against the wall. She followed through with a forward roll that left her on one knee, weapons held in front of her. The room was dark, but the heads up display on her contact showed a low-light image of an old apartment. A sofa lay on its side against the back wall, a flat screen television lay on the floor, its screen broken beyond recognition and the wall was broken through in so many places it was more Swiss cheese than sheetrock.

Two wide picture windows overlooked the ruins below and the distant lights of Old Manhattan glittered on the horizon, a beacon to those in the wastes. One of the windows was broken, but there was no sign of the creature she'd been chasing.

Angel straightened and brought up her thermal vision. "Come out, come out wherever you are!"

There was no sound save the wind blowing through the window. Angel cross-stepped into the room with her weapons aimed at the window. Angels of Decay had wings, but they were small, could they actually fly?

She reached the window and looked out. She'd followed the Angel of Decay all the way to the thirtieth floor after finding it feeding on wastelanders a few blocks away. The wastelanders were goners, all of the disease the AoD carried had been conveyed to them, but Angel intended to make sure they got to rest easy with their killer sent back to hell where it belonged.

Below she could see the fires of wastelanders and survivors, those deemed unfit to live within the walls of a sanctuary. They scraped out a living bringing recyclables and tech to the gates, where the assayers gave them food and water. Theirs was a difficult existence, one many gave up on in favor of taking their chances in the bitterly cold north or crossing the Howling to the west.

The Howling. That was a place no one with the brains of an average housecat ever went. The official word was that a series of nuclear weapons had opened a fissure that had caused the Great Quake. It was a radioactive pit that would roast human flesh alive in a matter of minutes.

The truth was far worse. A nuke had, in fact, detonated on the spot, but the shockwave hadn't opened a fissure or fault line, it had opened a crack in reality through which all manner of creatures appeared. It wasn't their only access to the human realm, but it was the largest and easiest way through. Angel had been through the darkwood to the Howling more than once, but she had dreaded it each time.

She raised her eyes and took in the other tall buildings across the street. More fires burned and she could see figures huddling around them for warmth, but there was no sign of the AoD. If it was down there, it would be feeding already.

Her danger sense warned her of the Angel of Decay's ruse a heartbeat before it threw her out the window. She ducked aside and rolled to come up firing. The Desert Eagles spat slugs designed by the Academy to destroy creatures never intended to live on the human plane.

The Angel of Decay was a tall, thin almost emaciated figure with black skin and stringy white hair that fell down his back to mingle with the feathers of his tattered wings. His eyes burned with hatred of all things humanoid and non-squishy and he held a short Deathblade in one hand. The blood-colored sword reflected Angel's attack and she rolled out of the way as the bullets punched holes in the floor where she'd been standing.

"Ye cannot kill me, child of man," Decay said. Its voice sounded like something stuck in the bottom of a clogged toilet with just a hint of timbre.

Angel came up on one knee and holstered her pistols. Her soulblade appeared in her hands a beat later and she smiled. "Watch me."

She rose and her blade slammed into Decay's with the sound of a thousand angry bees and a shower of red and purple sparks that threatened to set what was left of the drapes on fire. Decay countered by bringing them body to body. Angel could smell his fetid breath, taste the mold and filth that clung to his putrefying flesh and she nearly gagged.

"Gaia, you smell like an outhouse, how do you sneak up on anyone?"

Decay snarled and spun a roundhouse flurry of attacks that Angel blocked without difficulty. Each counter, however, brought her closer to the broken window and the fall into darkness beyond. She could feel the bitter nuclear wind biting at her back, tugging at her hair.

"Into each generation is born, blah blah...You're going to die, slayer!" Decay crowed, bringing his blade back for a final blow.

Angel glanced into the abyss behind her then looked back at Decay. "Does Joss know you steal his shit?"

Decay's blade descended and Angel ducked beneath, only to come up with her own whirling blade. The crackling purple energy sliced neatly through Decay's body and he began to dissolve with a look of surprise on his face.

"We aren't slayers and we sure as hell don't fall to the blade of a stinking demon like you," she said as he burned.

Decay's skull bounced to the floor and she kicked it out into the void with the heel of her boot.

"Well done, Havoc," a voice said.

Angel whirled and spotted a figure standing in the shadows. A bright light burst into existence above his head and he smirked. "A bit slow, perhaps, but you got the job done."

Angel lowered her blade. "Michael. How long have you been standing there?"

Michael, a thing who called himself an archon, stood close to seven feet tall. He had milk-pale wings that folded into his back, the face of a supermodel and the body of a Ken doll dressed in a suit of white linen that left his tattooed chest bare. He was also a thorn in Angel's side so often she wondered why she hadn't yet cut him into tiny pieces and left him for the hounds.

"Long enough to be dismayed at your idiot banter. Your job is to kill hellspawn, not have discussions with them," Michael replied.

He stepped forward and knelt beside the pile of ash and burned goo that was all that was left of the Angel of Decay. "What is a Joss, anyway?"

Angel rolled her eyes and set about reloading her pistols. "You've been spying on me since birth and you don't know basic pop culture?"

Michael dusted off his hands and stood. "It wasn't spying, I was preparing you-"

"Why are you here?" Angel snapped. "You don't do social calls."

Michael frowned. "You are very rude, child. You are right, of course, I am not here to speak with you, I detest human interaction. There is a task."

A task. That was Michael's way of saying he had a job too dangerous for his regular flunkies to do. He wouldn't risk one of his worshippers when a Chosen was around to do his dirty work instead.

Angel turned toward the exit. "Fine, what is it and why can't you send one of your twerps?"

Michael followed, his bare feet almost soundless on the floor. "You know perfectly well why I can't send one of my flock, and you would do well not to call them twerps. Their gifts keep you in ammunition."

"Whatever. What's the job?"

Michael paused. "I don't know."

The stairs echoed beneath Angel's boots as she descended. She hadn't noticed the distressing odor of old urine and fecal matter on her way up, nor had she realized how dark the stairwell was. She could barely see a few feet in front of her, even with the glow of Michael's halo above her.

"What do you mean you don't know?"

"I mean what I said. I am unsure what this task will require, I only know it requires your attention. People are disappearing from the slums outside Manhattan. I see something dark afoot," Michael said.

Angel considered the puddle of foul brown goop at the bottom of the stairs. It looked as if something was growing out of a patch of blood and urine. "I see something dark afoot here. How do you know your missing peeps didn't just give up and head south?"

"They wouldn't, they weren't the type and they had the protection of the Sanctuary," Michael replied.

The street outside was almost deserted. Only a few pockets of survivors still tended fires or nursed jars of homemade hooch on the cracked tarmac. Angel looked at them and wished for the thousandth time she could do more. They were easy prey out here and the city didn't care.

Her bike, an ancient and modified Yamaha, sat at the curb. It was painted dull silver camouflage with two saddlebags and knobby tires to cross the wasteland without suffering damage or loss of traction. She slid into the saddle and pulled her pink stocking cap down over her blue hair.

"So...people missing. Can you vague that up?" she asked.

Michael looked at her motorcycle distastefully. "Why do you insist on riding this dirty old thing?"

Angel put on her sunglasses and glared at him. "The missing? I need some clues, Mikey."

"Try the Sanctuary, as I said. And don't call me Mikey," Michael said.

Angel started the bike and raised the stand with her foot. "Then stop calling me Chosen, Mikey."

She popped the clutch and accelerated away, guiding her bike around the cracks and potholes in the old pavement. The distant lights of Manhattan gave her a beacon to follow and soon she was beyond all the broken down cars and the ruins of New Jersey and crossing the bridge that led into the city. On the far side, the bridge itself led to the massive gates of the city while the last remaining exit ramp descended to the New York ruins. Most of the city collapsed after the Aftershock and what hadn't fallen was nearly destroyed by nuclear junk falling from the upper atmosphere. Survivors not allowed into the city had built their own city along the outside, using the Wall to support their shanty town. In the heart was an old church known as the Sanctuary. Michael and the other Archons preached from the pulpit and kept their flock safe. Or as safe as they could, given the circumstances.

The church itself was a three story affair with a steel-capped steeple and three heavy cast-iron bells that chimed the hour, night and day. The doors stood open and welcoming light spilled from within, calling the flock to safety even at this late hour. Angel parked her bike at the foot of the steps and hurried into the church. It was dark, lit only by candles that flickered in the wind. Rows of pews lead to the far end of building, where a pulpit and altar had been constructed in worship to the Christian god some still believed watched over them. A few souls huddled in the pews looked at her with a mix of fear and curiosity, but the Sanctuary was largely empty. Most of the flock would be bedding down on the second floor where there was warmth and safety.

"Are you... Havoc?" a woman asked.

Angel looked at her, she was small, with brown hair matted with sweat and dirt, and deep brown eyes so hooded it was clear she'd seen some things, things no woman should ever have to witness. She wore jeans and a sweater two sizes too big for her.

"Angel, Angel Havoc. Michael sent me," Angel said.

"Thank the maker! Michael says you are the answer to our prayers. I am Porsche, leader of the Lost Girls," Porsche said.

"Lost Girls?" Angel asked.

Porsche nodded. "We are a small tribe of women that has banded together to offer mutual protection."

Angel frowned. It wasn't abnormal for groups with similar interests to form communities, the waste was dangerous at the best of times. Numbers meant safety and pooled resources. But a group of all women was... odd.

"Michael said people were going missing."

Porsche sat on a nearby pew and motioned for Angel to join her. "Yes. Four of my friends, my sisters, have been taken in the last two nights. I can't find any sign of them."

Angel sat opposite and lowered her sunglasses. "Okay, so how do you know they didn't make it through the gates? It's been known to happen, especially with women. If the Caretakers find them worthy, they get passage with no time to write home."

Porsche shook her head. "We gave up on that fever dream long ago. They were taken from our camp in the dead of night, silently and without a trace."

"What makes you so sure?"

She knew the answer before Porsche opened her mouth. It was in her body language, the way she looked away before answering.

"One of the girls, Macy, was taken while she was lying beside me. Someone took her away from me, and I never even woke up," Porsche said.

Angel bit her lip. She could see the anguish in Porsche's eyes and she knew the same pain. The loss of a loved one you couldn't save.

"Okay, I'm on it. Where is your camp?"

Porsche stood. "I'll take you, follow me."

CHAPTER TWO

THE LOST GIRLS CAMP WAS situated a few miles west of the wall, in the ruins of Galaxy Tower. The women had cleared the lobby and turned it into a sort of fortified market with a handful of stalls selling foodstuffs, salvaged gear and pleasures of the flesh. A fire of wood and old tires was placed at the heart of the market, its smoke curling into the atrium above. A single unblocked staircase rose from the lobby to the living area above and two guards stood at the bottom. They held old but serviceable shotguns and looked like they knew how to use them.

Porsche lead the way through the market to the stairs, where they were greeted by one of the guards.

"Welcome back, Porsche. Who's your friend?" the guard asked.

They clasped arms in an old-fashioned grip. "This is Angel, she is the one promised by the Archons. She will find our missing sisters."

"Whoa, whoa! I said I would try to find them, no promises," Angel said.

Porsche smiled. "As you say. It is more than anyone else will offer us. Nissa, I would like to show her the sleeping area."

"Of course."

Nissa and her partner stepped aside, allowing Angel and Porsche past. The stairs wound past a burning oil drum on the landing to the second floor where old cubicle partitions had been used to create small apartments. Single women and small groups lay on pallets within, oblivious to Angel's presence. There were several cubicles that had the feeling of being empty. Not just vacant, but devoid of life, as if something had taken away the essence that makes a hovel a home.

Angel stepped into the first empty cubicle and knelt beside the pallet. The old straw mattress and sleeping bag carried the scent of woman, distinct from that of a male. She could also smell the coppery scent of blood and the cloying odor of death. She reached beneath the mattress and removed a strip of bloodstained cloth. It looked like it was torn from an old white tee shirt or a similar item of clothing.

"This belonged to one of the missing, a blonde girl with pale blue eyes."

It wasn't a question. Being a Chosen meant knowing things, whether you wanted to or not. Angel knew this had belonged to a woman, not much more than a girl, really, with blonde hair and eyes the color of a sunset sky. She could see the girl in her mind's eye, like a still-life drawn from the ether.

"Her name was Cadi, she was taken night before last," Porsche confirmed.

Angel straightened. "But nobody saw or heard anything? Your quarters are pretty close together."

Porsche shook her head. "No, no one. I can't explain it, it's like she just vanished."

"People don't vanish."

Angel looked at the ceiling, which was of the drop-style, with old foam tiles crumbling with age and moisture. No one could have come in the way without leaving a trail of white glop.

"What's above us?" she asked.

"The empty floors. No one can get up there without getting past this floor, and even then they would need a key," Porsche replied.

Angel slipped out of the cubicle and scanned the room. There were two hallways that lead out into the rest of the floor, both with access to the stairs. One of the stair doors was plainly visible and placed beside a security checkpoint guarded by another armed woman. The other lay in shadow, partially hidden behind a piece of cubicle wall. It was chained shut with an old but serviceable steel chain and padlock.

"Why aren't both doors barred?"

Porsche pointed at a pile of salvage, old computers, printers, televisions and other oddities of the 21st century. "We are scavenging on the upper floors. That junk buys us food and medicine, some of which we resell in our own marketplace. That door is the only unlocked access."

Angel frowned and started down the dark hallway. The first door was securely chained and didn't look as if it had been opened for some time. She continued into the gloom, moving past empty chambers that had once been offices. Why hadn't the Lost Girls occupied them? It would be more private than the cubicles.

"We plan to move into these someday," Porsche said, as if reading her mind. "We thought it would be safer to stay together until our numbers were greater, we only have a few weapon-trained guards and fewer weapons to arm them with."

That made sense. Weapons of any kind were at a premium outside the walls. They were the first thing anyone traded when their belly was rubbing on their backbone and starvation was their biggest threat. The second thing they traded was their virtue. Far too many young men and women served the brothels, inside and outside the wall. Most died worn out, poor and addicted to narcs.

At the end of the corridor was another access door. Though a chain ran through the handle and around an old fire-extinguisher, Angel found that the padlock was broken and could be opened easily from someone in the stairwell.

"This should be locked!" Porsche exclaimed.

Angel removed the lock and held it up to the light. Fingerprints were melted into the haft and the key mechanism was smashed beyond recognition.

"Magik. Someone used a spell to break the lock."

"But the guards, someone should have seen it!" Porsche yelled.

Angel set the lock aside and pulled the door open. "Someone got lax. Why walk all the way down here when you know the door is securely locked from this side? Most security breaches are laziness, not intent."

Porsche was vibrating with anger. "Whoever did this will pay!"

"Settle down, Porsche. Whoever did this was powerful and they did it from the other side of the door, you can tell by the position of the lock and chain. You need to tighten security, but whoever did this would have gotten in somewhere, if not here, somewhere else. Locks and guns wouldn't have helped," Angel said.

"Then what do we do? How do I protect my people?" Porsche cried.

Angel turned from the door and met Porsche's eyes. "You're doing it. You've kept them together and out of the brothels, which is better than most so-called leaders. You couldn't predict someone with power this great would be after your girls."

She pulled a slip of plastic with a purple effigy of an angel in flight on the front. "Tomorrow, when the market opens, take this to the Junkman and tell him you were attacked and need protection. He'll get you some magikal wards that should keep anything else from getting in."

"The Junkman? That crazy old man who has all the salvage from out in the waste?" Porsche asked.

Angel nodded. "Yes. His name is Jericho, he's with the Sanctuary."

She turned back and yanked open the door, which slid open noiselessly on recently-oiled hinges. Beyond was a stairwell dimly lit by moonlight filtering in from above. The stairs leading down were choked with debris, but the stairs heading up were clear, save that they'd fallen in several places, forming the blockage to the lower level. Nothing human could have entered without equipment and making enough noise to wake the dead.

"What could do this?" Porsche asked.

Angel looked up at the moon some twenty stories above. Even from here she could see that the roof and walls of the stairwell had been melted away, leaving streamers of blackened material that trailed down the walls.

"I don't know," she said. "But I plan to find out."

She closed the door and laced the chain back through the handle. When she was done, she took a breath and crushed the chain together, forming a makeshift knot that would hold against anyone trying to enter. She then took an old lipstick from her pocket and drew an elder sign of protection on the surface.

"The all seeing eye?" Porsche asked.

Angel shook her head. "That's the Illuminati. This is a pagan symbol of protection, it will keep the undead out until you get the wards."

She turned away, heading for the stairs that led back to the outer city. Porsche stopped her with a hand on her elbow. "Is that it? What about the missing women?"

Angel stared at the offending hand until Porsche let go. She then raised her eyes. "I haven't forgotten. We're looking for something than can enter from the sky, which limits the possibilities."

"So what are you going to do?"

Angel continued down the stairs. "Ask for directions."

CHAPTER THREE

IT WAS ALMOST DAWN BY the time Angel parked her motorcycle outside the small Order chapterhouse within the Manhattan wall. Getting through security had taken the better part of an hour, even in the middle of the night. She preferred to come and go through the secret entrances known only to the Order, but given she'd left through the official exit, it was necessary to return the same way.

The Order chapterhouse was a four story brick building that housed a liquor store on the first floor and apartments above. Angel parked in the alley between the chapterhouse and an old grocery store and slipped through the back door. The room beyond was choked with beer kegs, boxes and liquor crates, with barely enough room for her to get between to the stairs. The stairwell was dark, lit only by flickering nightlights that cast yellow shadows on the faded wallpaper. Stairs led upward to the three levels of apartments, but they held nothing for Angel, who instead descended the stairs to the sub-basement. At the bottom was what appeared to be an empty closet. Angel stepped inside and closed the door. She stood in darkness, impatiently waiting. After several seconds a green beam of energy lanced out and scanned her DNA.

"Welcome back, Ms. Havoc," a mechanical voice intoned.

"Thanks, Bishop. Library, please."

The lights came to life and the lift descended beneath the city. The catacombs below Manhattan had been there for centuries. Portions were used during World War II to house one of the country's first computers, a thinking machine pitted against the Enigma code. Further sections were turned into nuclear bunkers and storage facilities. Who had built them originally was still a mystery, all that was known is they predated Amer-Inds by about a thousand years.

The Order had occupied a section since the 70s and maintained it even after Skyfall. The elevator whined to a stop and Angel stepped out onto a metal catwalk that hung above a waterfall and impossible abyss from which steam billowed. The steam powered the geothermal generators that powered the chapterhouse. The catwalk emptied into a corridor of rough cut stone lit by candles that dripped in the cold.

The library was located one floor down behind a pair of doors so scarred they looked as if the demons of hell had tried, and failed, to fight their way through. It wasn't far from the truth. The librarian, Malachi, was seated in a leather chair beside a roaring fire that still failed to warm the room. He was old, and his age showed in his lined face and fading fringe of hair reminiscent of Franciscan monks. He wore brown corduroy pants and a threadbare cardigan with patched sleeves that hung onto his hands. He set the pipe he'd been clenching in his teeth aside and looked at Angel.

"You're up late. What does Michael want this time?"

Angel perched on the end of the table and crossed her legs. "I need to know about flying undead, particularly ones that can cast spells and like nubile young women."

Malachi sat forward. "Nubile, you say? I don't suppose you have pictures..."

Angel made a face. "Yuck. Be a perv on your own time. Spill, what am I looking for?"

"Perv? I haven't been called a perv since, well before your time," Malachi said. He stood and crossed the room, leaning heavily on a cane as he walked. He reached up with a gnarled hand and pulled down a book heavy with silk marks.

"There are few undead who can use magik, they just aren't smart or in touch with the world enough. Most make do with dark sorcery. Are you certain it was magik?" he asked.

Angel leaned back on the table so she could see what was in the book. "It didn't feel like sorcery, it was more subtle and didn't smell like sweaty feet."

Malachi slammed the book onto the table and tapped the page. It showed a charcoal drawing of a winged creature standing in a cemetery. It was skeletal, with emaciated flesh and a bare skull with flame-filled eyes. Written below was one word. Wraith.

"What the fae is a wraith?" Angel asked.

Malachi adjusted his spectacles. "Wraiths are dark undead from the very pit of Hades. They are swift, intelligent and still connected with the living world through their bones."

Angel spun the book so she could see it more clearly. "Which means they can do magik. What's all this scribbling? Couldn't the ancients write English?"

Malachi took the manuscript back. "It's Aramaic, you heathen. Dollars to donuts, you're looking for a wraith."

Angel slid off the table. "Great, where do I find one and how do I kill it?"

They like cemeteries, graveyards and charnel houses."

Angel was halfway to the door. She stopped and looked back, irritated. "Can you be a little less vague, Mal? The city is surrounded by cemeteries and charnel houses, there are a few million corpses moldering out there!"

Malachi dropped back into his chair. "Wraiths do not work alone, they are lackeys of something stronger. Why are they on your hit list?"

Angel took off her cap and ran her hand through her hair. "He or they are kidnapping women from the Lost Girls, a tribe outside the wall. Does that help?"

"I'm too old for this," Malachi groaned. "Nubile, young, wraiths, my guess is a ritual. Female blood is a preference among the dark magik set."

"I figured that out on my own, Mal."

She continued out the door, pulling her hat back on as she walked.

"Where are you going?" Malachi asked.

"I've got an idea," Angel called, not caring if he heard or not.

* * *

The cruise ship Magellan was one of the first casualties of Skyfall. A nuclear weapon launched from a Chinese submarine had detonated just outside the tube. The resulting explosion created a tidal wave that rolled the cruise ship with over ten thousand passengers on board. It was towed into the harbor as salvage, but still hadn't been cleared. Ten thousand corpses in one small place was Angel's best guess at a charnel house that would be disgusting enough to attract wraiths from the pit.

Angel stood on the dock and looked up at the rusting hulk. The massive screws of the engines dripped algae that glowed in the dark and what looked like blood stained the hull. It ran down the sides and stained the harbor the color of heart's blood. The side doors where vacationers once rented jet skis and power boats stood open. Lights flashed from somewhere inside.

The inside wasn't an improvement over the outside. The walls were spattered with burned blood and charred flesh that smelled of death and decay, worse than anything Angel had experienced. She choked back bile and hurried down the steps, letting her instincts guide her into the bowels of the ship.

"Come out, come out wherever you are," she muttered.

The access-way emptied into a corridor. This was stained and spattered with offal like the rest of the ship, but the bodies were missing. It was as if they'd gotten up and walked away. Or were carried away. She turned her head to read an upside down sign and followed the arrow leading to the ballroom. The stories said a party was in full swing when the weapon hit, and most of the passengers were there. That meant the wraiths would be there.

As she neared the center of the ship, the aroma of death and blood rose, combined with the scent of harbor water, an experience unto itself. She passed piles of skulls arranged in unholy symbols matched with dark blood and symbols chalked on the walls.

The corridor emptied into the ballroom, a scene right out of hell. Harbor water filled the lower half where the atrium and balconies had once been. Bodies floated in the water, thousands upon thousands, so many that they could be used as stepping stones were someone of a crazy or disgusting enough bent to try.

In the middle of the room stood six women lashed to poles made from human bones. A fire burned between them tended by a tall figure dressed in a long robe. He was chanting in a language Angel didn't understand and casting herbs of some kind into the flames.

On the edges of the ritual space were the wraiths, shadowy figures clad in skin and bones beneath leathery wings that hung around them like capes. They stood holding fiery swords that flickered in time with their eyes, awaiting their next command.

Angel raised her pistols and aimed at the lead figure in front of the fire. "Did I catch you bastards at a bad time?"

The figure turned and Angel could see Porsche's face beneath the shroud. "Welcome, Miss Havoc. Thank you for closing the circle."

Angel started down the steps, weapons ready. "You kidnapped your own people?"

"Lord Asmodeus demands a holy sacrifice before opening the gate-"

Angel shot her in the face with both weapons. The bullets punched through Porsche's beautiful face and she fell backwards. "I really don't care what your stupid ritual is for. You're just another bottom-feeding demon trying to get home. If your boss wanted you, he'd install a revolving door."

Porsche stood, holding what was left of her face together with her hands. Green blood spilled between her fingers and dripped on the floor, where it fizzed and sparked.

"Kill her!" she screamed.

The wraiths came alive and rose into the air on leathery wings that trailed flame as they flew. Angel dropped to her knees beneath their strafing run and opened fire. Her pistols spat blue flame and heaven-sent bullets that found their final resting places in wings and bodies as they passed. Three of the creatures exploded and burned with holy fire before crashing to the floor, the others spun away to gain height, circling over the flames as Porsche chanted.

Angel took a knee and began to reload, dividing her attention between the distant wraiths and Porsche.

"I'm curious, P-girl, why did you want me?"

Porsche glared with eyes that were no longer human. "Asmodeus demands the blood of a Chosen to slake his thirst. I knew the Archon Michael would summon you."

The slides on Angel's pistols clicked home and she started running toward the water at the base of the room. "Want my blood? Come and get it!"

The wraiths followed, trailing smoke and flame, their swords whirring angrily. Angel felt the heat of their blades and ducked just in time. She felt her hat catch fire and paused to throw it into the water.

"That was my favorite hat, dammit!"

She baseball slid to one knee and started firing again as the wraiths returned. Her bullets found their marks and two more of the wraiths crashed and burned, sending ash into the water and making it boil. The corpses bobbed and bounced in the superheated water and the stench of hell rose.

Angel's nose wrinkled. "Can this day get any worse?"

Porsche whirled and sent twin pillars of flame at Angel, fire that crackled and heated the air as it screamed toward her. Angel rolled out of the way, fighting the pain rising from the skin on her back. Though the flames hadn't touched her, the heat was enough to char her jacket and her flesh.

"Okay, its worse."

She fought to her feet and was yanked into the air by the remaining wraith. She had just enough time to take a breath before it let go and she was thrown into the wall with enough force to knock the breath from her lungs and make her ribs crack. She fell to the ground and landed on one knee, fighting for breath. She saw Porsche's boots appear in her vision and looked up. Where Porsche's beautiful face should have been was the twisted visage of a demon, with black skin, red eyes and horns made of stone.

"You are overconfident, girl. This is too easy!"

The demon grabbed her throat and raised Angel to eye height.

"I'm going to drain you dry and suck the marrow from your bones!" the demon continued.

"Are you a demon or a giant?" Angel choked. "What's next, fee-fi-fo-fum?"

She slammed her face into the demon's nose then kicked out with her foot. She felt bone crack on both impacts and ripped herself free when the demon howled in pain and rage. Angel fell to one knee again then rose, summoning her soulblade. It came to life in her hand, a blade of pure purple energy held in a haft of bone and steel.

Porsche wiped her face on her hand and stepped back. "Do you think your pathetic soul magic will save you?"

Angel spat blood and stepped forward. "If it is so pathetic, why are you backing away?"

She attacked, a wide sweep of her blade. Porsche backpedaled and conjured a blade of black stone and blood that blocked her attack and showered them both with sparks. Angel attacked again and again, forcing the demon back toward the fire. With each swing, sparks fell and the blades howled like angry flies circling one another.

As they neared the fire, Porsche's blade snaked out and cut Angel across the arm, spilling her blood onto the flames. It sizzled where it hit and the flames rose, turning from crackling orange to flickering green edged with purple. It was accompanied by screams and the howling of the damned. It was a cacophony that set her teeth on edge and made her skull ache.

"Do you hear that, girl? The gate is opening!" Porsche yelled.

Angel dodged and spun a kick at the demon's head. "Good, go through it and get the hell out of my face!"

Porsche sneered and lashed out again, forcing Angel onto the defensive. "I'm not going home, home is coming here."

"Have you looked outside lately? Billions dead, the world cracked, monsters like you walking the Earth, hell is already here," Angel replied.

She was getting tired and keeping her soulblade on this plane was burning energy. She needed to end the fight and close the gate before anything else got through. She rolled away from another riposte and threw her blade, sending it humming through the air end over end. The demon ducked and Angel charged. She powered into Porsche and lifted her from the ground. The demon howled in fury and Angel cried out as she felt the demon pounding on her already charred and peeling back.

"Let go of me, foul creature!" Porsche howled.

"Not a chance, sister, you've got an express ticket across the bridge!"

She raised the demon over her head and threw her into the fire with all her strength. Rather than burning, the demon vanished screaming into the void. Angel sank down beside the fire and felt the gateway pulling at her hair.

"Why isn't it closing?" she asked the world at large.

"The innocents," Michael said behind her.

Angel pulled herself to her feet and looked at Michael. "What?"

Michael nodded at the kidnapped girls who hung in their restraints like wet rags. "The innocents, their energy is feeding the gate."

"Fine, I'll free them and we can all go for Icees."

She was stopped by Michael's hand on her shoulder. "It won't work. Their threads must be cut."

Angel gaped at him. She knew what he was saying, but she couldn't believe what she was hearing. Threads meant the tenuous thread that connected all living things to their souls.

"I'm not going to kill them, they're innocents!"

Michael pointed at the fire, where Angel could see demons amassing. It wouldn't be long before they possessed the courage to cross over. "You have no choice, it's innocent blood or demons possessing all the corpses on this ship!"

Angel swallowed. Ordinary undead was one thing. Zombies, skeletons, vampires, they could all be dealt with. Demons were another story. Porsche was a handful by herself, thousands would take over the world. But these were lives, real people just trying to survive.

"I can't!"

Michael grabbed her shoulders and shook her. "You must! It is them or the world, Angel!"

Angel looked into his eyes then at the girls. They were awake now, and struggling for freedom.

"No."

She cut them free, one at a time and pushed them toward the stairs. "Follow the signs to the boat dock and get out!"

"Angel, what are you doing?" Michael asked.

"The right thing," Angel replied.

Once the girls were safely away, Angel sheathed her blade and closed her eyes. She could feel it, the soul magic that created her blade and made her a Chosen. Malachi had said it could do more, but she'd never bothered to try. Until now. She visualized a shield, a dome of violet energy covering and smothering the flames of the gateway. It rose before her, humming loud enough to drown out the distant screams and the cackle of demonic laughter. When it was complete, she closed her eyes again, visualizing her soul, a shard of purple crystal that glowed with violet inner light. She reached out and broke a piece of the crystal free, a gesture that caused pain to lance through every fiber of her being. She screamed in pain and anguish as a piece of her soul tore free. She held it in her hand, a tiny fragment of what made her who she was.

"You can't," Michael said. "That is your soul!"

Angel gazed at the pulsing piece of crystal. It was beautiful, radiating purple light that sang to her, a gentle, calming tune that belonged inside her.

"Better mine than theirs."

She placed the crystal at the base of the shield and melded them, making them one.

"You will feel it the rest of your days, Havoc. You will be the lesser for it," Michael said.

Angel collected her pistols and holstered them. "Maybe. But I am better for not killing six innocents."

"It was an equitable sacrifice," Michael said.

Angel turned for the exit. "Only if you're a heartless Archon. This is a human fight and I'll fight it my way."

* * *

Michael watched her walk away, then turned to the shield. It was a crude, human thing, but effective. And so very much Angel.

"At last, one of the Chosen understands."